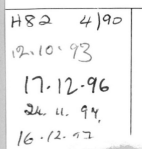

BLACK IS THE COLOUR OF MY TRUE LOVE'S HEART

Young singers and musicians are gathered for a folk music course that will occupy a weekend in the fantastic country mansion called Follymead. Most come only to sing or listen, but one or two have non-musical scores to settle. When brilliantly talented Liri Palmer sings:

'Black, black, black is the colour of my true love's heart! His tongue is like a poisoned dart, The coldest eyes and the lewdest hands...' she clearly has a message for one of the audience. Passions run high; there is murder brewing at Follymead.

Among the music students are Tossa Barber and her boyfriend Dominic Felse. When disaster strikes, Dominic can privately enlist the aid of his father, Detective Inspector George Felse, to unravel the tangle of events.

BLACK IS THE COLOUR OF MY TRUE LOVE'S HEART

BLACK IS THE COLOUR OF MY TRUE LOVE'S HEART

by
Ellis Peters

MAGNA PRINT BOOKS
Long Preston, North Yorkshire,
England.

British Library Cataloguing in Publication Data.

Peters, Ellis, *1913—*
  Black is the colour of my true love's heart.
  Rn: Edith Pargeter   I. Title
  823'.914 (F)

  ISBN 1-85057-741-2
  ISBN 1-85057-742-0 pbk

First Published in Great Britain by William Collins Sons & Co.
Ltd., 1967

Published in Large Print 1990 by arrangement with Macdonald
& Co. (Publishers) Ltd., London.

Printed and bound in Great Britain by
Redwood Burn Limited, Trowbridge, Wiltshire.

CHAPTER 1

The girl with the guitar-case was standing alone at the Belwardine bus-stop when Arundale parked the car before the station entrance, and went in to collect the records Professor Penrose had left behind. She was still standing there when he came back and stowed the battered box under the bonnet of his grey Volkswagen. She had the green-railed enclosure to herself. She didn't know it, but the Belwardine buses were independents, and waited for neither man nor train, and there wouldn't be another for more than half an hour.

Arundale was not a man who went out of his way to offer people lifts. It was the guitar-case that stirred his sense of duty; but for that he would hardly have been aware of her at all, for only one woman really existed in his life, and that was his wife. This girl was perhaps nine-teen or twenty, tall, slim, and of striking appearance. Her face was thin, richly coloured, with long, fine-drawn features and large, calm, fierce eyes as blue as steel. Her great fell of heavy brown hair coiled and spilled round her

9

face with a dynamic life of its own, and was gathered into a waist-long braid as thick as her wrist, interwoven with narrow strips of soft red leather, as though only tethers strong enough for horses could confine it. She had a duffle bag slung over her left shoulder, and wore a duffle coat carelessly loose over a charcoal-grey sweater and skirt of deceptively plain but wickedly expensive jersey. She stood carelessly and splendidly at ease, but her face was intent and abstracted. She looked like a fate in the wings, imperturbably waiting for her cue; and that was what she was. But all he saw was a long-haired girl with a guitar, and an inescapable and rather tiresome duty. He had delegated this course to his deputy; it was annoying that he should be obliged to ferry in the strays.

She looked at him, and found him looking at her. Without hesitation and without mercy, as the young will, she took all decisions out of his hands.

'Excuse me,' she said in a voice unexpectedly cool and limpid, the voice of a singer off-duty, 'could you tell me how often these buses run?'

She could pitch that superbly soft and confident note clean across the station approach at him, but he had to move nearer in order to reply without a sense of strain.

10

'I'm afraid they're not very frequent. In the evening there's a forty-minute interval. Perhaps I could be of service to you. I'm going that way myself.'

'I've got to get to a place called Follymead,' said the girl, measuring him without haste or prejudice. 'It's a sort of musical college, they're having a week-end course on folk-music. Maybe you know the place.'

'I know it,' he said. Who could know it better? But for some reason, or for no good reason at all except lack of interest in her, he didn't tell her how closely he was connected with that curious foundation. 'I can take you there with pleasure. It would be much quicker than waiting for the bus.'

She gave him the quick scrutiny wise girls do give to middle-aged gentlemen offering lifts, but it was a mere formality; his respectability, his status, and the store he set on keeping it, were all written all over him. He was fifty-five, and still an impressive figure of a man, even though his frequent games of tennis and squash could no longer keep his weight down as low as he liked it. He had a businessman's smooth-shaven face and commanding air, but a don's aloof, quizzical, slightly self-satisfied eyes and serious smile. He thought well of himself, and knew that the world thought well of him. She

11

couldn't be safer.

'Really? I shouldn't be taking you out of your way?'

'Not a yard, I assure you.'

'Then thanks very much, I'll be glad to accept.' And she let him take the duffle bag from her, but she held on to the guitar-case, and herself stowed it carefully on the rear seat of the car before she slid into the front passenger seat with an expert flick of long legs. 'My train was late. I only made up my mind to come at the last moment.'

'You're not actually taking part in this folk-music course, then?' he asked, casting a glance behind at her instrument as he started the engine.

The girl followed the glance with a thin, dark smile. 'Oh, that! I just happened to have it with me when I made up my mind to come. No, I'm not on the programme. Just one of the mob.'

'You came to study the form?' he suggested helpfully. He was surprised, all the same, for the guitar-case was old and much-carried, and her speaking voice promised a singing voice of quality.

The small smile tightened, burned grimly bright for an instant, and vanished. 'That's about it,' she agreed, her eyes fixed ahead. 'I

12

came to study the form.'

'But you *are* a folk-singer?'

'I'm a ballad-singer,' she said, with the crisp and slightly irritable intonation of one frequently forced to insist upon the distinction.

His eyebrows rose. Rather dryly he said: 'I see!'

'I'm sorry,' she said, softening, 'I didn't mean to sound touchy, but it's a sore point with me. I've never claimed to be a folk-singer. I'm not even sure I know exactly what a folk-singer is, and I'm dead certain too many people use the term to mean whatever they want to persuade the world *they* are. About a ballad-singer you can't be in much doubt, it's somebody who sings ballads. That's what I do, so that's what I call myself. How far is it to this Follymead place?'

'Nearly five miles. We'll have you there in a quarter of an hour.'

The streets of Comerbourne slid by them moistly in the April dusk. Neon-lit shop-fronts, all glass and chrome, gave place to the long, harmonious Georgian frontage of Crane Place, and that in turn to the two smoky lines of hedges streaming alongside like veils, just filmed with the green of new leafage, and the sinewy trunks of beeches, trepanned with metal reflectors. April had come in cold, angry and

13

wet, trampling and tearing the heavy late snow with squalls of rain, and bringing the flood-water rolling down the Comer brown and turgid from the hills of Wales. But this evening had fallen quiet and still, with a soft green afterglow in the sky, and a hazy, glow-worm look about the first side-lights wavering along the road.

The girl gazed ahead steadily, her fine brows drawn together, her profile intent and still. She watched the budding hedges swoop by her, and the compact villages come and go, and made no comment. Her mind, somewhere well ahead, grappled already with the unknown realities of Follymead; but when it came it was none the less daunting.

A deep half-circle of grass swept inward on their left, the tall grey-stone wall receding with it. The drive swung in towards huge, lofty gate-posts that almost dwarfed a tiny hexagonal lodge. The wrought-iron gates stood wide open, and on either side, on top of the yard-thick posts, an iron gryphon supported a toppling coat of arms. Beyond, acres of park-land stretched away in artfully undulating levels that owed very little to nature.

'This is it?' asked the girl, staring out with astonished eyes at the monsters pole-squatting ten feet above the roof of the car.

14

'This is it.' He had already turned the car inward towards the open gates.

'Oh, just drop me here at the entrance. I can walk up to the house.'

'With your luggage? It's nearly a mile. In any case, this is where I'm going. I should have told you before,' he said, condescending rather complacently towards apology. 'My name's Arundale, Edward Arundale, I'm the warden of the college.'

'Oh?' She turned her head and gave him a full, penetrating look, probing with candid curiosity, and some distrust. 'I see! Then it was you who arranged this course?'

'Not exactly, no. My deputy's running this one. I've got some outside engagements that are going to take me away for most of the weekend. In any case, this isn't really my field. My wife's the enthusiast for folk-music. And your lecturer is a don from our parent university, Roderick Penrose. No, I'm staying strictly in the background. Penrose forgot a case of recording tapes at the station, that's why I offered to run in and fetch them for him, otherwise I shouldn't have had the pleasure of offering you a lift. The guitar, you know. As soon as I saw it, I thought you must be headed for Folly-mead.'

'Lucky for me,' said the girl, 'that professors

15

live up to their reputation for absent-mindedness.' She peered out unbelievingly at the fantasies of Follymead unrolling along the drive. The dusk softened their outlines and colours, but there was no missing them. In a clump of cypresses on top of a hill too artfully rounded to be natural, the pallor of a Greek temple gleamed, a hotch-potch of Doric, Ionic and Corinthian in flaking plaster. Distant on the other side of the drive the tamed park gave way to a towering wilderness of crags, with the mouth of a cave neatly built in at a high level, no doubt for the hermit without whom no Victorian poetic landscape would be complete. A coil of river showed in angry silver among the folds of greensward, an arched bridge where certainly no bridge had been necessary before the landscape gardeners got busy. Somewhere ahead, on a still higher viewpoint, the jagged outline of a ruined tower posed self-consciously against a sky now darkening to olive-green.

'No pagoda?' said the girl disapprovingly; and suddenly there was the pagoda, prompt to its cue, peeping out of the trees behind the heron-pool. She laughed abruptly and gaily. 'Who in the world built this place? Beckford?'

'It was built by a highly-respected family named Cothercott.' The tone was a reproof, for all its forbearance, and all the chillier because she had surprised him by knowing about Beckford, and had got the period exactly right. Follymead was within ten years or so the same vintage as Fonthill Abbey and Strawberry Hill and all its neo-Gothic fellows; and she hadn't even seen the house yet. 'They had more money than was good for any family, and spent it on building their private world, as so many others were doing. And like most of their kind they dwindled away for want of heirs, and the last of them left Follymead to the county, about twenty years ago. With a very good endowment fund, luckily, or it would have been impossible to use it. As it is, by charging a fairly economic fee for board and tuition, we can contrive to keep out of the red. The place is considered a very fine example of its period,' he said forbiddingly, lest she should be in any doubt where he stood, 'and the grounds are justly famous.'

The girl was as capable of delighting in fantasy as anyone else, but she had not, until then, been disposed to take Follymead seriously. She took a sidelong look at the regular profile beside her, the austere cast of the lips, the smooth-set, humourless eyes; and she saw that Edward Arundale took it very seriously indeed, perhaps not for its own sweet sake, perhaps because it was an appurtenance of himself, and

17

sacred accordingly.

'So they turned it into a residential music college,' she said. 'I shouldn't have thought there'd be enough demand for that sort of thing.'

'There wouldn't be, locally, but from the beginning I've made it my policy to turn the place into a national asset. We draw on the whole country. We've got adequate space for conferences and festivals, as well as providing our own courses and recitals. It's taken a few years to establish us properly, but I think I can say we've achieved national recognition now. International, even.'

His voice had taken on the smoothness and richness of an occasion; she felt herself acting as audience to a lecture, and remembered the time-table:

5.0 p.m. to 5.30 p.m.   Students assemble. Tea will be available on arrival.

5.30 p.m.   Conducted tour of the house, optional.

6.45 p.m.   Assemble for dinner. The warden, Dr Edward Arundale, M.A., F.R.C.M., will welcome artists and students to Follymead.

She wondered if it was always the same address of welcome, suitably modulated, or if he ever made allowances for the sceptics, and admitted to the possibility that this kingdom he inhabited was a monstrosity. And yet, was it? She found herself almost tempted to enjoy a fantasy so uninhibited, as somebody had enjoyed creating it. Not reverently, like the warden, but exuberantly, with all the abounding energy and ingenuity of the eighteenth century, no holds barred. And who cared what a plethora of turrets might be jangling overhead, as long as the acoustics in the music rooms were right?

'It was particularly suitable to use it for music,' said Arundale, unbending a little. 'It so happens the Cothercotts were a musical family, and they left us a very fine collection of instruments with the house. We had to restore the organ, but the other early keyboard instruments are splendid.'

Clearly this *was* his field; he still sounded like a lecturer, and perhaps he always would, but at least there was the warm flush of enthusiasm in his voice now. But he didn't enlarge; she was merely one of the folk-singing clan, he could hardly expect her to be interested in the Cothercott virginals and the perfect little table spinet by Holyoake. And in any case, the car was just rounding the final, planned curve of the long drive, and the house would be waiting to take the stranger's breath away, as it had been

19

designed to do.

Here came the curve. The bushes shrank away on either side, the great, straight, levelled apron of lawn expanded before them, and the house, nicely elevated on its three tiers of terraces, soared into the dusk and impaled the sky with a dozen towers and turrets and steeples and vanes, tapering from steep gables above row upon row of mullioned windows silvered over with the faint afterglow, as calculated and stunning as some monstrous stage-set at curtain-rise. There were tall, glazed oriels, rounded rose-windows, tight, thin arrow-slits; there were battlements, and pediments and conical roofs, and galleries, and even gargoyles leaning darkly from the corners of the towers. It was so outrageous as to be almost beautiful, so phoney that it had its own kind of genuineness. For one thing, it hadn't happened by mistake, or through sheer over-enthusiasm. The effect it produced was the effect it had been made to produce, and no chance horror. And it had been built well, from a lovely light-grey stone, and with a certain assured symmetry. There had been a mind behind its creation, as well as money, and an individual, cool and sinister mind at that. The owner or the architect?

The girl sat silent, staring in fascination and

disbelief, tensed in resistance, as the car approached along the pale ribbon of tarmac between the planed acres of grass, and the pile of Follymead grew taller and darker and vaster with every yard.

'Impressive, isn't it?' said Arundale, aware that she hated being impressed by mere stone, mortar and glass; he could feel how furiously she was bracing herself against it. 'Walpole stayed here several times. He described it as a house where drama was a permanent upper servant, eccentricity a member of the family, and tragedy an occasional guest.'

'And comedy?' said the girl unexpectedly. 'They named it Follymead, not Nightmare Abbey. Maybe it took them by surprise, too, when they saw it finished.'

He drew the car round to the foot of the sweep of stone steps that led to the terrace. Lights winked on, one by one, along the great glazed gallery on the first floor, running the whole length of the house-front. Through the windows they saw a gaggle of people passing slowly, peering round them with stretched necks; earnest elderly ladies, bearded, shaggy young men with pipes, ascetic students in glasses, broad-barrelled country gentlemen with time on their hands and a mild musical curiosity, eager girls peering through their

21

curtains of limp long hair.

'They're just taking parties round on a tour of the house,' said Arundale, opening the door for his passenger. 'Leave your luggage, I'll bring it in when I've run the car round to the yard. You just trot in and join them. Formalities later.'

She reached in again for her guitar, all the same, and straightened up to look at the lighted windows above them. The party passing had halted for a moment, all their faces turned up to some painting hung very high on the inner wall. Only their guide faced the windows as she went through her recital; a very young girl, surely no more than fifteen or sixteen, slight and pale, with wings of mouse-brown hair framing a serious and secretive face, a face full of doubts and hesitations and flashes of uneasy animation, as early-April as the weather outside, and her own difficult season. Something in the fine, irresolute features, the set of the eyes and carriage of the head, made the newcomer turn and look again at Arundale; and she was not mistaken, the likeness was there, allowing for the years and the toughening and the entrenchment, though maybe he'd never possessed the possibilities of passion which the girl in the gallery certainly had, and didn't know yet what to do with.

'That must be your daughter, surely?'

His face stiffened very slightly, though he gazed back at her with polite composure. 'My niece. Unfortunately my wife... We have no children.' He snapped off the sentence briskly, like a thread at the end of a seam. A sore subject, she was sorry she'd embarked on it, however innocently. She was just wondering how to ride the punch, and whether his voice was always so constrained when he spoke of his wife, when he turned his head to look along the necklace of lighted windows, as willing to evade complications as she, and said in a very different tone: 'Ah, there is my wife now, with the next party.'

She had thought him without passion, but evidently he had one. This was quite another voice, warm and proud and soft, heavy with unguarded affection. No, his wife's childlessness was only a shared sorrow, not at all a count against her, or a shadow between them. The girl looked up, following his devoted, secret smile, and saw a woman caught for a moment under the full brilliance of one of the chandeliers. She was slender and fair and elegant in a plain dark dress, with pale hair piled on her head, and a swimming, wavering walk that seemed to balance the silvery coils like a conscious burden. Her eyes were dark and large,

23

her colouring richly fair, her face bright and animated almost to the point of discomfort. She talked and gestured and passed, and the medley of students and guests passed after her, consolingly ordinary, unhaunted and content.

The girl stood fixed, watching her go without a smile, and for some moments without a word. When the pageant had passed she stirred, and moistened her lips.

'She's beautiful,' she said at last, with deliberation.

This time she had said the right thing. She felt the evening filled with the glow of his pleasure.

'Some excellent judges have thought so,' he admitted, a little pompously, more than a little proprietorially.

'I have a feeling that I've seen her somewhere before,' said the girl in a cool, distant voice.

'It's quite possible. You're a ballad-singer. Audrey has some close friends in folk-music circles.'

The girl with the guitar-case suppressed a faint and private smile. 'Yes...yes, I'm sure she has,' she said gently, and turned from him and ran up the stone steps towards the great doorway.

Miss Theodosia Barber, Tossa to her friends,

was an implacable hater of all humbug, and a merciless judge of all those who seemed to her tainted with its unmistakable sweet, self-conscious odour. At rising nineteen she could afford to be, her own proceedings being marked by a total rejection of falsity. She had weighed up the celebrated Dickie Meurice, disc-jockey, compère and television personality extraordinary, before they had even reached the armoury and his third questionable joke. Give him an audience of twenty or so, even if they were by rights young Felicity Cope's audience, and he'd have filched them from under her nose within minutes, and be on-stage. Doubtful, rather, if he was ever off.

'Licensed clown,' said Tossa fastidiously into Dominic Felse's ear, as they followed the adoring giggles of the fans into the long gallery. 'All *he* ever goes *anywhere* for is to advertise the product. I bet he cracks wise in his sleep, and has a built-in gadget to record the level of applause. What's more, he won't stop at much in the cause. Watch out, anybody in the business here who has a reputation to lose.'

'Could be several people in danger, then,' said Dominic critically, eyeing the group that surged amorphously before them, and seeing celebrities enough. And this was only one party of three perambulating the house on this conducted tour. Over by the window shone the cropped red heads of the Rossignol brothers; less vulnerable, perhaps, by virtue of being French, identical twins, and tough as rubber, not to say capable of considerable mischief themselves if they felt like it, but all the same this folk-music business was an international free-for-all, these days, and no one could count himself immune. The new young American, Peter Crewe, stood close to his guide, earnestly following everything she had to say, and turning his bright, weathered face faithfully from portrait to portrait, staring so solemnly that if there was anything to be discovered about the Cothercotts from those calculated approximations, he would surely discover it. Malice might well bounce off such innocence as his, but it might also take a strip of hide with it at every rebound. There was Celia Whitwood, the harp girl—the second witticism this evening had been at her expense, and she hadn't relished it. And yet this licensed clown, as Tossa called him, could draw the fans after him with a crook of his finger, and have them hanging on his lips ready to laugh before he spoke. An extraordinary force is television for building or destroying public figures, without benefit of talent, desert or quality.

'I wonder who was the genius who thought

we needed a compère for this week-end?' said Tossa, sighing.

'Somebody shrewd enough to know how to fill the house,' said Dominic simply. 'He fetched the fans in, didn't he?'

And he had, there was no doubt of that; but not only he, as Tossa promptly pointed out.

'You think all those kids fawning round Lucien Galt came for the music?'

'*I* wouldn't know, would I?' responded Dominic crisply. 'Did *you?*' The slight edge to his voice, and the faint knife-prick of disquiet that went with it, startled him. He was accustomed to immensely secure relationships in which jealousy would have been an irrelevant absurdity, and the indignities a lover can inflict on himself came as a surprise to him, and an affront. As for Tossa, she wasn't yet used to the idea that someone could be in love with her, and she wasn't alert to possible pitfalls; she missed the smarting note and took the question at its face value.

'Idiot!' she said cheerfully. 'Are you lumping me in with that lot? Not that I can't see their point,' she added honestly, studying the lofty male head islanded among hunting girls. 'At least he looks and sounds like a real person. Take his microphone away, and he's still *there.*'

27

Lucien Galt certainly could not easily be ignored, even thus hemmed in at close quarters by his unkempt admirers. The black head tossed impatiently, the lean, relaxed shoulders twitched, like a stallion shaking off gadflies, and for a moment his face was turned towards the two who discussed him. Dark as a gypsy, with heavy brows and arrogant eyes, built like a dancer, light-framed and quick in movement, intolerant of too close approach, and scornful of adulation as of any other stupidity, he carried his nature in his looks, and took no trouble to moderate its impact. He slid from between the ranks of his fans and put the width of an inlaid table between himself and them, leaning with folded arms and braced shoulders against the damask-pannelled wall. He had put Felicity off her stride by the abrupt movement; he caught her eye, and apologised with a brilliant, brief smile that transformed his saturnine face for an instant. And that was the only move he had made to charm, and no more to him than a brusque gesture of politeness.

He was twenty-three years old, and already an artist on a world scale. In what other field can you climb the peak so fast? Or so suddenly slither all the way down it again and vanish? Or, once vanished, be so completely forgotten?

'You couldn't say he went out of his way to

please, could you?' whispered Tossa. 'He as good as tells them they're a bore and a nuisance, and they lap it up and come back for more. And just look at the other one, working at it every minute, ladling out the honey like mad. He must just *hate* Lucien.'

Considering she had never set eyes on either of the pair before, it was a fairly penetrating observation; but all Dominic noticed at the time was the easy way the name Lucien came to her tongue. The popular music world deals in Christian names, of course, and there's no particular significance in it; still, he noted it, and was annoyed with himself for the resulting smart. Ever since he'd brought his girl home from Oxford with him for the Easter vacation, to meet his parents for the first time, he'd been discovering in himself nervous sensitivities he'd never suspected before, like broken nails forever ready to snag in the fine threads of this most difficult of all relationships. It wasn't doing his vanity any good.

'Theirs is a cut-throat world,' he said sententiously. 'Still, he looks as if he can stand it.'

'Oh, I should think he's pretty tough,' she agreed serenely.

'With a name like that,' said Dominic, involuntarily rubbing the sting, 'he'd have to be.' Who knew better than he did the hard training to be derived in early school days from having an unusual and provocative name? As if being a policeman's son wasn't enough in itself to keep a boy on his toes!

'From what I read somewhere, he was brought up in an orphanage, right from a baby. His parents were killed in the buzz-bomb raids on London at the end of the last war. They say he thinks the world of his home, though, and goes back there regularly. Not at all a deprived child type. And yet you never know.' said Tossa thoughtfully, 'maybe that does account for the way they say he is.'

'*I* haven't been reading him up,' said Dominic patiently. 'How *do* they say he is?'

'Oh, like he looks. You-be-damned! Terribly independent, won't compromise, won't pretend, a real stormy petrel. The way I heard it, his agent and the recording people, and all the ones who have to work with him took to calling him Lucifer instead of Lucien.'

Lucifer leaned with folded arms against the wine-coloured damask panelling of the long gallery, under the carved black ceiling and the Venetian chandeliers. Rankly dramatised Cothercott portraits hung cloaked and hooded about him, the expensive, perilous and eclectic accumulations of generations of Cothercott collectors were elegantly displayed along

30

the walls at his back, their often lovely and sometimes repulsive furniture fended off teenage girls from too close contact with him. The dark, rich, Strawberry Hill colours, the heavy gilding, the assured and lavish use of black, all framed him like one of the family pictures. He looked at home here, and in his element, a little sinister, a little dangerous, treacherously winning, like the house itself.

'Now you can't,' Dickie Meurice was saying persuasively, his incandescent smile trained at full-tooth-power on the warden's niece, 'you really *can't* ask us to believe that all these characters were models of industry and virtue. Just take a look at 'em!' He waved a hand towards the family portraits deployed along the wall, and indeed half of them did look like romantic poets and half like conspirators. Even the ladies appeared somewhat overdressed in conscious merit, as though they had something to hide. 'Every one of 'em straight out of the wanted file. There ought to be profiles alongside. Don't tell me they got the fortune that built this pile out of honest trade.'

'Ah, but I think that's just what they did,' said Felicity with animation, 'and just what they didn't want you to believe about them. They much preferred to put up on their walls something that looked like degenerate aristo-

31

crats who'd never done a day's work in their lives.'

She had abandoned her usual recital already, derailed by Meurice's facetious comments, and begun to indulge her own suppressed feelings about this formidable place; but it wasn't at Meurice she was looking, and it wasn't for him she was lighting up like a pale, flickering candle, her serious grey eyes warming into brilliance. She gazed wide-eyed at Lucifer, leaning there against the wall with his dark brightness dulling the painted faces on either side of his head, and her small, grave face reflected his slight, sardonic smile like a mirror. She was the teen-age fan with a temporary and precarious advantage, and she was using it for all she was worth, bent on catching and holding his attention now or never, and reckless as to how pathetically she showed off in the attempt. She had begun this tour, as on all the other similar occasions, very poised, very grown-up, a world-weary sophisticate aged fifteen and a half, but the first time he had looked at her the shell had begun to melt, and let in upon her all the hurts and all the promises of the untasted world of maturity, and from the time that he had smiled at her she had thrown away everything else and bent herself to make an impression. Once for all, and now or never.

She hated being fifteen, but she wouldn't always be fifteen. She looked rather more, she hoped, even now. And he was only twenty-three himself. She knew all about him, he'd been written up lavishly since he became famous, and she hadn't missed a single article about him if she could help it.

'Take this one—William Henry Cothercott the third. He looks like Byron turned bandit, I know, but he hadn't a line of poetry or an act of violence in him. He made a pile out of the early railway boom, and he had some ships that weren't too particular whether they carried slaves or not, when other cargoes didn't offer, but that's the worst we know about him. They even started collecting more curious things than harpsichords, just to give the impression they were a lot of romantic damned souls. There are some very naughty books you won't get shown, but I doubt if they ever really read them. And all these rapiers and knives and things, here along the wall—those are part of the effect, too, just theatrical props. That fan—you wouldn't know it had a dagger in it, would you? And this silver-headed walking-cane—look! The head pulls out, like this...' She showed them, in one rapid, guilty gesture, six inches of the slender blade that was hidden inside the ebony sheath, and slid it hurriedly back again. 'Straight out of "The Romantic Agony",' she said, purely for Lucien's benefit, to show him how well-read she was, and how adult. 'Only it doesn't mean a thing, they were still nothing but stolid merchants. Not a mohawk among the lot of 'em. They never stuck so much as a pig.'

'And yet somebody put the devil in this house,' said Lucien with detached certainty.

'Maybe somebody here among us,' suggested Dickie Meurice, turning the famous smile on him, 'brought that aura in with him.'

Lucien turned his head and looked him over again at leisure, without any apparent reaction. He knew who he was, of course. Who didn't? He had even worked with him on two occasions. It couldn't be said that he had ever really noticed him until now, and even now he wasn't particularly interested. In such a narrow gallery, however, you can't help noticing someone who is so full of quicksilver movement without meaning, and makes so much noise saying nothing. Lucien, when not singing, was a dauntingly silent person, and spoke only to the point.

'I doubt it,' he said indifferently. 'This is built-in. More likely to have been the architect. What was he like? Who *was* he? Do they know?'

34

'His name was Falchion. Nobody knows much about him, there are only two other houses known to be his work. We think he must have died young. There's a story,' said Felicity, recklessly improvising, and looking even more passionately truthful and candid than usual, 'that he was in love with one of the Cothercott daughters. *That* one...' She pointed out, with deceptive conviction, the best-looking of the collection, confident that no one would notice that she belonged to a later generation. 'She died about the time the house was finished, and he was broken-hearted. They used to meet in this gallery while he was working on the features in the grounds, and she's supposed to haunt here.'

She had Lucien's attention, and she didn't care whether he knew she was lying or whether he believed her. Maybe it would be even more interesting to be seen to be lying. In many ways this whole set-up was a lie, even though Uncle Edward was a genuine scholar and a genuine musician, devoted and content with his sphere. In a sense, only what was utterly and joyously false had any right to exist in this setting, phantasms were the only appropriate realities in this shameless fantasy.

'She comes in daylight, not at night,' said Felicity, loosing the rein of her imagination, but holding fast to Lucien Galt's black and moody stare. 'She comes to meet him, and she doesn't know she's dead, and she can't understand why he never comes. She's still in love with him, but she's angry, too, and she's only waiting to meet him again and take it out of him for leaving her deserted so long...'

'She's making it up as she goes along,' said Tossa very softly in Dominic's ear. 'What a gorgeous little liar!'

'It's this place,' Dominic whispered back. 'It would get anybody.'

'Has anyone actually seen her?' asked Peter Crewe, round-eyed.

'Oh, yes, occasionally, but it only happens to people in love.' Felicity turned, and began to pace slowly and delicately towards the great oak door at the end of the gallery; and they all caught the infection and walked solemnly after her, their steps soundless in the deep carpet. 'You may be walking along here some day, just like this, going to put fresh flowers in that stone vase there on the pedestal. Not thinking about anything like ghosts. With the sun shining in, even, though it could be just at dusk, like this. And you're just approaching this door when it suddenly opens, and there she is, confronting you...'

And suddenly the oak door opened, flung

wide by a hand not accustomed to doing things by halves, and there she was confronting them indeed, with head up and eyes challenging, a tall, brown, imperious girl with a great plait of dark hair coiled like an attendant serpent over one shoulder, and a guitar-case in her hand.

Felicity rocked back on her heels, startled into a sharp and childish giggle of embarrassment. The procession at her back halted abruptly, with a succession of soft, clumsy collisions, like a Bank-Holiday queue of ambling cars suddenly forced to brake sharply. It would all have been a little ridiculous, but for the composure with which the newcomer marched into the gallery and looked them over, undisturbed and unimpressed. Her glance passed over the whole group in one sweep, riding over their heads and rejecting all but the tallest. She found Lucien, alert, dark and still against the wall. There she fixed, and looked no farther.

Tossa, watching from the fringe of the group, literally saw the flash and felt the shock as their eyes locked, and her fingers reached for Dominic's sleeve. The tension between those two set everyone quivering, even those who were too insensitive to understand why. And yet they could hardly have maintained a more stony assurance, calmer faces or stiller bodies.

Only for the briefest instant had the daggers shown in two pairs of eyes now veiled, and cool. The girl's face wore a newcomer's polite, perfunctory smile, she was looking clean through Lucien and failing to see him, she had excised him from her field of vision. But the pressure of Tossa's fingers, alert and excited, directed attention rather to Lucien himself. So far from crossing the stranger out of his notice, he was staring at her frankly and directly, trying to see deep into her and read some significance into what he saw; but if he was getting much information out of that closed and aloof face, thought Tossa, he must be clairvoyant. The glint in his eyes might have been alarm, or animosity or, curiously, elation. He might, for that matter, be the kind of person who would find a certain elation in the promise of a stand-up fight.

The instant of surprise and silence was gone almost before they had recorded it. The girl with the guitar turned to Felicity, and was opening her lips to speak when the high, self-confident voice of Dickie Meurice gave tongue smoothly and joyously:

'Well, well, well! Just look who's here!' And he danced forward with arms outspread, took the girl's hands in his, guitar and all, and pumped and pressed them enthusiastically. Her

38

dark brows rose slightly, but she tolerated the liberty without protest.

'Hullo, Dickie, I didn't know you were going to be here.'

'I didn't know *you* were. For goodness sake, why didn't they have your name on the prospectus?'

'They didn't know I was coming, and I'm not here to perform. I came as a student, like anybody else.'

'Come off it!' said Meurice, laughing, and tapped the guitar-case. 'You think you're the sort of girl who can take her harp to a party without anybody asking her to play? Not while I'm around!' He laid an arm familiarly about her shoulders, and turned her to face the company. 'Don't you know who we've got here? Just about the greatest ballad-singer this side of the Atlantic, that's who. Ladies and gentlemen, I'm proud to present to you none other than the great Liri Palmer.'

CHAPTER 2

Edward Arundale made his speech of welcome in the small drawing-room before dinner, against the sombre splendour of black, white and heavy gilt décor that might have been specially designed to render him more impressive. He expressed his pleasure at having so intelligent and enthusiastic a company beneath the roof of his college, outlined the origin and history of the Follymead foundation, wished them a very pleasant and productive week-end, and deeply regretted that he himself wouldn't be able to enjoy the whole of it with them, since tomorrow afternoon he had to leave to fulfil two speaking engagements in Birmingham, and would not be back until Sunday evening. After this evening, therefore, he would be handing over direction of the course to his deputy, Henry Marshall,—Mr Marshall, who was young, anxious and only too well aware of being on trial, smiled nervously—and Professor Roderick Penrose, whose name and reputation were certainly known to everyone interested in folk-music. Mr Arundale wouldn't

40

claim that folk-music was the professor's subject; he would prefer to describe it as his passion and if he held some unusual and controversial opinions on it, the discussion during the week-end would be all the livelier.

Professor Penrose, who was seventy-five, bursting with energy, and just beginning to take full advantage of the privileges of age, notably its irresponsibility and licence, grinned happily, fluffed up his clown's-tufts of grey hair with eager fingers, and licked his lips in anticipation. He couldn't wait to get his carnivorous teeth into all the sacred cows of the cult.

Then they trooped in to dinner in the neo-Gothic vaulted hall, still hung with Cothercott tapestries and lit by great torches (electric now) jutting from the gold and scarlet walls. Audrey Arundale, dazzlingly fair in her plain black dress, sat beside her husband, looked beautiful, kept a careful watch on the conversation, and said and did all the right things at all the right moments. That is what the wives of the Edward Arundales are for, though they may also, incidentally, be loved helplessly and utterly, as Audrey was loved.

She was fifteen years his junior, and looked even younger. He had never grown tired of looking at her, never lost the power to feel again

41

the knife-thrust of astonishment, anguish and delight that possession of her beauty gave him. He still hated to leave her even for a day.

'I wish you were coming with me,' he said impulsively in her ear. The young people were getting into their stride, you could gauge the potential success of a course by the crescendo of noise at their first meal together. He smiled at her quickly and reassuringly. 'No, I know you can't, of course. I wouldn't take you away from this, I know how much you're going to enjoy it.'

'It's just that I really began it,' she said apologetically. Her voice had something of the quality of her eyes, hesitant and faintly anxious, as though even after twenty years of backing him up loyally, first as the revered head of Bannerets and now here, she was still in doubt of her own powers, and still constantly braced to please. 'I've really got to see it through, after getting Professor Penrose and all those others into it, haven't I?'

'Of course, my dear, I know. But I shall miss you. Never mind,' he said, letting his hand rest for a moment on hers, 'let's enjoy this first concert together, anyhow. It looks as if you're going to have a success on your hands, by all the signs.'

The noise by then was almost deafening but

there were those who observed that Lucien Galt wasn't contributing much to it, and neither was Liri Palmer.

'Tomorrow,' said Professor Penrose, rubbing his hands, 'will be time enough to begin haggling about all the usual questions, such as definition and standards, what's permissible and what isn't, who has it right and who has it wrong. Tonight we're going to enjoy ourselves. We have here with us a number of recognised artists in the field, whose judgement of their material *ought* to command respect. Let's ask them, not to tell us, but to show us. We'll get them to sing their favourites, songs they take as beyond question or reproach. And then we'll examine the results together, and see what we find.'

'Now you got me scared,' said Peter Crewe plaintively, and got a mild laugh from under Dickie Meurice's nose; but his time was coming.

'Mr Crew, you are probably the safest person around here. We shall see! Don't let me cast any shadows. I'm retiring into the audience as of now.' The professor, a born chameleon, was taking on colouring from his American artist without even realising it. 'Here and now I hand over this session to an expert

43

at putting people through hoops. Mr Meurice, take over.'

Mr Meurice rose like a trout to a fly, and took over gleefully. The professor retired to a quiet corner beside the warden and his wife, and sat on the small of his back, legs crossed, looking at his specimens between his skidding glasses and his shaggy brows, and grinning wolfishly.

'There's really no need of any introductions at all tonight,' said Dickie Meurice, beaming. 'If you people down there didn't know all about all these people up here, you wouldn't be here at all. All they need me for is to name them in order, and you could tell me everything I could tell you about them. Maybe more! I dare say there's something even I could learn, this weekend. So let's not waste time listening to me, but get on to the music. Ladies first! Celia, will you lead the way? You all know Celia Whitwood, the girl with the harp. It makes a change from guitars, doesn't it?'

It got a ripple of delight from his fans, but it was a very gentle joke for Dickie Meurice. 'I thought he'd be cruder.' Tossa confided in a whisper.

'He probably will,' returned Dominic as softly, 'before he's done. Just feeling his way. He's no fool. This needs a different approach from a disc-jockey session.'

Celia Whitwood settled her instrument comfortably, and sang 'Two Fond Hearts' and 'By the Sea-Shore,' both in Welsh, translating the words for those who did not know them. She had a small, shy voice, and at first was uncertain of the acoustics in the great yellow drawing-room, but by the end of the first song she had the feel of the space about her, and was using it confidently. She followed with 'The Jute—Mill Song,' and made her harp do the mill noises for her. Peter Crewe sang 'Times are Getting Hard,' 'I'm Going Away' and 'The Streets of Laredo'; Andrew Callum contributed two Tyne-side colliery songs and 'The Bonny Earl of Moray' from across the border. And Dickie Meurice continued bland, bright and considerate, as though his judgement, too, was on trial.

'*All* playing safe,' remarked Tossa disapprovingly.

The Rossignol twins began with a ballad-like thriller, grim and dramatic, 'Le Roi a fait battre tambour.' They were twenty, flame-headed, of rather girlish prettiness but more than male toughness and impudence, and decidedly disturbing to watch, for one of them was left-handed, and one right, and they amused themselves by trading on this mirror-image appearance to such an extent that it had now become second nature. They followed with a lullaby in a dialect so thick it was plain they felt sure not even Professor Penrose would understand a word of it. 'Quarrel with that!' said their innocent smiles. Then they consulted each other by means of two flicks of the eyebrows, cast a wicked glance at the professor, and broke into the honeyed, courtly melody of the fifteenth-century 'L'Amour de Moi.' They sang it like angels, with melting harmonies as gracious as the flowers they sang about. The professor nodded his ancient head and continued to smile.

'Well, they trailed their coats, anyhow,' said Dominic.

Lucien Galt began with 'Helen of Kirkconnell.' There was no doubt from the opening that here was an artist of stature, first because nature had given him a voice of great beauty, a warm, flexible baritone that would have been attractive even without art, and second, because he had the rare gift of total absorption in what he did, so that he lost them utterly while the song lasted. He *was* the bereaved lover hunting Helen's murderer along the water-side, and hacking him in pieces for her sake. The voice that had beeen all honey and grief over her body could find gravel and hate when it needed them. He was all the more compelling because everything he did was understated, but the passion vibrated behind the quietness with an intensity that had them holding their breath. He seemed surprised when they applauded him; probably for the duration of that experience he had forgotten they were there.

Next he sang 'The Croppy Boy,' a venturesome choice for somebody without a drop of Irish blood; nor did he attempt to put on the Irish. He sang it like an Englishman possessed by the guilt of England past, and with an unexpected simplicity that made the child-soldier's last innocent confession almost unendurably touching:

' "I've cursed three times since last Easter Day,
At Mass-time once I went to play,
I passed through the churchyard one day in haste
And forgot to pray for my mother's rest".'

By the time he reached:

' "Good people who dwell in peace and joy,
Breathe a prayer and a tear for the Croppy boy",'

he had several of the teenage girls in tears.

That startled him, too, but he was disarmed. It was the first time Tossa and Dominic had seen him look kindly at his fans.

'And what's the third one to be?' asked Meurice amiably.

Lucien thought for a moment, his lip caught between his teeth, his fingers muting the strings of his guitar. He looked across at the rows and rows of expectant students, and Dominic, turning his head to follow that glance, caught a glimpse of Liri Palmer's chiselled profile and great coil of brown hair. She sat at the back of the assembly, attentive and still. There was no reading anything in her face.

Lucien began to sing. They all knew the air as "Believe me if all those endearing young charms," but that was not what he was singing.

' "My lodging is on the cold, cold ground,
And hard, very hard is my fare,
But what doth me the more confound
Is the coldness of my dear.
Yet still I cry, O turn, love,
I prithee, love, turn to me,
For thou art the only one, love,
That art adored by me.
I'll twine thee a garland of straw, love,
I'll marry thee with a rush ring,
My frozen hopes will thaw, love,

And merrily we will sing.
Then turn to me, my own love,
I prithee, love, turn to me,
For thou art the only one, love,
That art adored by me'','

'That ought to fetch her,' whispered Tossa,
shaken, 'if anything can.'

Dominic was astonished. He hadn't noticed
this incalculable girl of his following any significant glances, and yet it seemed she knew very
well what was going on. He wished he did.
There was certainly something, and there was
a tension in the air that threatened more; yet
nobody else seemed to have noticed anything.
Maybe all the girls took that declaration to
themselves, and applauded it accordingly; and
it was just possible—wasn't it?—that that applied to Tossa, too.

'Now hold your horses a minute,' beamed
Dickie Meurice, fanning down the applause.
'We haven't finished yet. Oh, yes, I know
that's all we promised you, but we've still got
a card up our sleeve, you'll find. Some of you
know it already, but to most of you it'll be great
news. Do you know who's been modest enough
to come along to this course as a student? She's
right there among you at this moment, maybe
some of you talked to her at dinner and never

realised. Liri...Liri Palmer! It's no use trying to hide back there. I know where you are.' She hadn't moved, not even a muscle on her disdainful face. She didn't want to be haled out of her anonymity, but she certainly wasn't hiding even from the crack of doom.

'Yes, folks, that's the whole secret. Liri Palmer is here among us. There she sits! Now you give her a big hand, and maybe she'll surrender.'

He was growing by the minute, expanding to fill the twenty-one inch screen that wasn't there, to dominate the cameras, the emotions and the events of this evening. This was what he'd been waiting for.

'Come along, Liri, don't cheat us. You can't blame us for wanting you. Come up here where you belong, and let us hear from you.'

Every head had turned by this time, even the slowest of them had located her, even those who knew nothing about her had identified her by the glutinous stares of the others. Someone began to applaud, and all the rest took it up like a rising wave.

'Come on, Liri, we're all waiting just for you.'

She rose from her chair, but only to gain a hearing. 'I came to listen, you must excuse me. And I haven't got my guitar down here.'

50

'Lucien will lend you his guitar, I'm sure. Come on, you can't disappoint everyone. Lucien, don't just sit there, help me out. If *you* ask her, I'm sure she'll come.'

Lucien Galt was seen for once out of countenance, and that in itself was astonishing. He sat shaken and mute, staring across the array of hopeful faces to where Liri stood braced and annoyed, her brows drawn down in a formidable scowl. It was Lucien who flushed and stammered.

'Yes, Liri, please do. You'd be giving everyone so much pleasure.'

There could have been no milder invitation, but what happened next was more like the formal acceptance of a challenge.

'Very well,' said Liri abruptly, 'since *you* ask me.'

And she walked fiercely up the gangway between the goggling fans, and stepped up on to the concert dais in the great window-embrasure, where the artists sat. She took the offered guitar, sat down on the forward edge of Dickie Meurice's table, and stroked the strings, frowning. There was a moment of absolute silence, while she seemed to forget they existed, and only to be gathering herself for a private outburst. Then the whole drawing-room shook to the shuddering chords she fetched out of Lucien's instrument, and she lifted her head and poised her silver-pure entry with piercing accuracy, like a knife in the heart:

' "Black, black, black, is the colour of my true-
    love's *heart!*
His tongue is like a poisoned dart,
The coldest eyes and the lewdest hands...
I hate the ground whereon he stands!

' "I hate my love, yet well he knows,
I love the ground whereon he goes,
And if my love no more I see
No one shall have his company!

' "Black, black, black, is the colour of my true-
    love's *heart...*" '

An achingly sweet voice, so rending in its sweetness as to corrode like an acid when she used it like this, as if all the frightening possibilities of her nature, for good or evil, could be molten in the furnace of her feeling, and pour out in that fine-spun thread of sound and purify or poison. She sang with such superb assurance that they all accepted it as the only rightness, only realising afterwards how she had changed words to her own purposes, and torn the heart out of the song to leave it the antithesis of what it was meant to be. As if she turned the coin of love to show hate engraven in an almost identical design.

The silence was unnerving, but it did not unnerve her. She stood up, and the applause began, noisily and violently, with almost guilty fervour, to cover the pause which should not have been there. She laid down the guitar on the table.

'It doesn't sing properly for me. I'll use my own tomorrow, if you don't mind.' There was an empty chair behind the semi-circle of artists; she slid by them and took it, abdicating from public notice before they had stopped approving her, and giving them no acknowledgement.

The incident was over before half of those present fully grasped that there had been an incident. But with the end of the applause the numbness wore off, and the shock reached them all.

In the front row old Miss Southern, as innocent at seventy as she had been at seventeen, leaned anxiously to her neighbour. She had come to this course in the hope of hearing again 'Early one morning,' 'The Oak and the Ash,' 'Barbara Allen,' and all the songs she had been taught at school—sometimes in bowdlerised versions!—and nobody could put anything over on her where the canon was concerned.

'But she got it wrong,' she whispered. 'It's *hair*. 'Black is the colour of my true-love's *hair.*' Do you think we ought to tell her?'

'*No!*' hissed her neighbour, appalled. 'For heavens' sake!'

'But perhaps she got it from one of these degraded variants, you know. I learned it at school. It's *'hair,'* not *'heart.'* Shouldn't we...?'

Half the front row had heard this last agitated utterance. Professor Penrose came up off the small of his back with the agility of an ageing monkey, but without any appearance of haste or concern, and demonstrated his right to be in charge. His old voice had all the power and command it needed, and he, at seventy-five, was not innocent at all.

'Well, I'll admit I did issue a sort of challenge,' he said, scowling amiably round the half-circle of tense and quiet singers, 'to our young friends here, and they certainly took it up. We'll go into details tomorrow morning. All I'll say now is that we've just had a very ingenious demonstration of one of the essentials of folk-song, and that is its ability to change and renew itself. Folk-music is organic. It adapts itself to answer the needs of expression of those whose natural music it is. Once

54

it becomes static it has begun to die. One of its chief functions is to be the voice of the otherwise inarticulate, and don't you forget it. As for you,' he said severely, wagging a finger at the Rossignol twins, who gazed back at him with benign smiles, 'I'll deal with you tomorrow. Toss a sophisticated little court-pastoral melody at me, would you, and hope for me to fall over my own feet telling you it isn't a folk-song! Of course it's a folk-song! The people took what they wanted where they found it, as well as creating it for themselves, but don't doubt it became truly theirs. From the court, was it? So was the *carmognole!* So was the *Ca ira!* Go collecting in the more rural parts of Bohemia, and you'll find themes of Mozart sung to folk poems, and if you go back far enough you'll find they were genuine folk-songs almost before Mozart was dead, and those who heard them carried from the distant towns and took them for their own use never knew or cared what seed they were cultivating. And don't think you can faze an old hand like me by bouncing off into Auvergnat *patois*, either. I knew that lullaby before you were born.

'All right, let's break off there for tonight, and think over what we've heard. Tomorrow I hope you won't be afraid to disagree with me, there's room here for a lot of different opinions.

55

If you think "My lodging is on the cold ground" can't be a valid folk-song because the words are by John Gay, and have the ring of the theatre rather than the village, you stand up for your views. We probably shan't come to any firm conclusions, but we might uncover some very interesting ideas. As well as hearing some very fine singing and playing. I may say, if they live up to tonight. And now let's all adjourn to the small drawing-room for coffee.'

And they went, swarming out of the great room and along the corridor, so bemused by his persuasive tongue that they were almost convinced nothing fiery and violent had ever passed between those two people now silently following. Just a clever bit of impromptu theatre, to show that folk-music was alive and adaptable to a human situation today, no less than two hundred years ago. All the same, there was something still quivering in the air, electric and disquieting; something that moved the left-handed Rossignol twin to murmur to the right-handed Rossignol twin, as they climbed the staircase:

'Do you know, *mon vieux*, I think perhaps this week-end is going to be not so boring, after all.'

She hadn't reckoned fully with his ruthless ability to rid himself of unwanted company, and had supposed that if she hung back until all was quiet he would be swept into the small drawing-room and the coffee conversation by the crowd of eager fans that swarmed about him, enthusing, flattering and angling for position. But when she came to the turn of the stairs, alone, treading on the fringes of the distant clamour, he reached out from the folds of the velvet curtains and caught her by the arm, pulling her to a stand-still face to face with him.

'Liri, I want to talk to you.'

His voice was taut and very low, his face flushed and dark and convulsed with pride. She tried to wrest her arm out of his grasp, and instinctively gave up the attempt, knowing she could not do it by force and he would not let her go.

'*I* don't want to talk to *you*. Let go my arm.'

'Liri, don't be like this, I tell you I've *got* to talk to you...'

'You did talk to me,' she said through her teeth, 'just now. You talked and I answered, and I've said all I've got to say to you. Now get away from me.'

'I don't believe it! If that's all you've got to say to me, why did you come here at all?'

'Why shouldn't I?' she demanded fiercely.

'I came as a student, like anybody else...'

'That's a lie,' he said bluntly. 'You came because you knew I should be here, you must have, you couldn't have known the course was on at all without knowing I was part of it. You followed me here. Why, if you've got nothing to say to me now you're here?'

'You!' she said, suddenly rigid with quiet fury. 'You think the world goes round you. You think you can play what tricks you like, and no one has the right to kick. You wouldn't know what I have against you, would you? Oh, no! Listen just once more, and then I never want to see you or hear your voice again. I'm finished with you! I don't know you, I don't want to know you, you mean nothing to me, and you never will mean anything again. Now take your hands off me.'

'The devil I will, till you listen to *me*...'

Lucifer blazed, and the answering fires burned up in Liri's eyes. She would have liked to swing her free palm and hit him resoundingly in the face, but in the quietness where they were, and sharp above the still ferocity of their voices, it would have brought the curious running as surely as a pistol-shot. There were other ways. She stooped her head suddenly, and closed her teeth in his wrist.

He never made a sound, but his startled

muscles jerked, and in the instant of surprise when his grip relaxed she tore herself free, eluding the recovering lunge he made after her, and slipped away from him up the staircase.

By one of the coffee-tables in the small drawing-room—they were just getting used to applying the term to an apartment about as large as a tithe-barn—Dickie Meurice had gathered his court about him, and was exerting himself to be at once king and court-jester. He, at least, was having a successful evening. Things were shaping up very nicely. He didn't miss Liri's entry, or fail to hug himself with satisfaction at sight of her high colour and burning eyes; but he let her alone. So far from having anything against her personally, he was just beginning to find her interesting. She might be a tigress, but she had looks and style; she made most of the girls look like mass-produced dolls. There might be a bonus in it for him if he could make certain that her separation from Lucifer was permanent.

Lucien Galt came into the room with his usual long, arrogant step, his head up, his brows drawn together into a forbidding line. He crossed to the coffee-table and helped himself without a word or a look for anyone, and then stood balancing the cup in his hand

and looking round until he found Liri, in a group surrounding Professor Penrose, in the far corner of the room. He watched her frowningly, attentively, without a thought for all the curious, covert glances fixed on him. It was like him not to bother to dissemble for them; the most offensive thing about him was that he made no concessions to his public. In Meurice's catalogue of sins that was blasphemy.

And, damn him, here came the girls, just the same! He could stand there and look through them as though they didn't exist, and they came edging in on him like cats, purring and rubbing themselves against his knees. The Cope kid among the first of them, of course; she'd got it badly. Pale as death, tight as a bowstring, swallowing her deserate shyness in still more desperate bravery.

'Mr Galt, you were wonderful! I know you must be tired of hearing it, but I do mean it, I really do!'

'Fabulous! I mean, that Irish song...I *cried!*'

'I always listen to your broadcasts...I've got *all* your records. But to hear you *live*, that was just out of this world. Mr Meurice, wasn't he *marvellous?*'

Dickie Meurice slid unobtrusively nearer, merging his own adorers into the rival group; that way, there was always a hope of annexing them all, or at least being credited with them all, when Lucifer lost his patience and swooped away, picking his feet fastidiously out of the syrup of their idolatry like a hawk ripping himself loose from birdlime. He was certain to do it, sooner or later.

'He was indeed,' said Dickie sunnily, and smiled into Lucien's frowning stare. 'If anybody got the message tonight, he did!' The bright, hearty, extrovert voice pushed the small, private barb home, and felt it draw blood. 'Nice performance, Lucien, boy, very nice.'

'Yours?' said Lucien laconically. 'Or mine?'

'Now, now! No bitchery between colleagues, old boy.' His blue eyes, wide and hard and merciless as a child's, fixed delightedly on Lucien's lean brown wrist, the one that supported the coffee-cup. The oval of tiny, indented bruises, strung here and there with a bead of blood, marked the smooth skin with an interesting pattern of blue and purple. 'Well, well!' sighed Meurice, shaking his blond head. 'And I was always taught that eating people is wrong!'

Lucien looked down at his own battle-scar, and raised his brows in sheer astonishment. He had felt nothing since she ran from him, and never even looked to see if she'd marked him.

Observing the evidence, and hearing the small, indrawn breaths and the blank, brief silence, he would have hidden his wrist if he could, but it was too late for that. He let it sustain the sudden, avid weight of their curiosity, and looked over it at Dickie Meurice with a cool indifferent face.

'Really? You must have quite a job reconciling that with the tone of your TV programme, I should think. The only time I watched it, it was pure cannibalism.'

The circling girls shrank and gasped. They looked from Lucien's stony composure to Dickie Meurice's fair face, suddenly paling to bluish white, and as abruptly flushing into painful crimson. If there was one point on which he was sensitive, it was his programme. There was no parrying that straight stab with a joke, and the killing stroke didn't come to him.

'Except that some of the meat you were gritting your teeth on was carrion,' said Lucien with detachment, 'so I suppose the term hardly applies.'

He turned at leisure and laid down his cup, wasted a polite moment for any come-back, and hoisted an indifferent shoulder when none came. Without haste he walked away, weaving between the shifting groups of people; and

Felicity Cope turned like a sleep-walker, and followed him.

'I never invited him to be my guest,' said Meurice, collecting himself. 'Maybe that colours the view.' And he offered them his quirky smile and intimate glance, and got a slightly embarrassed murmur of response; but it was too late to repair the damage, and he knew it. He had been discomfited before his loyal and scandalised fans, something no public personality can ever be expected to forgive. Something heroic would be needed to restore his authority.

'Between you and me,' he said, his voice earnest, confidential and sad, 'we have to forgive Lucien almost any crudity just now. God knows I wouldn't want to score off the poor devil while he's all knotted up the way he is over Liri. Don't spread this, of course, but I think it's as well if some of you know the facts. You can help to smooth the way if you understand what's going on.' His tone was all warmth, consideration and kindness; and no one could do it better when the need arose. 'You see,' he said, 'up to a couple of weeks ago Lucien and Liri...'

His voice sank to a solicitous whisper, drawing their heads together round him like swarming bees to their queen. He made an artistic

63

job of it, and sighed at his own cleverness. 'What a situation! And here we are over the week-end, stuck with it! No, don't misunderstand if I let Lucien get away with murder just now. I figure he's got more than enough on his mind, without my turning on him as well, just because he takes his soreness out on me. My shoulders are broad, I can take it.'

They shifted and glowed, worshipping. They murmured that it was really big of him to look at it that way. They promised faithfully that they'd keep his confidence. And within minutes they were dropping off from the edge of his circle to spread the news.

The girl with butterfly glasses peered through the brick-red fringe that came down to the bridge of her nose, and her short-sighted eyes glistened. She had relayed the tale four times already, and it got better every time. Her fellow-missionaries were circulating with equal fervour round the room, avoiding only the august vicinity of Edward and Audrey Arundale, whose position, among this largely under-twenty assembly, remained very much that of the headmaster and his wife, and effectively froze out gossip. The only other islands immune from this industrious dirt-washing were where Lucien Galt moved aloof, abstracted and tense, with Felicity faithful at his elbow, and where Liri Palmer sat withdrawn and alone. Every other soul in the room must be in the secret by now.

'…madly in love,' said the girl breathlessly, 'and then it all blew up in their faces, just two weeks ago. They had a terrible row. *She* broke it off, but *he* was just as mad with her. Well, you can imagine what a fight between those two would be like. So they parted, and they haven't seen each other since, not until today. And now suddenly she turns up here, where *he's* got an engagement for the week-end. Just as if she's following him…'

'How do you know all this?' asked Tossa sceptically.

'Dickie told us. He knows them both well, he's worked with them before. You can be sure it's quite true. If you ask me, she's come to make mischief if she can.'

'She certainly didn't seem to be in any conciliatory mood,' admitted Dominic, 'when she laid off just what she thought of him, tonight.'

'She didn't, did she?' Delighted eyes blinked behind the butterfly glasses and the curtain of hair. 'It's thrilling, really, because when you come to think of it, she actually *threatened* him! She said if she couldn't have him, nobody should. And did you know!—they had some sort of a brush before they came in here. No, honestly, I'm not making it up! She *bit* him!'

'Oh, go on!' said Tossa disbelievingly. 'People don't go round biting each other, not even the folk element.'

'All right, if you don't believe me, take a look at his left wrist. You'll see the marks there, all right.' Her voice sank to a conspiratorial whisper, drunk with the pleasures of anticipation. 'You don't suppose she really came here to try to *kill* him, do you? I mean, she as good as *said...*'

'No,' said Dominic flatly, 'I don't suppose any such thing. One minute you're telling us she gave him the push, and the next that she's carrying a torch for him, and will see him dead before she'll let anybody else have him.'

'Well, they could both be true, couldn't they?' said the girl blithely, and went off to spread the news farther.

'And the devil of it is,' said Tossa, looking after her with a considering frown, 'that she could very well be right. They're getting good value for their tuition fees this time, aren't they?'

'Now don't you start!' protested Dominic. 'Don't forget this has all come from Dickie Meurice, and you said yourself he must hate Lucien, so what's odd about his drumming up

66

all the trouble he can for him? But it's just a load of personal spite. It won't come to anything.'

The Arundales, dutifully circulating among their guests, were approaching this quiet corner by easy stages, the image of a successful, efficient, socially accomplished college head and his eminently suitable and satisfactory wife. 'Now I ask you,' said Dominic, low-voiced, 'how on earth could melodrama muscle in on any party of theirs? It would never get past the secretary's office.'

Half an hour later he was not quite so certain.

The party broke up early. The warden had no way of ensuring that his houseful of young people would stay in their four-bedded rooms, even when he had got them there, but he could at least set a good example, and hope that they would take the hint and follow it. Felicity had already been detached unwillingly from Lucien Galt's side and edged away to bed. A few of the other people had drifted off to their rooms, and more were on their way, pausing to nose along the library shelves for bedside books. The Arundales completed their tour of all the groups left in the drawing-room by half past ten, said a general good night, and strolled out along the gallery towards their own rooms. And so powerful was the compulsion of their authority that Lucien Galt, who happened to be with them at the time, fell in alongside and left with them, and half a dozen others wound up their conversations and followed.

'Not that I shall get to bed for an hour or so yet,' observed Arundale with a rueful smile. 'I've got to address the Vintners' annual dinner tomorrow night, on adult education in general and Follymead in particular, and I haven't got any ideas in order yet. We're hoping to get an annual grant from them, of course! And on Sunday afternoon there's a conference of clerical and lay educationalists, on the use of leisure—a big subject, and very much in the news just now. I'm afraid it must all sound rather boring to you,' he said, glancing across his wife's fair head at Lucien Galt, with more of patronage than apology. 'At your age the problem of leisure is largely a matter of getting enough of it—no difficulty in filling it.'

'I don't find it boring at all,' said Lucien politely. And indeed, the dark profile he turned to the view of Dominic and Tossa, strolling a yard or two behind, did not look bored; the tight lines of it had eased and warmed, his colour was high and his eyes soft and bright. A slightly hectic gaiety touched him, perhaps from the salutary effort of making conversation, perhaps from the secret activity of his mind. He looked at Audrey Arundale, walking between them, and from her to her husband, and said with warmth: 'I think what you're doing here is fine, and I'm glad to be associated with it.'

Mrs Arundale turned her head a little at that, and her dutiful, acquiescent smile, which seldom left her lips and never lost its faint overtone of anxiety, flushed into something proud and animated with pleasure.

'I'd like to think it's fine,' said Arundale, accepting the bouquet. 'I know it isn't enough. I can only hope it has some effect.'

At this point Dominic's thumbs pricked, surely quite unjustly, as he told himself. But who had ever heard Lucifer go out of his way to pay a compliment to anyone before? He sounded quite sincere, and probably he was, but even so it didn't seem in character that he should say it. And the slight prick of wonder and curiosity suddenly reminded Dominic of that alleged mark on Lucien's left wrist. That was why he happened to glance down at the right, or perhaps the wrong, moment, and see what Tossa failed to see.

The three in front were walking close together, the flared skirt of the woman's dress rustling softly against her escorts as they

69

moved. Lucien's left hand, carried loosely at his side, suddenly uncurled its long fingers, and delicately and deliberately touched Audrey's hand between their bodies, and in instant response she opened her fingers to accept him. They clasped hands ardently for an instant, and as quickly and smoothly drew apart again. Their steps had never faltered, their faces had not quivered; only the hands embraced and clung and separated with passion and resolution, as though they had an independent life of their own, or had drawn down into themselves, for one moment, all the life of these two people.

In an unexpected but natural reaction, Dominic looked round hastily and almost furtively, to see if anyone else had been watching and seen what he had seen. But Tossa, thank goodness, was looking up at the elaborate pendants of the Venetian chandeliers, now turned down discreetly to a quarter their full power, so that the long gallery was almost dim, even in its open walk; and the view of anyone coming along behind must have been blocked completely by their bodies. No, nobody! He was almost relieved as if he had risked being caught out in some embarrassing misdemeanour himself, and by luck rather than desert survived undetected.

Then a minute, sudden refraction of light drew his eyes sharply to the deep alcove where one of the Cothercott portraits hung. Someone was sitting there, so still that but for the ring she wore he would never have found her. But when he had once found her, her eyes burned brighter than the reflection from her ring. She sat motionless, the long, heavy plait of hair coiled on her shoulder. Her face was as fixed as ice, her nostrils flared wide. She was neither surprised nor disconcerted. She had seen only what she had been prepared to see, something against which she was forewarned and forearmed; but it was at the same time something she would never forget or forgive, and something she would not endure without retaliation.

They moved on, and Liri Palmer watched them go, and never moved. No one saw her but Dominic; no one but Dominic knew what she had seen.

CHAPTER 3

'I hope,' said Professor Penrose, casting a lightning glance at his watch, which showed twenty minutes past twelve, and lifting the tone-arm delicately from his precious disc of Moravian Slovak recordings, 'that we've at least established a basis for the *name* of our subject. I hope we can agree that it should not be merely "folk," but "music," too. Beware of the fanatic who finds everything phoney that isn't sung without accompaniment by an eighty-five-year-old in a public bar...without voice, too, as a rule, and who can wonder at it? No, we've disposed of that. We've surely demonstrated that there are places in the world where performances of the utmost virtuosity can be truly "folk," because the heritage of that particular people is a musical sensitivity which we, here in England, associate only with privilege, training and sophistication. Never lose sight of that humbling fact, and beware of subscribing to purely English standards—or should I say, British?' He cocked an eye at Andrew Callum, and grinned. 'But they're two

72

different things, as I'll show you this evening. The Celtic fringe has the drop on us poor English in so many ways, you'll find. Puritanism has a lot to answer for.'

He slammed shut the huge book of notes at which he never even looked, though he opened it religiously at the beginning of each session.

'Now be off with you and get ready for lunch. This afternoon is free, and I understand the deputy warden has arranged two excursions for us in the locality. I'll be going with one of the parties myself, so one of the coach-loads, at least, will have to behave. And the rest of you I'll expect here at five, fit and ready for action. Mind you're not late. Away with you, and wash! Gong in five minutes!'

They took their tone from him, and rushed for the doors in a furious babble of argument and controversy. It was becoming clear now that the professor, from the recesses of his own antiquity, regarded them all as eighteen years old at most, and liked them that way. They'd had a deliriously happy morning with him; the afternoon was to be in every sense a holiday, and the evening a continued delight. He had his class exactly where he wanted it.

The first coach, headed for Mottisham Abbey

and antiquities of West Midshire, and captained by the professor, hummed away down the drive prompt at two o'clock. Tossa and Dominic watched it go from the highest view-turret at the front of the house, up among the fantasy of chimneys and gargoyles and leads that lived a film-cartoon life of its own over the heads of the music-students. A scarlet beetle, scurrying along a thread of pale gravel, it rounded the planned bend in the drive, and vanished from sight. In a few minutes more the second, bound for the region of geological curiosities in the north-east of the county, followed it, Henry Marshall no doubt still anxiously counting his chickens. When it was gone, it seemed to them that the whole house had been evacuated, and they were alone with the fairy-tale threat that had driven the others away. Only then did they become aware of the large bird-population of Follymead, the inhabitants of this roof-world. The noise of starlings and martins and pigeons was all the music left to them. Somewhere in the park a green woodpecker was beating out his staccato rhythms like a drummer.

'You're sure you didn't want to go with them?' asked Dominic, shoulder to shoulder with Tossa at the open window.

She shook her head vehemently. 'No, this

74

is better. You know all those places, and we hardly know this at all. It's all ours now.'

'Oh, there must be a few others who chose to stay.'

They saw one of them at that moment, crossing the pale forecourt far below them, a tiny, foreshortened human creature, walking rapidly but progressing slowly. It was astonishing how long it took him to cross the open court and set foot on the grass path that led away into the park, downhill towards the river, glimpsed, in a few specks of silver through the trees.

'Lucifer was in no mood for excursions, evidently,' said Dominic.

The small, dark speck achieved form and proportion as it receded; it no longer looked as if it could be smudged out of existence, like a May midge, by the pressure of a finger. And in a moment a second figure came bounding down the steps to the gravel, and set off full speed in pursuit, a thin little figure with a child's long-legged and angular movements. She caught him up before he reached the trees. He checked and turned for a moment with a formidable suggestion of impatience, but then he set off again, and she fell into step beside him. They disappeared together where the trees engulfed the path.

'I shouldn't!' said Tossa in a warning whisper, and shook her head over what she certainly couldn't help.

'Maybe you would, if you were Felicity. Actually he's been remarkably forbearing with her so far, considering his reputation. She was under his feet all last night, and he stood it nobly.'

'It won't last. She'll be due for a shock pretty soon if she doesn't get out of his hair.' Tossa looked after them with perplexed sympathy. 'She's a queer little thing, isn't she? Rather sad, really. I was talking to that nice elderly maid in the buttery this morning. She says Felicity's mother is Mr Arundale's younger sister, she's a widow, not all that badly off, but the querulous sort, and it seems she's inclined to think her distinguished brother owes her a living. She farms the girl out on Follymead every holiday as a sort of junior secretary, and has her hang around the Arundales all the time she isn't at school.'

'Hoping she'll come in for whatever they've got to leave, some day?'

'Well, that's what Mrs Bremmer says, anyway. After all, they've got no children of their own, so it's a reasonable hope. And in the meantime, at least she's making them provide for her nearly half the year. But what a life!

I mean, it isn't as if she was dumb. She isn't at all, she's rather too bright, if anything, she must know very well what goes on. Not too good for an intelligent adolescent,' said Tossa, wise at nineteen, 'knowing she's being used to prise hand-outs out of her relatives, and her mother cares more for her prospects than her company. No wonder she's gone cagey. You can see right away that she's all the time waiting for the world to hit out at her. That's why she puts on the sophistication so thick, to pretend things don't hurt.'

Dominic listened to this with the more respect because not so long ago Tossa herself had been in a somewhat similar relationship with the world at large, and her actress-mother's procession of husbands in particular; and with the more tenderness and pleasure because her tone now indicated a quite remarkable degree of recovery. He was a little dubious of crediting himself with the change, but the fact remained that he had happened to Tossa just at the right time to assist the process. If she was right, then young Felicity Cope was all set to be a pushover for a grand passion; and if it went right it would liberate her for good, even if it afterwards went the way of most adolescent loves. But he couldn't persuade himself that she was going to get anything but

77

disaster out of Lucifer.

'Felicity!' he said thoughtfully, and made a wry face. 'Whoever christened her that has something to answer for.'

Tossa leaned out from the window to look down dizzily on to the terraces below. 'Look, there's Liri, too.'

'So she didn't want to go sight-seeing, either.'

Liri, in a red sweater bright as a drop of blood, crossed the terrace and walked slowly down the steps. On the drive she hesitated for a moment, and then set out briskly across the grass towards the distant hillock on which the fake ruin stood. She walked as one who has decided on an objective, rather than as one who is going somewhere with a purpose, and her chosen course was taking her steadily farther and farther away from the copse that had swallowed Lucien and Felicity. The damp grass showed the silvery line of her passing, lengthening along the sward; and it might also have been ruled there, it was so uncompromisingly straight.

'Let's go down and have a look at the grounds,' said Tossa, turning away abruptly from the contemplation of that lance-like wake, 'while we've got the place more or less to ourselves.'

They went down, and the house was wonderfully hushed and quiet about them. True, there were still one or two people around. The staff must be still washing up after lunch, Edward Arundale in his private quarters was collecting what he needed for his drive to Birmingham, there were two elderly ladies placidly reading in the gallery, and two more strolling between the flower-beds in the shelter of the enclosed garden; but with the withdrawal of some seventy people the whole house was changed, had reverted to its cat-sleep with eyes half-open, and lay deceptively still and harmless and helpless in the faint, stormy sunshine of April.

There was room in the grounds of Follymead to lose a thousand people, and still believe yourself alone. They walked away from the drive, turning towards the arched bridge that spanned the river in the distance. Crimson and orange alders showed the winding course of the stream, even when the flood-water itself was hidden from them. Clustering woods drew in to complete the picture like a blackcloth; and out of the trees, while they were still some hundred yards distant, came Felicity, her head down, her fleet, child's running muted to a stumbling, rapid walk. She didn't notice them until the sound of their feet whispering in the grass, and the hint of a shadow at the edge of her vision, made her fling up her head with a wild, wary gesture, like a startled colt.

She said: 'Oh!... Hullo!' and her face put on its armour, settled narrow, clean-arched brows and quivering, irresolute mouth into arduous but instant serenity. 'Going for a walk?'

'Why don't you come with us?' suggested Tossa impulsively, and her eyes signalled apology to Dominic for a rash generosity he might not approve. But the girl was so solitary and gauche, and her grey eyes looked out so defensively from behind the delicate, half-formed face, like lonely wild things in hiding. 'You know all the best places. We haven't seen anything yet.'

'I'd love to, thank you,...but I can't. I've got to go in now. I've got some jobs to do for my uncle in the office. I only came out to run down and have a look at the swans' nest. There's a pair nesting down there under the alders, on a tiny island.' She pointed rather jerkily, turning her face away from them. 'But be careful if you go to look, don't go too near, will you? The pen's all right, but if the cob's there he can be rather dangerous.'

'We saw you come out,' said Dominic casually, and saw the faint colour flow and ebb again in her solemn face, and the grey eyes in ambush flare into panic for an instant. 'We hoped you were going to have an afternoon off, you spend enough time indoors. Can't the work wait for today?'

But she did not want it to wait, that was clear. She began to sidle round them, intent on escape. 'No, I'd rather get it done. Things like the press-cutting book and the photographs get into arrears very easily, you see, and we don't just keep them for interest, the record's needed for reference. But, look, if you go on this way, along the river, you'll come to the summer pavilion, and from there you can work round through the woods to the pagoda. There used to be a heronry there at the pool, but the last pair flew away last year. You will excuse me, won't you?' She was backing away from them towards the house, ten yards distant before she stopped talking, and turned, and broke into a run. The feverish sound of her voice clung unpleasantly in their ears as she dwindled, sometimes running, sometimes walking hastily and unsteadily, her track a shaky line in the wet grass.

'It seemed only fair to let her know we'd seen her,' said Dominic dubiously, meeting Tossa's eyes. 'She hadn't said anything that *couldn't* be true, up to then.'

'I know, I was glad you said it. I don't think we'll go and look for the swan's nest, somehow, do you? It'll be there, of course. She's quick, she wouldn't give herself an excuse that could be knocked down just by going and looking.' Tossa stooped and picked up from the grass a couple of tiny, cross-shaped blossoms that had fallen from Felicity's hair as she combed it nervously with her fingers. 'Lilac...look, what a colour! So deep, and really almost pure blue instead of purple...'

She stood for a moment holding them, and then turned her palm and let them fall again sadly into the turf. 'I suppose he turned on her. Something happened.'

'I suppose so,' said Dominic. 'Probably told her to run away and play with her dolls.'

'Isn't it hell,' sighed Tossa, 'being fifteen?'

The coach parties came back hungry and in high spirits just after half past four, and tumbled up the steps into the hall for tea. The noise, now that they had sorted themselves out into congenial groups and had plenty to talk about, was deafening. Arundale, if he had been there to hear, would have been satisfied of the success of the course by the soaring decibel count. There were no clouds, no shadows, no disagreements, no clashes of temperament, and nobody even wondered why; until five o'clock struck, and Professor Penrose came in to hasten the laggards along to the drawing-room for his next lecture, and looking round the emptying room, suddenly asked:

'Where's young Galt?'

He was not with the other artists, already on station in the window-embrasure of the yellow drawing-room. He was not in the hall, lingering with the scones and tea-cups. And now that the question arose, he hadn't been in to tea at all.

'He wouldn't stand us up purposely, would he?' asked the professor shrewdly, and in a tone which required confirmation of his own views rather than information.

'Surely not,' said Dominic, abandoning his self-imposed task of loading the huge tea-trolley; and: 'No!' said Liri Palmer at the same instant, and still more positively, even scornfully.

'No, that's what I thought. Boy's a professional. No, I don't think he'd welch on a session. So *where is he?*'

There was a dead silence. No one had anything to volunteer. There were only a handful of them left there, in the strewn wreckage of tea, a china battlefield.

'He didn't come out with us this afternoon,' said Henry Marshall. 'Was he with your party?'

'No.' The professor sounded a little testy. Lucifer was not the kind of person who could pass unnoticed on board a coach.

'He stayed here,' said Dominic. 'Tossa and I saw him go out, soon after the coaches left. He started off towards the river, by that path that dives into the trees.'

'And you haven't seen him since?'

'No. Felicity just might have. She was down that way this afternoon, we met her coming back.' No need to say she'd followed Lucien from the house; she knew that were others who knew, she'd be able to answer questions and keep her secrets, too.

'Shall I go and find Felicity?' offered Tossa, to fend off any other messenger.

'If you wouldn't mind, my dear. No need to broadcast anything—not yet, anyhow.' The professor smiled at her, but he was not quite easy in his mind, even then.

'No, I won't.' And in a few moments she returned from the drawing-room with Felicity. The girl was pale, her eyes huge and opaque as grey glass, her mask slightly and frighteningly out of drawing.

'Felicity, we've lost Lucien Galt.' The professor was placid and gentle. 'Maybe he's just loitering about somewhere with a stopped watch, maybe he's gone to sleep in the

84

summer-house, or something daft and simple. But we'd better have a look for him, perhaps, just in case. I hear you were down by the river this afternoon, did you see anything of him? I'm told he'd gone that way.'

'I...we went out together,' said Felicity in a thin thread of a voice. 'He was just ahead of me when I went out, so I caught him up and we went together. We went downstream on the other side, but only as far as where the paths cross. You know, by the baby redwood tree. Then he went on across the loop, I think... anyhow, I crossed over again by the stone bridge, and left him there.' She looked from the professor to Dominic and Tossa, and moistened her lips. 'I met Miss Barber and Mr Felse when I was coming back.'

'And you weren't out again? And you haven't seen Mr Galt come back to the house?'

She shook her head vehemently. 'No. I was indoors all the rest of the afternoon. I had some work to do for Uncle Edward.'

The whip of the warden's name stung Henry Marshall into full awareness of his responsibilities. Arundale was in Birmingham by now, and the whole load of Follymead came down on his deputy's shrinking shoulders. The social load was enough, but that he was prepared to tackle. This was something that hadn't been

85

on the agenda, and he didn't know what to do.

'He must be in the grounds,' he said unhappily. 'Apparently he simply went out for a walk. I suppose there's always a possibility that he may have had an accident, just an ordinary fall. It's not so difficult to break an ankle, or something like that, along the river-banks. Professor, I really think you'd better get on with you lecture, and try to manage without him, if you can, while some of us have a hunt through the park for him.'

'I think I had,' agreed the professor dryly, one ear cocked for the rising noise of conversation drifing in from the distant drawing-room. 'I'll tell them nothing about this. Better keep it to the few of us here, until we know what we're about.'

They agreed, in a subdued murmur.

'You find the lad,' said the professor, swooping towards the door. 'I'll keep this lot quiet.'

When he was gone, there were just five of them left in the room, Tossa, Felicity, Liri Palmer, Dominic and Marshall. It wasn't the party they would have chosen. Three of them women, and two of those tense and anxious already. Liri was unquestionably durable, but Felicity looked brittle as glass, ready to shatter. Dominic touched her hand lightly, and urged her with a frown and a silent shake of his head to leave the search to them. Nevertheless, they were still five when they went out in the green, misty, pre-evening light to quarter the grounds for Lucien Galt.

The path by which Lucien and Felicity had vanished in the early afternoon sank itself deep in groves of diverse trees, artfully deployed, and reached the river at some distance from the house. A narrow footbridge with a single handrail brought Dominic to the other side. The largest of the three weirs that controlled the passage of the Braide through the Follymead grounds lay upstream, and here the waters rolled brown and high and fast, seamed with currents, and tossing twigs and branches from hand to hand as it rushed along. The spring rains had been heavy after heavy snows, the sodden grass of the banks fermented with brownish foam, and strained at its roots, streaming out like dead hair along the taut surface of the water. On the other side the path turned downstream, at first close to the bank; but in a little while it plunged into woodland again, and left the waterside to take a short cut across one of the artificial loops into which the Braide had been contorted by Cothercott ingenuity.

Dominic turned with the path. Almost certainly Lucien had come this way with Felicity this afternoon, just as she had said. She had reappeared from the copse on the other bank, having recrossed by the arched stone bridge two or three loops downstream, the bridge which was designed as a part of the Follymead stage-set, to be seen in exactly the right place in that elaborate landscape when viewed from the drawing-room windows. Somewhere between this spot and that bridge she and Lucien had parted company. Dominic walked the widening ride, fenced off now on the water side by a barrier of old, ornate iron posts and fine chains, and his feet were silent in last autumn's rotting leaves.

It didn't follow, of course, that Lucien need be anywhere in this quarter now; in the time between he could have been anywhere in the grounds, or even several miles out of them. There was so much of Follymead that the five of them had had to spread themselves out singly in order to cover it all; and it was hardly surprising that Felicity had set off, at first, in this direction. But she had drawn back when she had seen Dominic heading the same way, and gone off voluntarily to thread the shrubberies and gardens on the other side of the house. Liri and Tossa were patrolling the more open ornamental park-land, one on either side the drive to the lodge. Where Marshall was he didn't know; probably in the distant preserves which were going to be the worst job of all if they were forced to make a real search of it.

The river was out of sight now, somewhere away on his right hand; but here came a small cleared space where another path crossed his, and the right turn here must surely close in on the Braide again, and bring him to the bridge. And here was Felicity's baby redwood, just inside the railed enclosure, an infant of about fifty or sixty, probably, with the characteristic spreading base and narrow, primitive, aspiring shape. He leaned over the chain fence and stuck his thumb into the thick, spongy bark. So here it had happened, whatever had happened between them...here or somewhere close by, she wouldn't bother to be accurate to a few yards. And after that nobody had seen anything of Lucien again. Though there was always the comfortable possibility, of course, that he had simply decided to be irresponsible this evening, and gone off to the pub in the village to see what entertainment was offering locally.

Dominic would have liked to believe it; but whatever Lucien Galt might not have been, he seemed to be a conscientious professional who delivered his promises. And again, and more disturbingly, the prosaic solution didn't chime with the atmosphere of this fantastic place.

He hesitated at the crossing of the two paths, and then turned right, as Felicity must have done when she took her broken heart and hurt pride in her arms and ran away from the débâcle. And twenty yards along, with the chain fence still accompanying him on his right, he came to an enormous scrolled iron gate in it, massive with leaves and flowers, twice as tall as the fence. Evidently the gate was a survival from some older and far more solid fence, long taken down for scrap. To judge by the gate itself, it dated from the high days of iron, maybe around 1800 or even earlier, stuff that could go neglected for centuries before it even began to corrode seriously. It hadn't been painted for a long time, and it sagged a little on its hinges, but swung freely when he pushed it. The bracket into which the latch should drop was still fixed immovably to the gate-post, as big as a bruiser's closed fist; but there was no latch hanging now in the wards.

The elaboration of the approach suggested that this patch of woodland by the river bank enshrined one of the features of the grounds. He went through the gate on impulse, and down to the riverside. He could see the distant gleam of sullen light on the water in broken glimpses between the trees; and the belt of woods thinned suddenly and brought him out on an open stretch of grass, ringed round every way with shrubs. Even across the river the woods lay close here, the alders leaning over the bank. A nice, quiet, retired place, carefully made, like everything here. Nature had abdicated, unable to keep up the pace. The cluster of rocks that erupted on the bank had been placed there by man, artfully built up to look as natural as the eighteenth century liked its landscape features to look. Dominic crossed the thirty yards or so of open meadow that separated him from it, and found that the face the rocks turned towards the Braide was hollowed into a narrow cavern, with a stone bench fitted inside it. The inside walls were encrusted with stucco and shells, and overgrown with ferns, and there had once been a small spring there, filling a little channel in the stone floor and running down to the river. There was only a green stain there now, and a growth of viridian moss.

He looked round the grotto dubiously, and was turning to leave it when he saw, between the stone and the river, the first raw scars in the grass. The ground was soft and moist, the grass still short, but lush enough to show wounds. Feet had stamped and shifted here, with more pressure and greater agitation than in mere walking. Close to the edge of the flood,

91

gathering in concentrated force here before leaping the third weir, there was a patch of grass some two yards across that had been trampled and scored, the dark soil showing through. Here someone's foot had slipped and left a slimy smear.

Dominic approached cautiously, avoiding setting foot on the scarred place. Close to the water the grass shrank from a bare patch of gravel and stone; and there were two darker spots on the ground, oval and even and small, a dull brown in colour. He stooped to peer at them. It had rained briefly in the morning, but not since. These were therefore more recent than that rain; and they looked to him like drops of blood. He went down on one knee carefully to look more closely, and put his supporting hand on something hard that shifted in the grass. He made an instinctive movement to pick it up, and then took out his handkerchief, and handled his find delicately through the linen. A small silver medal, worn almost smooth, some human figure, maybe a saint, on one side, and on the other what seemed to be a lion rampant. From the ring that pierced it above the saint's head a thin silver chain slid away like a snake and slipped through his fingers; he caught it in his other hand, and saw that it had not been unclasped, but broken.

He had seen it before, or at least something so like it that in his heart he knew it was the same; round, worn, plain, of this very size, why should there be two such in Follymead at the same time?

This morning, at Professor Penrose's lecture, Lucien Galt had worn an open-necked sweater-shirt, and several times he had leaned forward to attend to the professor's record player for him. He had been wearing this medal round his neck. Dominic had noticed it because it had seemed at first out of character; and then, and more acutely, because it was entirely in character, after all, that he should wear it as he did, without a thought for either display or concealment, as naturally as he wore his eyelashes. And the thing itself had an austerity that made it singularly personal and valid, like a silver identity bracelet round a sailor's wrist in wartime. Not for show, but not to be hidden, either; something with a right to be where it was.

He stared at it in the fading light, and he knew it was the same. He looked at the sky, which was ragged with broken clouds, and then went and found some large leaves of wild rhubarb from the waterside, and laid them over the drops that were possibly blood, and the trampled ground, in case of rain. He found a sharp stone and drove it into the turf where he had picked up the medal. That was all he could do.

Then he went to find Henry Marshall.

'I'm not sure about the blood,' said Dominic for the fourth time. 'I *am* sure about the struggle. Two people—or more than two, but it looks like two—were fighting there. And *this* was in the grass, and Liri says it was his, and I say so, too. And that's all we've got, between the five of us.'

They were in the warden's office, with the door tightly shut. Dinner was over, without them; they had sandwiches and coffee in here, but no one had done more than play with them. Liri sat bolt upright, pale and calm, her mouth tight and her eyes sombre. Felicity, mercifully, had been manoeuvred out of the council by Tossa, and driven in to the evening session, where she would have to mingle and be social and keep her mouth shut. She didn't even know exactly what Dominic had found, though maybe she guessed more than was comfortable. Someone would have to keep an eye on her, and it looked as if the someone would have to be Tossa. But Felicity had resources of her own, and whatever she couldn't do yet, she could keep secrets. At fifteen it's an essential

94

quality; one's life depends on it. She wouldn't give anything away.

'We can't leave it at that,' said Dominic reasonably.

'No, I realise that, of course.' Henry Marshall was barely thirty, none too sure of himself after four months under Edward Arundale's formidable shadow, and at this moment in an agony of indecision. 'But we have no proof at all that anything disastrous has happened, no proof of a crime, certainly. And you must understand that this establishment is in a curiously vulnerable position. If a scandal threatened our reputation it might cut off funds from several sources, as well as frightening away our actual student potential.' He dug his fingers agitatedly into his straw-coloured hair, and his black-rimmed spectacles slid down his long young nose. 'A bad period of some weeks could close us down. It would be cataclysmic. As long as we run steadily on a moderate backing we're perfectly safe. But any interruption of any long duration would finish us. And that would be a real national loss. I know we must follow this up. But I must protect Follymead, too. It's what I'm here for.'

'I still think we need the police,' said Dominic. 'For that very purpose. You want to avoid scandal, of course, but it would be a worse scandal if you concealed what turned out to be a criminal matter. To cover Follymead, I'm afraid you've got to hand this job over to the proper people.'

And that was the whole crux of the matter, the thing that was tearing the deputy warden apart. He was terrified of calling in the poiice, perhaps to find it had all been unnecessary, and even more terrified of bearing the responsibility for not calling them in, should the affair turn out to be serious after all. Above all he was afraid of trying to contact Edward Arundale, and for good reason. Arundale was a man of decision, who would know how to deal with every situation, and he would be highly intolerant of any deputy who couldn't handle affairs himself in an emergency. Marshall hadn't been here long, this was his first assignment on his own responsibility; and he wanted, how he wanted, to keep his job.

'We have so little to go on,' he said in agony.

'We're not competent,' said Liri Palmer tersely, 'to say whether it's little or much. That's the whole point.'

Dominic looked at Tossa, and found her looking at him, with the clear, trusting, eager look by means of which she communicated her sense of adoption into his family. He knew what she was thinking, and what she wanted him to do and say. It was having lost her own father so early, and suffered such frustrations and vicissitudes with stepfathers since, that had made her attach herself so fervently and gratefully to Dominic's beautifully permanent, stable and reassuring parents. And especially to George Felse. He wasn't at all like her adored professor father, but he gave her the same sense of security. She would have taken all her own problems to him, it was natural she should think of him immediately in this crisis. Even if he hadn't been a policeman, she would have wanted him; but he was, and that was the solution to everything.

An exchange of glances like that, radiant with confidence, could turn Dominic's bones to water with gratitude and astonishment. He had brought her home in the common agonies every man feels in bringing together two jealous and valued loves; he wasn't yet used to the staggering bliss and relief of his total success.

'If I could make a suggestion,' he said, with all the more care and delicacy because of his own conviction of undeserved grace, 'I could get my father to have a look over the ground.' He caught Tossa's glowing glance, and trembled; he still couldn't quite believe in the accumulation of his luck. 'He's a detective-inspector in the county C.I.D. I'm sure he'd be willing to come out here, if you'll let me call him. Then you'd have covered yourself and the college, in case there *is* something in this. And we could ask him to treat it as a quite private matter until he's satisfied that there's a case for official investigation. In either case, you'd be protected.'

Henry Marshall took his head out of his hands, and gaped unbelievingly but gladly at his salvation. Arundale himself couldn't do better than this.

'You think he'd come? On those terms?'

'I'm sure he would. It's better for them, too, if they have notice of these things in time to judge. If it turns out to be something quite harmless and on the level, so much the better. May I call him?'

'Please do,' said Henry Marshall thankfully. 'Perhaps you could meet him at the lodge, when he arrives? You *do* drive? Take the station wagon down and wait for him. I'll talk to Professor Penrose, and see to everything here. We shall be most grateful. *Most* grateful!'

CHAPTER 4

George Felse swore, but with resignation, listened, and came. Dominic was not in the habit of going off at half-cock; he had been a policeman's son too long for that. If the affair turned out to be a mare's-nest after all, there was no harm done; and if it didn't, far better to take a close look at the circumstances as soon as possible, rather than after the scent had gone cold.

'Save it,' he said, cutting off the details. 'I'm on my way, we'll have all that when I come.' It took him twenty minutes to drive from Comerford to the Follymead gates; there wasn't much on the roads at this hour, and the going was good. The college station wagon was parked just behind the lodge, already turned to point back up the drive, with Dominic and Tossa waiting beside it.

'We thought it might be better if you leave the car here at the lodge,' said Dominic. 'Just in case there's somebody who knows it.'

'In that case,' said George reasonably, 'the somebody would be more likely to know me.'

'Yes, but we hope you'll be able to stay out of the general view. There's only a handful of us know what's happened. If anything *has* happened. And that way, if it all turns out to be nonsense, there's no fuss, and nobody's made to look a fool. It seemed the best thing. It's this second-in-command, you see, he's left holding the baby, and he's terrified of calling the police, and terrified of not calling them. Whatever he does is probably going to be the wrong thing.'

'So I'm the working compromise. He realised that if there does turn out to be anything in it, it becomes an official matter?'

'If there's anything in it, the fat's in the fire, anyhow. Yes, of course he understnads that. Even Arundale couldn't help that.' Dominic climbed into the driving seat of the station wagon, and set it rolling up the long, pale drive, bordered now, by fitful moonlight and scurrying cloud, with phantoms of Cothercott ingenuity even more monstrous than by day. 'Is Bunty very mad at me? I'm sorry about it, but honestly, this business...I don't like the look of it.' He had only recently taken to calling his mother Bunty, and it didn't come quite naturally yet, but using the old, childish form of address had suddenly become as constricting to him as a straight-jacket. He'd never so much as given it a thought until Tossa entered the house; but it still hadn't occurred to him to work out the implications.

'Not with you. Maybe with your missing folk-singer, for his bad timing. Cold, Tossa?' She was between them on the broad front seat, shivering a little in spite of the camel-coloured car coat in which she was huddled.

'No, it's just tension, don't mind me.' She relaxed against George's shoulder, reassured by his presence. There were going to be times when Dominic would feel a little jealous of George, who, after all, was only forty-five, and tall and slim, and not that bad-looking as middle-aged men go. 'I'm glad you're here. I don't like this much, either. There are too many over-developed personalities around, things *could* happen.'

'Well, let's hear it.'

Dominic told it, as succinctly as he could, and Tossa added an occasional comment. There was no time for all the background detail now, only for the facts. Nevertheless, glimpses of personalities emerged, and they were seen to be, as Tossa had said, a little distorted, drawn from a world where bizarre and improbable things could happen. The moon came out and silvered the pagoda roof, beyond the heronry where there were no herons, and picked out like a lance-thrust the black entrance of the hermit's cave, distant in its concrete rocks. Anything was believable here.

'With a house full of about eighty people,' said George, 'he thinks he's going to be able to keep this secret?'

'If it has to be a fullscale investigation, no. But long enough for you to have a look at the set-up and judge, yes, I reckon with luck we might. Because almost everybody was right away from here all afternoon, you see, with these two coach-parties. They left before we saw Lucien Galt go out into the park. And they came back only just on time for tea, and came milling in all together. They're out of it. They *can't* know anything.'

'That leaves how many? More than enough.'

'Not really, because the staff were working indoors as usual, and they're sure to be O.K. Mostly they'd be in pairs or more all the time, what with washing up after lunch, and then preparing for tea and dinner. We were here, of course, you know about us. Then there's Felicity, that's the young one I told you about, Arundale's niece. And Liri Palmer...she was in the grounds, too, we saw her start off towards that phoney ruin, over that way. And we four, and Mr Marshall, are the only ones who know about what I found by the river, so far. Then there's Professor Penrose, he knows about Lucien being missing, but he doesn't know the rest yet. He'd just got them all into the drawing-room for his after-dinner session when we came back to the house.'

'And you think all that lot can be trusted to keep it dark?'

'We can only try. Yes, I think we might'

'Even the girl? This Felicity?'

'Yes,' said Tossa positively. She cast a quick glance at Dominic, and went on, encouraged: 'She had a special reason for keeping quiet. Dominic didn't tell you quite all about her afternoon. Oh, he told what we know, but not what we *think* we know. You see, she's an odd child. But no, it *isn't* odd to be like that, not at her age, it's not odd at all. She's awkward and tense and self-conscious, and she's a sort of poor relation here, and things are pretty much hell for her, even though everybody means well. And this week-end she's gone right overboard for Lucien Galt, that's all about it. That's why she followed him out this afternoon. And when we met her coming back, we felt pretty sure he'd got fed up with having her round his neck, and sent her off with a flea in her ear. So if she seems to be covering up, that's what she's covering. And whoever tells more than they need about this afternoon, it won't be Felicity.'

'I see,' said George, touched by what she had omitted rather than what she had said. 'Don't worry, I'll leave her her dignity.'

'I know,' said Tossa warmly.

'What about the mere fact that one of the artists has missed two sessions? I suppose he should have appeared in all of them? Aren't quite a number of people going to wonder about that? Even if they don't notice *your* absence from the audience.'

'I don't think we need worry about that. We sit wherever we happen to find a place, it's liable to be different every time, and if you're not along there now, why shouldn't you be somewhere at the back? They won't wonder about us, among so many. But about Galt it is rather different. We left that to the professor. Unless he saw a need, I don't suppose he's told them anything at all, just sailed on as if everything was just as it was meant to be. But if he thought they were beginning to do some serious wondering, I bet he could hand them an absolutely first-class lie.'

'He may have to. Keeping it quiet suits me, too. I don't want seventy excited people tramping all over the place and getting in the way, any more than the county or the warden want their cherished college to get the wrong sort of advertisement. Will they still be in at the lecture now?'

'Should be. We ought to have half an hour yet.'

'We'll go down to this grotto of yours first, then. Can we slip in by a back door afterwards, and dodge the house-party?'

'Yes, easily, from the back courtyard, where the garages are. There's a covered passage to the basement stairs, and the warden's office is quite near the top of the staircase. The front's all gilt and carpeting and ashlar, but the back stairs is a little spiral affair. Pity,' said Dominic, 'about the light. But there's a huge torch in the glove-pocket here.'

'I want to take a look at the marks tonight, lift a sample, if possible. It's going to rain before morning.'

'He covered them,' said Tossa, promptly and proudly.

'I should hope so,' said George; but he smiled.

They swept round the dramatic bend in the drive, and the house rose superb and staggering in the bone-white moonlight to take their breath away. The long range of the drawing-room windows blazed with light, flooding the lowest of the terraces; the class was still in session.

Dominic drove round the wing of the house

and into the courtyard, and there they locked the station wagon and left it, taking the torch with them. The whiteness of moonlight on the pale, complex shapes of stone here was hard and dry as an articulated skeleton, the windows glared like empty eye-sockets. Dominic led the way down to the footbridge, and in the spectral, half-fledged woodland he switched on the torch. The great, gaunt gate towered in its inadequate fence, a few yards beyond the redwood tree. They came out on the blanched greensward by the grotto. The noise of the river, more deadly than by day, reached for them, a humming, throbbing, low, ferocious roar, a tiger-cat purring, and just as dangerous and beautiful.

Carefully Dominic circled his ring of rhubarb leaves, and lifted them. The little pool of the torch's light moved in deep absorption all around the area, an eye of warmer pallor in the cold pallor of the moon.

'All right, cover them again,' said George at length. 'Where's this stuff that may be blood?'

The two heavy drops seemed to have shrunk since early evening, but even by this light they were there, clearly visible. They had no colour now, only a darkness without colour; but they had a clear form. Liquid had dripped, not directly, but in flight from a body in motion.

One was flattened on open stone, immovable; but the second was on hard ground. George took a pen-knife to it, patiently and carefully, and pared it intact out of the ground, while Tossa held the torch for him. He had brought pill-boxes with him for such small specimens as this.

'Tomorrow morning, early, I'll go over all this open ground. Maybe Mr Marshall can find me a tarpaulin, or something to drape over this. Now where was this medal and chain you found? Yes...I see.'

Behind them the river roared as softly as any sucking dove, and they felt it there, and were not deceived into believing it harmless. The sound had a curious property, it seemed to be one with the vast outer silence which contained it. At night, in the grounds of Follymead, Pan and panic were conceptions as modern and close as central heating, though what they distilled was a central chill. Dominic folded his arm and his wind-jacket about Tossa, and felt her turn to him confidingly. She wasn't afraid; she only shook, like him, with awareness of chaos, braced and ready for it.

'All right,' said George, in a soft, surprised and gentle voice. 'Let's get back to the house and talk to Mr Marshall.'

'We must have tests made, of course,' said George, installed behind the desk in Edward Arundale's private office at the top of the back stairs, 'but I think I ought to say at once that this is almost certainly blood.' The little pill-box with its pear-drop shape of dull brown on fretted gravel lay in his palm; he shut the lid over it and laid it aside. 'I needn't tell you that blood in that quantity could come from the most superficial of injuries. But we're faced with the fact that Lucien Galt has not reappeared or sent any message. Those who know him say he wouldn't cheat on the commitment. I regard this as good evidence. They know what to expect of him; they didn't expect this, and they don't accept it. He was regarded as in many ways a fiendishly difficult colleague; but he didn't give short weight once a bargain was struck. We must also face the fact that the Braide in flood ran a yard or so from where these tell-tale marks were found. If there was a struggle there, as appears to be the case, then the loser may only too easily have gone over the weir and down the river. I am putting, of course, the gravest possible case, because we can't afford to ignore it. We must take into account *all* possibilities.'

Henry Marshall licked his dry lips and swallowed arduously. 'Yes, I realise that. I...

may I take it that you will assume responsibility for whatever inquiries are necessary? I want, of course, to co-operate as fully as possible.'

'I should prefer to keep this inquiry quiet, as long as that's possible. I gather you feel the same way. Let me have this office for my own use, and keep the course running. Can you do that? I've already talked to Professor Penrose, he's quite willing to work them as hard as possible, and it looks as if they're enjoying it. Concentrate on helping him, and keep the course afloat between you, and we ought to be able to get them out of here on Monday evening none the wiser about what's been occupying us. They'll have enough to think about.'

'I shall be very grateful,' said Henry Marshall, in the understatement of the year. 'You understand my position...this is the first time I've been left to run a course singlehanded. It would be disastrous if we allowed our students to panic and the course to disintegrate. Not only for me. I'm worried about myself, naturally, I don't pretend I'm not. But I'm honestly worried about Follymead, too. We *are* worth an effort, I give you my word we are.'

He was an honest, decent, troubled young man, not very forceful, not very experienced, but George thought Arundale might have done very much worse.

'I'm sure of that. I want to use discretion, too. But you understand that if there has been a tragedy here, if there has been a crime, that can't be suppressed. The moment I'm convinced that it's a police matter, it will become official.'

'I couldn't, in any case, agree to anything else,' said Marshall simply. 'I'm a citizen, as well as an employee afraid for his job. But there's no harm in hoping it won't come to that.'

'None at all. I've got the list of people who stayed here this afternoon, instead of joining one or other of the sight-seeing parties. Tell me if there's anyone who should be added.' He read off the list. It included four elderly ladies, all local, and therefore all acquainted with the local antiquities, and disposed to vegetate in the Follymead libraries or gardens rather than to clamber over castles; but they had booked in in pairs, and almost certainly had hunted in pairs this afternoon. With luck there would be no need to involve them. A little casual conversation—Tossa might help out here— would eliminate them. 'I realise that Mrs Arundale will have to be told, eventually, about this inquiry. Is there anyone else who stayed here?'

'Yes,' said Marshall. 'Mr Meurice should have gone with my coach this afternoon. He

110

cried off at the last moment. I may be wrong, but I got the impression that he changed his mind because he found that Miss Palmer was staying.'

'It wouldn't be such an unheard-of thing to do,' agreed George. 'No one else?'

'Not that I can think of.'

'Then as time's getting on, I wonder if you'd get Felicity Cope in to me first. I won't frighten her. I believe she knows already about Mr Galt's disappearance.'

'She knows,' said Marshall, pondering darkly how much, indeed, Felicity did know. 'You won't frighten her. She's a very precocious young woman.' It sounded like a warning; it also sounded, paradoxically, as if he felt sorry for her. George made a mental note to beware of that attitude; it might, he reflected, be the most demoralising thing in the world to feel that everyone was sorry for you.

'I know I'm difficult,' said Felicity, in a very precise and slightly superior tone. 'I *have* difficulties. I don't know how much you remember about being my age?' She gave him a sidewise look, and was arrested by the nicely-shaped growth of the grey hair at his temples; it gave him a very distinguished look. He had nice eyes, too, deep-set and quiet; it would be

111

hard to excite him. It must be so restful, she thought, clutching at distant, desirable things to suppress her memories of anguish, to be with people who've known nearly everything, and can't get feverish any more.

'More than you'd think,' said George earnestly. He was on the same side of the desk with her, almost within touch; he knew quite a lot about making contact. 'And I have a son— that's going through it again, you know, only with one experience to build on. Not a daughter, I wasn't that lucky. My wife couldn't have any more children. We badly wanted a girl.'

'Really?' said Felicity, side-tracked. 'Uncle Edward is terribly unhappy, too, about Aunt Audrey not having any children. He's extremely fond of her, but it's always been an awful disappointment to him.' She tightened suddenly, he saw her face blanch. Her eyes, momentarily naked and vulnerable, veiled themselves. No one can be more opaque than a girl of fifteen, when she feels the need to defend herself. Why did she? From what?

'You know Lucien Galt's gone missing,' said George practically. 'It looks as if you were the last person to see him, here at Follymead. He didn't say anything to you, did he, about running out? After all, something could have happened to call him away.'

'No,' said Felicity, with a fixed, false smile. 'He didn't say anything about leaving. Nothing at all like that.'

'What did you talk about on your walk?'

'Oh, about the course, and the songs we had in the morning session. Just things like that.'

'Miss Barber and my son were a little disturbed about you...did you know? They had a feeling you were unhappy...upset...when they met you this afternoon. They'd have felt better if you'd agreed to go with them. *Was* there anything the matter? You know, it's a kindness to confide in people. We *do* worry about one another, that's what makes us human. Tossa's had her difficulties, too, you mustn't be surprised if she has a feeling for other people's crises.' Careful, now! She had shied a little at the word he had chosen; her eyes, blankly grey, fended off his too great interest distrustfully. 'I'm not being clairvoyant,' he said patiently. 'You told me a moment ago you have difficulties. You wouldn't have mentioned them if they hadn't been on your mind.'

She looked down into her lap, clasping and unclasping her hands in a nervous pressure. The small, thin, beautiful fully-boned face was subtle and still, but it was a braced and wary stillness.

'I made my mistake,' she said, in a dry and

113

careful voice, 'being born into a clever and distinguished family. It *is* a mistake, when you turn out to be the plain, dull, nondescript one. Uncle Edward—everybody knows how brilliant he is. And my mother—she's his sister, you know,—she has an arts degree, and she paints, and sings, and plays, she can do everything. It's only because of her ill health, and because she happened to make a rather unfortunate marriage, that she didn't become a scholar and celebrity like him. Aunt Audrey isn't an intellectual, like them, of course, she doesn't come from such an intellectual family. Her people were tradesmen who'd just got into the money. She went to a terribly select boarding school, and all that—Pleydells, I expect you've heard of it?—but she didn't get any great distinctions, they took her away before her final exams. I've never understood why. Maybe they weren't interested in academic success, all they wanted was the cachet. But she was everything else, you see. It's enough to be so beautiful, don't you think so? She's beautiful, and she knows how to do everything beautifully, even if she doesn't do it so terribly well. Me, I'm well-read, and I'm not stupid, but that's all I've got, and in our family it just isn't enough. Even things I can really do well, I find myself doing so badly... It's...a personal thing. I try too

114

hard, and over-reach myself. It isn't easy, being the one without any gifts at all. I can't see any future ahead of me, except playing second fiddle all my life to someone. I *know* I have moods! Wouldn't you have moods?'

Most of which was her mother speaking; and the faithful repetition of the threnody of complaint only went to show the helpless and vulnerable affection she had for her mother. She hadn't yet turned to doubt any of that, or pick it to pieces as some young people can and do, and find all the flaws in it. There was a lot of undeserved loyalty wrapped up in this rather pathetic package.

She caught his eye, and her pale cheek warmed a little. She liked the thick, strongly marked eyebrows that yet stood so tranquilly apart, with none of the menace of those brows that almost meet over the bridge of the nose. She minded his penetrating glance less than she had expected, and yet she was afraid of it.

'I suppose I'm a psychiatric case, really,' she said rather loftily, 'only nobody's done anything about it, so far.'

'On the contrary, I think you're a completely normal adolescent who has suffered from rather too much adult companionship,' said George candidly, and smiled at her astonished, even affronted stare. 'Abnormalities *are* the norm,

115

when you're struggling out of one stage and into another. Let's face it, Felicity, you're not grown-up yet, you're only growing up. I haven't forgotten how damned uncomfortable it is. I've seen it happen to others. You're not doing too badly. Just don't take any of your elders too seriously. Above all, don't take any of them as the gospel. Not even the psychiatrists, some of them need psychiatrists too. Is that what was troubling you, this afternoon?'

He had brought her back to the matter in hand none the less firmly for the gentleness of his manner; but she didn't hold it against him, she knew she had to face it. The long, fair lashes lay on her cheeks. Her face was set, and she wasn't going to show him her eyes.

'It makes it worse that I have been so much with grown-ups. I still am. They expect me to act like an adult, and yet they don't treat me as one. They get the work out of me, and then expect me to be in bed by ten. I did try to confide. I...I didn't choose very well. He hadn't got time to listen to me. I thought...he's only twenty-three, and women are so much more mature...I thought we could be contemporaries but he...I saw it wasn't any good,' said Felicity with dignity, 'so I went away and left him. But you'll understand, I didn't want to talk to anyone after that.'

'I do understand. You left him...where?'

'Just under the redwood tree,' she said firmly, 'where the paths cross.'

'You took the path to the bridge? And left him standing there?'

'Yes,' she said, with the flat finality of a slab of stone being laid over a grave.

'Let me be quite certain...he was then at the crossroads, and outside the fence that rails off the riverside enclosure with the grotto?'

'Yes,' she said, with the same intonation.

'You didn't look round to see where he went from there?'

'I didn't look round at all. I'd been dismissed, I went,' said Felicity, with completely adult bitterness.

'And that was the last you saw of him? You don't know where he went from there?'

'I do now,' said Felicity. 'I didn't then. That was the last I saw of him.'

She looked up. Her eyes were enormous in fear and grief, greedy for reassurance. Of this terror and this hope there was no doubt whatever. 'Mr Felse, do you think something happened to him? You don't...you don't think he's...?'

'I don't think anything yet,' said George. 'I hope he's simply suffered a crisis of his own, and run away from whatever was on *his* mind.
117

Don't think he's exempt at twenty-three. Maybe he was so full of his own problems he couldn't spare any consideration for yours. If we can find him, be sure we will. Now you go to bed, and leave it to us. If you've told me all you know, there's nothing more you can do.'

'I've told you all I know.' She got as far as the door, and looked back. Her face was mute and stiff, but her eyes were full of haunted shadows. 'Good night, Mr Felse!'

'Good night, Felicity!'

And all that, thought George, watching her go, sounds like truth, and nothing but truth. But he still had an uneasy feeling that truth, with Felicity, was an iceberg, with eight-ninths of its bulk under water.

'I'd better tell you at once,' said Dickie Meurice, settling himself at his ease and spreading an elbow on Edward Arundale's desk, 'that of course I've realised what this is all about, even if there's been no official admission that anything's wrong. Old Penrose has given the impression that everything's proceeding according to plan, and he had no intentions of using Lucien Galt in tonight's lectures. Without even saying so, which is pretty good going, but then, he's a deep old bird. But I know too well what Lucifer costs. If they

118

bought him at all, they wanted him on-stage the whole week-end. And I know *him* too well to miss the moment when he absents himself from among us. He went off, voluntarily or otherwise, between lunch and tea. And *you're* here to cover the management, in case it turns out he didn't disappear voluntarily. Solicitor? Or private trouble-shooter?'

'County C.I.D,' said George without expression but not without relish, and saw with satisfaction the instant recoil, quickly mastered but not quickly enough.

Dickie Meurice tapped his cigarette on the arm of his chair, and stared, and thought so hard that his blond countenance paled. He said carefully, lightly: 'You don't mean you've found him? You've got a genuine police case? This is official?'

'Not yet. If everybody co-operates it may not have to be. No, *we* don't know yet where Lucien Galt is. Do *you*, Mr Meurice?'

'Why should *I* know?' The smile a little stained now, the voice demonstrating involuntarily its disastrous tendency to shrillness.

'You had, it seems, about the same chance of being the last to see him, this afternoon, as any of the others who passed up the sight-seeing trips and stayed at Follymead. Were you?'

119

'Look,' said Meurice, persuasively, leaning forward with the look of shining candour that meant he was at his most devious, 'if this is on the level, if it's a police job, of course I'll co-operate.' He had made up his mind rapidly enough where his interests lay, and that they were already involved; tweak that string occasionally, and he'd co-operate, maybe even a bit too much. 'Tell me what you expect of me, ask me whatever you want to know, and I'm with you.'

'I expect you to keep this strictly to yourself until, or unless, publicity becomes inevitable. Only a handful of people know about it, and it's better for all concerned that it should remain that way. Better for Follymead, better for all these people attending the course, better for the artists involved, and better for me. Publicity may be very good business in your profession, of course, but only the right kind of publicity. And as you happen to be one of those who stayed at home today... Though of course, you may be able to account for every minute of your time, and provide confirmation of your account...'

The artless, concerned smile became more winning and anxious to help. So he couldn't account for his time; and he would play ball, though perhaps not strictly by the rules.

'I don't need that kind of publicity, I can't use it. I'll keep it quiet, don't worry. What can I tell you?'

'You were going on one of these coach-trips, I gather, originally. What made you change your mind?'

'I thought I could use my time better here. There's no chance to talk seriously to anyone at this sort of affair, with seventy or eighty people milling around in a communal spree. And there was someone I wanted to talk to. And she didn't go, so I didn't go.'

'Liri Palmer?'

'That's right. I thought there might be a good opportunity of cultivating her company while the place was virtually empty.' He was being very frank, very open; an honest man would have looked less eager, and sounded a good deal less forthcoming. 'I like Liri. She's wasting herself on a heel like Lucien Galt, whether she loves or hates him. I wanted to tell her so, and get some sense into her. I don't know whether they've told you what's in the background between those two, or what happened last night?' He didn't wait to be answered, he told it anyhow; no one could do it better. Maybe he wanted it on record officially that someone, and not himself, had threatened Lucien Galt's life; if, that is, you cared to

121

take that impromptu revision of a song as a serious threat. He liked Liri Palmer—or did he?—but he liked Dickie Meurice a lot better.

'I see you don't exactly love Galt, yourself,' observed George.

'That's no secret. Why should it be? He's treated Liri badly, and the rest of his profession didn't christen him Lucifer for nothing. But I didn't set eyes on him all this afternoon,' he said firmly. 'The last time I saw him was at lunch.'

'But you did see Liri?'

'Yes, I hung around in the gallery until she went out, and gave her five minutes start. Just after two o'clock, that would be. She made for that artificial ruin on the hillock across the park, and I came along shortly afterwards and found her there. I tried to get her to write off Galt and spend her attention on something better worth it—me!' A gleam of apparently genuine self-mockery shone in his eyes for an instant; it was the nearest he had come to being likeable, but in all probability he was merely experimenting to find out what attitudes would recommend him to George.

'Was she amenable?' asked George, with a wooden face.

'Metaphorically speaking, she spat in my eye. Nobody was going to put Liri off her grudges or her fancies.'

'And which was this?'

'At that stage, I'd say practically all grudge. She'd been badly hurt, and she can be an implacable enemy. I saw I was getting nowhere, so I gave up and came away. There was hardly anybody about, I'm afraid, I can't bring witnesses, but I give you my word I was back in the walled garden soon after three o'clock, and I didn't leave there until I came in to tea. There are archery butts there. I was practising all by myself until four, and then I came indoors to wash. And that's all. Not a very productive afternoon.'

'And you left Liri there at the tower. When would that be?'

'Maybe about twenty minutes to three. She was sitting there alone, nobody else in sight that I noticed.'

'You wouldn't see very much of the river's course from there?'

The winsome blue eyes lit with a flare of intelligence that was not winsome at all. 'Well, not from the ground, that I do know. There are tall trees in between, all you see is a gleam of water here and there. But there's a stairway up that tower,' he added helpfully. 'I haven't been up there, but I should think you'd get a pretty good view with that added height. Not that she showed any signs of making use of it,' he concluded fairly, 'while I was there.'

'Well, thank you, Mr Meurice, you've been very helpful. If we should have any difficulty in filling in the details of the afternoon, I'm sure you'll do your best for us again. And you will keep the matter confidential?'

Give him his due, he could take a double-edged hint as well as the next man. He promised secrecy with almost unnecessary fervour, and departed, having done his level best to plant the suggestion that, if something had really happened to Lucien Galt, Liri Palmer had made it happen. Who else, after all, had threatened his life?

George sighed, grimaced, and sent for Liri Palmer.

'Oh, he was there, all right.' Liri crossed her long and elegant legs, and declined a cigarette with a shake of her head. 'He was doing his best to make up to me, but I wasn't having any. What it adds up to is that he was inviting me to join in an all-out attack on Lucien's professional position. A lot of dirty work goes on in the record business, and popular disc-jockeys have a lot of influence. With a few like-minded assassins as dedicated as himself, Meurice could ruin a man.'

124

'And you were not interested?'

Her lips curled disdainfully. 'If I decide on assassination, I shan't need any allies. I told him where he could go.'

'Yesterday, I hear, you made what could be considered as being a threat against Galt, about as publicly as possible.'

'Oh, that!' A tight, dark smile hollowed her cheeks, but she was not disconcerted. 'Dickie made sure you knew about that, of course. He needn't have worried, I'd have told you myself. Yes, it's true. I did that.' She sounded faintly astonished now in looking back at it, as though it had become irrelevant and quite unaccount able in retrospect.

'Did you mean it?' asked George directly.

'Did I mean it...Yes, at the time I probably did. But even then what I really had in mind was not action so much as a declaration of my position. All the rest of them just happened to be there,' she said, with an arrogance Lucifer himself could not have bettered. 'It was nothing to do with them.'

'Then you didn't act on it, this afternoon?'

It was the first direct and deliberate suggestion that Lucien Galt might have suffered a murderous attack, might, in fact, be dead at that moment. She received it fully, thoughtfully and silently, and betrayed neither surprise nor any other emotion. What she thought, what she felt, she kept to herself. Like her private communications in song, they were nothing to do with anyone else. This was a young woman accustomed to standing on her own feet, and asking no quarter from anyone.

'I didn't see Lucien this afternoon. He never came near me, and I didn't go looking for him. I sent Dickie Meurice away, and stayed up there at the folly until it was time to come in to tea.'

'Not, I feel, without some sort of occupation?'

Her smile warmed a little, but remained dark and laden. 'I was wrestling with an idea for a song. It didn't work out.'

'Miss Palmer, I've gathered—and not only from Meurice—that a little while ago your relations with Lucien Galt were very close indeed. Would you mind telling me the reason for your break with him?'

'Yes,' said Liri, directly, firmly, 'I would mind. It's a private matter between him and me, and I want it to stay that way.'

He accepted that without question. 'Then, if you're good at keeping things private, keep this interview, this whole investigation, between the few of us. This week-end may as well run its course without a general alarm, if it can.

126

And there's one more thing I'd like to consult you about.'

He laid upon her knee the small box in which he had placed the silver medal and chain. 'My son found this at a certain spot by the river. Maybe you've already seen it.'

She took up the box in her palm, and touched the little disc gently with one long finger. 'Yes, I've seen it. Dominic showed it to us— the few of us who knew. It's Lucien's. He always wore it.'

'Always? As long as you've known him?'

'Yes, from the first time I met him. He said he's worn it ever since he was a child. It was the one thing he had that belonged to his father.

'He told you that himself? And how long have you known him?'

'Just over two years now. Yes, he told me himself.' There had been confidences between them then, and confidence. He was not, by all accounts, a person who talked about himself, or indeed much of a talker on any subject. 'He wouldn't have much left from his parents, obviously, after their shop was flattened by a buzz-bomb. You know about the Galts? They had a newsagent and tobacconist business in Islington. It was one of the last bombs of the war that got it. Both his parents were killed. He grew up in a children's home.'

'I know what's been published about him,' said George.

'That's all most of us know. He loved his foster-parents at the home, though, there wasn't any warping there. He still goes back there pretty regularly.' She looked up suddenly; her face was pale and still. 'He *did,*' she said, and closed the box carefully over the silver medal.

'Mr Marshall has told me,' said Audrey Arundale in a low, constrained voice, 'about this affair, and about your great kindness in coming here privately to help us. We're very grateful to you. My husband would wish me to thank you on his behalf, as well as my own. I feel— you'll understand and excuse me—terribly lost without him.'

She stood in her own rose-and-white sitting-room, herself a white rose ever so slightly past her most radiant bloom, fair and frightened and gallant, terribly lost without Edward. She was used only to things that went smoothly; things that went hideously off the rails bewildered and confused her.

'Please sit down, Mr Felse. I feel so guilty at making use of you in this way, when we have really nothing to go on. Is there anything you want to ask me?'

'As a matter of form, I should like to know

how you spent this afternoon, whether you saw anyone, and what time your husband left. I want to form as full a picture as possible of the hours between lunch and tea.'

'I understand, yes. I was indoors all afternoon. Edward was here with me until just before three o'clock, then he went out to the car, to load it for his trip. I can't say exactly what time he got off, because I didn't see him go. I think he wanted to pick up some books from the library, but that wouldn't take long. I should think he was away by a quarter past three. After he left I was in here writing letters.' She made a faint gesture of one hand towards the neat little pile of them, lying on her writing-desk. 'I didn't go down to join the party at tea, I had it in here. I didn't realise that Mr Galt was missing, though I noticed, naturally, that he didn't take part in the five o'clock session. He hasn't come back, of course.' Her anxious face hoped against hope for reassurance.

'He hasn't. On the contrary, we've found certain traces which suggest that we have a serious matter on our hands.'

'May I know?' she asked hesitantly, 'What they are?'

He told her. She turned half aside from the mention of blood, and seemed for an instant to want to withdraw absolutely from this place and these events, which obeyed no rules in her ordered existence, and made chaos of her security. She reached out blindly and briefly with one hand for Edward, who had always been there, but Edward wasn't there. She said, though with dignity and quietness, exactly what George had felt sure she would say:

'Don't you think we ought to contact my husband and tell him what's happened? I wouldn't think of suggesting it in any normal circumstances, when Harry's in charge, but these aren't normal circumstances. This is more than the mere responsibility for the present course, it's a question of the responsibility for Follymead as an institution. Edward can't delegate that, not in such a serious matter.' She looked across the room at Henry Marshall, who had sat silent throughout this exchange. 'I'm sorry, Harry, I ought to have left it to you even to make the suggestion. I knew you would have done.'

No mistake about it, that fancy boarding school of hers had done pretty well by the tradesman's daughter, even if she hadn't distinguished herself in examination, like Felicity's illustrious kin. No wonder Marshall looked at her with something like devotion.

'Mr Felse and I have already recognised the need to put this matter on a proper footing. Obviously I hoped and believed we should have some word from Mr Galt, or that he would turn up again with his own explanation, but after so many hours without news it becomes rather a different case. Yes, I think we should call Dr Arundale.'

'I think perhaps I'd better do it,' said George, 'if I may. Where will he be at this hour?'

The clock on the desk said ten-forty. 'It's a guild dinner,' said Audrey. 'He's staying overnight with the chairman afterwards, but they won't be very early. I should think they're still at the Metropole. I have the number here.'

George dialled and waited for his connection. It was very quiet in the room; even the clock was almost silent.

'Hotel Metropole? I believe you've got the Vintners' annual dinner there tonight? Is the party still in session? Good! Would you ask Mr Arundale to come to the phone? That's right, Edward Arundale—he's their speaker tonight.' He waited. Audrey felt behind her for the arm of a chair, and sat down very slowly and silently, never taking her eyes from George's face. It felt so still that she might have been holding her breath.

'Hullo, is that...? Oh, I see. No, I didn't know that.' There was a long, curious pause while he listened, and the faint clacking of the distant voice that was, surprisingly, doing all the talking. 'At what time was that?' And again: 'You're sure? You'd know that voice? No, that's all right, I'm sorry to have disturbed you, I'll contact him there. Thank you! Goodbye!'

He cradled the receiver and held it down in its rest, and over the hand that pinned it in position he looked up gently at Audrey.

'Mrs Arundale, I'm afraid this is going to be a surprise to you. Even a shock. Mr Arundale isn't there. That was a nan named Malcolmson speaking to me, the president of the Vintners' Guild. Mr Arundale cancelled his engagement, they had to whip up a substitute speaker at a minute's notice.'

'But...that's impossible!' she said in a soundless whisper. 'Why should he cancel it? He said nothing to me. He took his notes...and the references he needed for tomorrow...everything. I didn't know anything about this...I didn't know...'

'All the same, he did it. There's no doubt at all about this. He says Mr Arundale rang up to explain and apologise, this afternoon, just about three o'clock. He says he's known him

132

for eight years, he knows his voice on the telephone too well for any possibility of mistake. It was your husband himself who called. An emergency, so he told him, here at Follymead, that made it impossible for him to leave as planned. Naturally Mr Malcolmson didn't question it, however inconvenient it might be for him.' He lifted the receiver again; distant and staccato, the dialling tone fired its dotted line of machine-gun bullets into the silence. 'Can you give me the number of someone who'll know about this conference tomorrow? The secretary?'

She got up from her chair and moved to the pedestal of the desk like a creature in a bad dream. Her fingers fumbled through the pages of a notebook, and found the entry. The secretary was the vicar of a suburban parish, and his voice, when he answered, sounded young and crisp and agile.

'I'm sorry to trouble you at this late hour, but I'm clearing up a few arrears of business for Mr Arundale, and the notes he's left me don't make it clear whether he managed to call you about the conference tomorrow. Have you already heard from him today?' No need to sound the alarm yet; this would do better than candour.

'Yes, he telephoned this afternoon,' said the

distant voice promptly. 'We're very sorry indeed that we shan't have him with us tomorrow, after all, it's a great disappointment. But I know he wouldn't have called it off if he could possibly have avoided it.'

'No, of course not. About what time did he ring you?'

'Oh, I suppose shortly after three. It might even have been a little earlier.'

'Thank you,' said George, 'that's all I wanted to know.'

The telephone clashed softly in its cradle.

'He telephoned there, too, and cancelled his engagement. Wiped out all his arrangements for the week-end. And yet he took the car and left, at about the time he was expected to leave, and without mentioning to anyone that he'd changed his plans. So where has he gone? And why?'

Marshall let his hands fall empty before him; there was nowhere he could get a hold on this, and no way he could make sense of it. 'I don't know. I don't understand anything about it.'

Audrey stood motionless, her eyes enormous in shock and bewilderment. In an arduous whisper she asked: 'What must we do?'

'I don't think we have any choice now. We still have no real evidence of anything either criminal or tragic, but we have two unexplained disappearances, occuring at much the same time, and we can't ignore them, and we can't afford to delay. Lectures had much better continue as though nothing's happened. If we can get through the week-end without making this affair public, we'll do it. There'll be the least possible obtrusion. But I've no alternative now,' said George, 'but to inform my chief. From now on, this becomes an official police matter.'

CHAPTER 5

As soon as he was back in Edward Arundale's office, with the door closed on the distant and cheerful din of the house party and the close and fearful silence of the warden's apartments, George telephoned his chief. Detective-Superintendent Duckett was Midshire born and bred, with all the advantages of having come up from the uniformed branch the hard way. It meant he not only knew his job and his own subordinates, but also all the complex social pressures of a conservative country; sometimes, in his less tolerant moments, he called it a feudal county, and nobody had a better right. The first thing he said was: 'Thank God your boy was there!' And the second: 'Can you still keep this dark?'

'Yes,' said George, with fair certainty that he was telling the truth. 'We've no body, no proof of a crime, only a very, very fishy situation that still may confound us by coming out blameless. Let's hope it does. In the meantime, we've every right to behave as if nothing had happened, on the surface, provided we dig like moles underneath. Only seven people know anything about my being here to investigate Galt's disappearance, though they must all know by now that he's gone. That can't be helped. Only Marshall and Mrs Arundale know that Arundale's apparently run out.'

'That suits me, and it'll suit the Chief Constable still better. He's a prime backer of that outfit at Follymead. The place balances its budget and fends off the taxpayers by luck, faith and act of God. What can we dig for you?'

'It's going to be pretty sticky,' said George honestly, 'in any case. Don't forget one of the parties concerned is the warden. What we're going to find is anybody's guess, but what I've got here is a nasty situation in which two people have vanished, one apparently without warning and involuntarily, the other with evidence of premeditation. No bodies, no known motives

136

for any violence, but some evidence that there *was* a struggle, that there *were* injuries. If there's a link between these two people, I want to know about it. I'm not so simple as to believe that they could both take off into the blue at the same moment, and no connection between the two events. It's against the law of averages. Now, these two are public persons. I'd like reports on their backgrounds. I want to know if there could be a link between them, and if so, what it is. And brace yourself, in case what comes out goes against Arundale. Because *he's* the one who planned his departure, not the boy.'

'If he slung the kid in the river,' said Duckett with admirable directness, 'neither you nor I can get him out of the resultant mess, George, my boy. With luck we might get Follymead out of it. Knock off fifty per cent for over-enthusiasm, and still the place is worth preserving.'

'I think so, too. All right, at first light I'm going down to look over the ground again, carefully. I hope to have some specimens for the lab boys, and I don't care if we do have to pull 'em back from their Sunday hobbies.'

'Right, and first thing tomorrow I'll have Scott turned loose on their histories.' He was silent for one pregnant second. 'How's the flood level?'

'High,' said George. 'I reckon anything that went in there would bounce that last weir like a cork, and be out of the grounds long before now. We're past the fancy curves at that point. The next real check is the bend by Sandy Cliff, the other side of the main road. Anything can happen with this sort of spring flow, but I should start dragging there. That's where he's most likely to come ashore.'

George went down to the riverside in the first light of morning. The threatened rain had fallen in the small hours, while he had slept uneasily and briefly in Arundale's office, declining the bed Marshall had offered him. The dawn sky was tattered with filmy clouds and fitful brightness, and the grass was saturated and silvery against the river's turgid brown. Slanting light picked out in deep relief the wounds in the turf, still dark, fresh and soft from the protection of Marshall's plastic car cover. George went over the ground carefully, inch by inch. There was only one clear print, and that of only the sole of a shoe, stamped into the raw clay, a composition sole crosscut in sawtooth grooves for grip. A well shaped shoe with a good conservative toe, maybe size nine; the kind two thirds of the men in the house probably wore, half of them in this size. All the rest of the tracks were trampled over, crossed and blurred by the resilience of the grass, but in sum they were there, and their implications unmistakable.

He found one other thing. One of the stamping feet, driving in a heel deeply, had left behind in the print one of last autumn's leaves from the ride, one of the old ivy leaves, rubbery even in decay, that drop with their naked, angular stems, and lie long after the rest of the woodland loss is mould. This one had been cupped round the edge of the shoe's heel, and remained so, pressed into the turf; and something that was not water, something hardly visible at twilight against its brown colouring, had splashed into it later, and gathered in the cup. Warm and sheltered under the plastic sheeting, it had remained moist. Not so much of it, maybe, as they take from your thumb for a blood test; but possibly as much as the lab boys would need in order to group it.

George extracted the moulded leaf gingerly, and found another little box for it, propping its edges with cotton wool and keeping it upright. There was nothing else here for him. He covered the bruised ground again, and prowled along the very edge of the water; it seemed to him that it had risen a shade higher in the night with the new rain, but he had seen it last night only by moonlight and torchlight. Certainly in this green, moist dawn, full of the drippings and whisperings of water, that concentrated brown flood was impressive. No finding anything in that without dragging, or going down into it; not until chemistry did its work, and it surfaced again, and judging by the force of this current that would be miles downstream. The coiled curve by Sandy Cliff just might bring it ashore, as he had said to Duckett; but even there the water would be over the summer beach and burrowing hard under the cliff, and whatever it carried might continue downstream with it.

George made his way thoughtfully back to the house, mapping this part of the Follymead grounds mentally as he went; and in the warden's office Dominic was waiting for him.

'Hullo!' said George with unflattering surprise. 'Whatever got you up at this hour?'

'I thought of something that may be important. I meant to be up earlier, but I had to be careful. I've got the Rossignol twins in my room, and they can hear the grass growing. I didn't want to bring the whole hunt down on you. But it's all right,' Dominic said in hasty reassurance, 'I left them dead asleep.' He looked from his father's face to the small box carried so carefully in his hand. He didn't ask any questions about it, and George didn't volunteer anything.

'All right, what's on your mind?'

'It was on my mind, too, half the night. You know how it is when you know you've seen something before, and can't for the life think where or when? I woke up suddenly this morning, and I'd got it. That medal...could we have another look at it, and I'll show you.'

The pillbox that contained it was locked into the top drawer of Arundale's desk. George extracted and offered it. Dominic remembered to turn it with the tip of a ball pen when he wanted to refer to the reverse, as he had remembered not to handle it directly when he first found it. He shivered a little with clinging sleepiness and the chill of the morning.

'You see here, this side, that formalised figure in armour, with a nutshell helmet like the Normans in the Bayeaux tapestry, and a long shield with a sort of spread eagle on it...? I suddenly remembered where I'd seen it before. You can't mistake it once you do get the idea. That's Saint Wenceslas. Yes, I'm quite sure. He always looks like that. You ask Tossa, she'll tell you the same, we got to know the form last year, when we were in Prague on holiday. And the other side...' He turned it

141

delicately to show the lion rampant with a fork-
ed tail. 'This I *can* show you, right here. I
should have known it on sight if it hadn't been
quite so worn. Look! By pure luck I happened
to have this still in my jacket.'

He held it out triumphantly, a small badge,
questionably silver, the same rampaging lion,
with feathery fringes like a retriever, and
double tail bristling.

'Lieutenant Ondrejov gave me that, before
we left Liptovsky Pavol, last year. You see, it
is the same. This is the Czech lion. And Saint
Wenceslas is the chief of their patron saints,
and doesn't belong to anyone else. I bet you
anything you like this medal originated in
Czechoslovakia.'

George measured the two small heraldic
creatures, and found them one. 'Now, why,'
he wondered aloud blankly, 'should Lucien
Galt be wearing a Czech medal?'

'I wish I knew. But that's what this is.'

George stared, and thought, and could not
doubt it. This was, according to Liri Palmer,
the one thing Lucien had that had belonged to
his father. That didn't, of course, determine
to whom it might have belonged earlier. It was
wartime, Galt could perfectly well have some
chance-met friend among the self exiled Czechs
who formed, at that time, the most articulate,

142

the most reticent,—the two were compatible!—and the most nearly English component of the European armies in Britain. Maybe they swopped small tokens before the unit moved out for D-Day; and maybe the medal acquired value because its giver didn't come back. There were such things, then, unexpected friendships that went deeper than kith and kin.

'Well, thanks very much for the tip. It's certainly curious.' George pocketed the trophy along with his other specimens. 'And since you are up, how about running me down to the lodge and bringing back the station wagon afterwards?'

'Yes, of course.' He brightened perceptibly at the thought of being useful. 'You're going in to headquarters? Is it official, then?'

'It's official, but it's still not for publication.'

'Shall I meet you at the lodge again when you come back?'

'No need. I'll drive up by the farm road at the back, and put my car in the yard there. I might need to get out and in quickly, later in the day.'

'Is there anything I can be doing?'

'Yes, but you won't like it much.'

'I still might do it,' said Dominic generously, 'seeing as it's for you.'

'Be on the spot here, then, attend everything,

and help to keep everybody occupied and out of our hair. Have a word with Professor Penrose, and ask him to lay on a session after lunch, too, even if it wasn't in the programme. Keep everybody's nose hard against this folk-music grindstone, and try to make the whole week-end pass off without anything of this business leaking out. Get the professor to ask Liri Palmer to take part in every session. If the stars back him up, the rank and file won't want to miss anything.'

'And in the meantime,' Dominic asked soberly, perceiving one answer for himself, and not much liking it, 'what *will* they be missing?'

'Maybe nothing. But I don't want them down by the river. They wouldn't get to the grotto, anyhow, I shall have a watchdog on duty. But I'd rather they didn't know that, either, so keep them hard at work here in the house.'

'We can but try. Anything else?'

'Keep your ears open. I'd like to know what sort of comments they're making. The professor will probably have to tell them some tale about Galt being called away, but, even so they'll have their own theories. I want to know what they are, and who starts them. And anything else you notice that may be of interest.'

'When shall I see you, then, to report?
144

Hadn't we better have an arrangement?'

'Come down to the grotto as soon after lunch as you can, and come on the quiet. If I'm not there, Price will know where to find me.'

'There it is, then,' said Duckett, shuffling the typed pages across the table, 'and much good it does us.'

And there it was, compressed, bald and completely barren, the fruit of Scott's interim researches into the past history of Edward Arundale and Lucien Galt. And nothing could be more above-board.

Arundale, only son of an illustrious academic family, one sister, five years younger; father a historian, mother a specialist in Oriental languages, both dead; his school, his college, his degrees, all listed, all impeccable; a distinguished teaching career, culminating in the headmastership of Bannerets, which he held for fifteen years, and after that this appointment as warden of Follymead. Married in 1946 Audrey Lavinia Morgan, only child of Arthur Morgan, of Morgan's Stores, a chain of groceries covering the south of England. The bride, it seemed, was then twenty years old, and Arundale, thirty-five. Her father's money was recent and plentiful, *his* father having merely run two modest suburban shops, and limited his ambition to getting elected to the local council. Arthur, or maybe Mrs Arthur, had bigger ideas for their offspring. Audrey had been sent to Pleydells, a good boarding-school in North London, though evacuated to Scotland during the war years, which must have been Audrey's period. It seemed that the Morgans were then on the climb, bent on equipping their daughter for an outstanding marriage. Maybe Arundale's was the kind of lustre they valued and wanted. No university career for Audrey, no mention of any special academic qualifications; just as Felicity had said, quoting, no doubt, her aggrieved, mother. Her upbringing had been aimed at marriage, not a career. Edward supplied all the scholarly distinctions necessary, she provided him with a hostess well trained, conscientious and lovely to look at. All very satisfactory, and nowhere a shadow on it. Their life at Follymead was constantly in the public eye, and the public eye doesn't miss much.

That was Arundale. And in the other file, this boy from a children's home, bright, handsome, aggressive, disdainful, intolerant of adulation, and single-minded about his art. Lucien Galt, born 1943, son of John James and Esther Galt, who kept a small newsagent's shop in Islington. Parents killed by a V-2, one of the last to fall on London, son taken into public care and brought up in one of a group of cottage homes in Surrey. Good school record, early development of musical ability, apparently well adjusted, never in anything worth calling trouble. Not interested in staying on at school, already set on music. Left at fifteen, and worked as a garage hand and mechanic until he broke into the record business, broadcasting and television, all in the same month, at the age of nineteen. Made a tremendous success as a folk-singer, several European tours behind him, heading for a South American tour very soon. Said to be still on the warmest terms with his former foster-parents at the home, visiting them regularly, and being credited with several gifts to the present household. Considered difficult in the entertainment world because there are songs he won't sing, engagements he won't accept, places he won't go, and indeed nothing he will do except what he wants to do.

And all they knew of him, to add to that dossier, was that he had worn a silver medal on a chain round his neck, that he had told Liri Palmer it was all he had of his father's, and that he had left it lying in the grass by the river when he vanished from Follymead.

'Not a thing in common between them,' said Duckett, 'and not a thing to show that they'd ever clapped eyes on each other before Friday night. How can you get to the point of murder in only twenty-four hours?'

'How do you even get to the point of being on fighting terms in only twenty-four hours? With their kind of contact and at that kind of place?'

'There's always the classic way,' said Duckett disgustedly. *'Cherchez la femme!'* He wasn't serious, of course; Arundale's past was so rigid with rectitude that the idea of connecting him with a *crime passionnel* managed to be almost funny. Besides, there was only one woman in his life, apparently, and that was his equally blameless wife, to whom he'd been married for twenty well-matched years. 'putting him on one side, just for argument, I gather there are others who might be capable of pushing this lad in the river?'

'Several, I'd say. The girl has all the necessary fire and guts, and Meurice hates him enough, given the opportunity. And either of them *could* have been there with him at round about the right time.'

Duckett breathed pipe-smoke heavily through his brigand's moustache, and drummed a thick fingertip on the edge of his desk. 'Well, I'll keep Scott on the job. If we take anything out of the river,' he said grimly, you'll be the first

to know about it. What can Scott most useful-
ly be doing for you?'

George considered, frowning at the meaningless pages that yet must hold somewhere a
more substantial image of the persons to whom
they applied. 'Seems to me that if Galt had
anything to confide, the people he'd turn to
would be his foster-parents, this housefather
and mother—Stewart, the name seems to be.
It might be worth a drive down there to see if
they can shed any light. With a lot of luck he
may have gone to them, or at least got in touch
with them—*if* he's alive, if this is some other
sort of trouble that's caught up with him. And
Scott could call in on this service garage where
the boy worked, that's another possibility, if
a thin one. Then there's his business agent, of
course. Send Scott down there, have him comb
out the lot, all the people he might have turned to if he's alive and in trouble.'

'Right, I'll see to that. We can't put out a
call for Arundale or the car,' said Duckett
reasonably, 'unless we do bring the body
ashore. It would be as much as my life's worth
to compromise that set-up for nothing, so let's
concentrate on finding the boy—dead or alive.'

George was smoking a cigarette moodily by the
river, watching a methodical sergeant take

casts—probably useless, of the one clear shoe-print and the indentation of the heel, when Dominic came to report. The dragging of the Braide had not yet reached the Follymead boundary, more than a quarter of a mile away; nor, so far, had it netted them anything more than driftwood, two long-abandoned eel traps, and an old bicycle frame. By the quantity and size of the driftwood you could gauge the violence and indiscipline of the spring. The Braide ran down to the Comer, which was a river with its feet in the mountains; this was a tamed park stream by comparison with what the Comer brought down out of Wales. Any more rain, and Comer water would be backing up from the confluence, churning up the muddy countercurrent until they both spilled out over the whole expanse of the low-lying fields. Lucien Galt might yet fetch up on somebody's doorstep.

George heard them coming through the trees, not one, but two, a boy and a girl talking briefly, in subdued and serious voices. He should have thought of that possibility, of course, but it came as something of a revelation that Dominic should have reached the point of taking it for granted that any privilege given to him automatically extended to cover Tossa, too. 'They' were to be deflected by any means from this area by the river; but Tossa was not 'they,' Tossa had become 'we.' It was not quite so clear whether she also took it as her right. The moment they emerged from the trees she slipped her hand from Dominic's and hung back, silent and tentative, but very much on the alert. She caught George's eye and moved nearer, encouraged. Under the ornamental trees that circled the grotto she halted; the tiny blue crosses of lilac blossom drifted down into her dark hair, as the branches threshed uneasily in a rising wind.

'Well,'said George, 'how are things going?'

'All O.K, so far. Everybody's come along to the lectures, and they all seem to be enjoying themselves. I told the professor what you said, and Mr Marshall, too. It's working smoothly enough up to now. Nobody's let anything out to the others, and they don't suspect anything's wrong. The professor made a sort of vague apology for Lucien's having to leave, but he managed not to say anything definite about the reason. But you were right about the rumours. There's a murmur that Lucien ran out because he couldn't take the Liri situation...You know, she'd followed him here with a grudge, and the atmosphere was tense, and he preferred to duck out. It makes good sense, and it tickles them, so they like it. And it lets the professor out, too, because of course the authorities would simply have to accept whatever excuse Lucien offered, even if they thought privately he'd run for cover from a situation he couldn't manage.'

'That ought to serve pretty well,' agreed George with a wry smile. 'Go along with it. Who started it?'

'Well, I'm pretty sure it came from Dickie Meurice in the first place. That way, you see, he makes a good show of helping you to keep the thing wrapped, and at the same time he churns up a little more dirt to stick to Galt when he does reappear. *If* he does reappear,' he corrected himself, very soberly.

'He will,' protested Tossa, her eyes fixed confidently on George's face. 'Won't he? This is just something quite stupid, that only *looks* like that sort of trouble, isn't it?'

'We hope so,' said George gently. 'You keep on thinking so. What about this afternoon?'

'That's all fixed. We're in session again at two-fifteen. We slipped out by the back way as soon as we got away from lunch, and came down through the trees. Nobody's any the wiser.'

'Good! Has Felicity attended this morning?'

'We sat with her,' said Tossa, 'the first time. I think she only came at all because nobody can talk to her while there's a lecture going on, or

152

people singing. She looks terribly wretched and sick. She dodged us in the second session, after coffee. And as soon as we're out of the music-room she goes off somewhere out of sight. I'm worried about her. But she doesn't want anybody, she only wants to be left alone.'

'Keep an eye on her,' said George, 'all the same. Did Mrs Arundale show up?'

'Yes. She looked pretty pale and anxious, too,' said Dominic, 'but she's keeping the thing rolling. It must be rather awful for her, having something like this happen, especially when the warden isn't here. I bet she'll be glad when he comes back tonight.'

George said nothing to that; there was no need to burden them with even more secrets to keep, however trustworthy they might be. As for accounting for Arundale's non-return this evening from those meetings in Birmingham, leave that bridge to be crossed when the time came.

His mind had been much on Audrey Arundale, ever since he had talked to Duckett this morning. *Cherchez la femme*, indeed, but what an unlikely woman to look for at the heart of a *crime passionnel*. And yet she had everything but the temperament; beauty, a gentle appeal about her, even youth—she was only forty, and older women have changed history in their time. Maybe this wasn't the first time *she* had met Lucien Galt.

No, it was crazy. He couldn't picture her in the role, however objectively he tried. Nevertheless, he found himself asking, with deliberate and crude abruptness: 'Have you seen any signs of a special relationship between Lucien Galt and Mrs Arundale?'

Dominic was too startled to side-step, and too shaken to hide his discomfort. He stood staring in consternation, seeing again the ardent hands tough and clasp, seeing Arundale, walk imperviously and majestically on his wife's left, while she gripped Lucien Galt's fingers on her right. The question was so unexpected, the incident had begun to seem so irrelevant, that the sudden attack took his breath away. After all, Arundale didn't enter into the affair they were investigating. He was the one person who was out of it, surely. The only person.

'I...what on earth has that got to do...I men, nothing, really, nothing of any significance.'

'Come on,' said George quietly, 'tell it, and we'll see.' Tossa was looking from one to the other of them, lost, a small, hurt frown contorting her brows. Whatever Dominic had seen had certainly passed her by.

'Well, I don't know...It was just that on Friday night, when we left the drawing-room after

154

coffee, and were walking along the gallery, we were behind the Arundales and Lucien Galt. Mrs Arundale was in the middle. They were talking, just like anybody else, and Lucien's hand brushed...' Dominic's voice baulked at that half-willing distortion, and backed away from it. 'He touched her hand, and she opened it, and they clasped hands,' he said grudgingly. 'Only for a moment, though.'

'But...warmly?'

After a moment of silent debate Dominic admitted: 'Yes.' He went on rapidly: 'But it needn't mean much, you know. Just big-headedness on his part, and maybe she felt a bit irresponsible for once...an accidental touch...'

'Did it look accidental?' asked George quite gently.

Reluctantly but honestly again: 'No.'

'And they went on making conversation to cover it?' No need to answer that, it was in his mutely anxious face. 'Did anyone else see this?'

Almost to herself Tossa said; '*I* didn't.'

'Yes, I think...I'm almost sure Liri saw it. She was sitting in a dark alcove in the gallery, quite still. I think she saw.'

Add about fifty per cent to that, and you might have some approximation of the ardour of that episode. Dominic had a very natural and

155

human reluctance to admit to having witnessed a show of affection between two people who thought themselves unobserved. And it was no more than a crumb of a connection, at that, though a very suggestive one.

'All right, don't worry, as you say, it probably means virtually nothing.'

But Liri had seen it, Liri of all people. Maybe the emerging pattern, after all, argued a man at the heart of it, not a woman. *Cherchez l'homme!* Women can be jealous, too, and dangerous.

'You'd better run,' said George, 'or you'll be late for your class. If you should want me later, I'll be in the warden's office.'

And they ran, Tossa looking back doubtfully at George for a moment with her chin on her shoulder. The lilac tree slapped a stray cone of blossom into her face as she turned, and she flung up her hand—Dominic had taken possession of the other—and brushed it from her. The twig broke, leaving the spray of falling flowers in her hand. She allowed herself to be towed along the leafy ride still holding it.

'You never told me!'

'You wouldn't have told me, would you? I never *wanted* to see it.' He wasn't happy. 'What put it into Dad's mind, anyhow? I don't get it.'

156

'I don't know. Maybe he thinks *Liri*...'

'What, just because of that?'

'But it isn't *just* because of that. Liri was already mad with him about something, what could it be but another woman?'

'You mean she followed him here because she knew about him and...? I don't believe it! It wouldn't be like Liri, anyhow.' He had never realised until now how firm an idea he was forming of Liri Palmer's character. 'If she'd broken with him, she wouldn't follow him around to *watch* him perform...not to torment herself, not to hit him again, not for anything.' They had reached the footbridge; their hurrying footsteps clopped woodenly over it, and the flood below sent up a low, hollow echo.

'To get him back, she might,' said Tossa without thinking, and instantly drew back from a statement so revealing. She shook the loose blossoms from her spray of lilac with unnecessary care. 'This must be a very early kind, look, dropping already, and it's only late April. Did you ever see lilac quite such a pure blue?'

Even then she didn't realise what she had said, it was simply a pleasant, superficial observation, something blessedly remote from the ugly mystery that was bedevilling this weekend. They were skirting the open meadow when the truth hit her. She halted abruptly, pulling back hard on Dominic's hand; he turned in surprise to find her gazing at him in consternation.

'Dominic...*she was there!* Don't you remember? I said then, how blue, really blue, not purple at all...'

She thrust the tattered cone of blossom at him, brandishing it before his astonished eyes.

'Have you seen this kind anywhere else? There's lilac by the drive, and up by the pagoda, too, but it's all white or mauve, and it's only in bud yet. Nothing at all like this. But Felicity had some fallen flowers just like this in her hair yesterday! Don't you remember, she was combing them out with her fingers?

'Good lord!' he said blankly. 'She had, too! *Just* like these!'

'I picked them up, afterwards. It was the *colour*...'

He remembered now with aching clarity how Tossa had turned her hand sadly, and let the small blue crosses float back into the grass.

'But she told Dad...she told *us*...'

'I know! She told us she parted from him where the paths cross. She said she left him there and came on over the stone bridge... She didn't know where he went afterwards, but *she* left him *there*. But she didn't,' said Tossa with absolute conviction, and very quietly. 'Because before she met us she was under that lilac tree. She was there by the river with him. *She knows what happened!*'

They looked for her in the libraries, in the drawing-rooms, in the gallery, but she was nowhere to be found. In the end they were forced to go in to the afternoon session without having spoken to her; and at the last moment she slid in from nowhere and took a seat in a dim corner, and sat through the two hours of song and argument and speculation with a pale face and haunted eyes. But that meant that at least they could corner her when the session was over, before she could escape again into whatever lair she used for her private agonies.

The afternoon meeting ended with a tour-de-force by Liri Palmer, a thirty-five verse ballad without a dull line in it, all about a traitorous nobleman who killed his king and usurped his kingdom, but suffered the pregnant queen to live, on the understanding that if her child turned out to be a boy, he should be instantly killed, but if it was a girl she should be allowed to live. But the queen managed to elude her gaolers for a short time when her hour was near, and hid herself alone in the stables to bear her son. When the wife of one of the courtiers found her there, the queen begged her to exchange her girl baby for the royal boy.

  ' "And ye shall learn my gay goshawk
      Right weel to breast a steed,
      And I shall learn your turtle-dow
      As weel to write and read.

  ' "At kirk and market, when we meet,
      We'll dare make no avow
      But: Dame, how does my gay goshawk?
      Madam, how does my dow?" '

Thirty-five verses, all to one unchanging tune, and mounting excitement with every verse. Liri Palmer was an artist, no question of that. It was partly the pure, passionate drama of her voice, and the latent acting ability that enabled her to people her stage with so many living characters, without breaking the melody or distorting the tone; and partly the virtuosity of her accompaniment, which varied with every verse, and produced the rattle of duels and the muted agitation of women's plotting as fluently as the hammer of hooves or the ripple of rain. They reached the point where the gay goshawk had grown up, and was hunting with his foster-father:

' "Oh, dinna ye see yon bonny castell
With halls and towers so fair?
If every man had back his ain,
Of it ye should be heir."

' "The boy stared wild like a grey goshawk:
"Oh, what may all this mean?"
"My boy, ye are King Honour's son,
And your mother's our lawful queen." '

Tossa looked at Dominic, and her eyes
signalled that they must be near the end of the
story now. She was next to the wall, and in a
quiet corner; she rose softly, and slipped back
into the shadows, to circle the room unobtrusively to Felicity's hiding place.

The goshawk had reached his apotheosis,
leaping the castle wall and confronting False
Foundrage in arms. Not all ballads have happy endings. This one did. The boy killed his
enemy, delivered his mother, and took the
turtledow as his bride. The entranced hush
broke, the moment the last shuddering chord
of Liri's strings had vibrated into silence.
Under cover of the applause Felicity got up to
slide out of the room: and Tossa's hand closed
on her arm.

'Felicity, come into the little library. We

want to talk to you.'

The tone was quiet and reasonable, but Felicity recognised its finality. Perhaps she had been waiting for someone to take the burden out of her hands, with even more longing than terror. She went with them, stiff and silent, not trying to escape now, except into the deeps of her own being, and even there hoping for little. They sat her down in a quiet corner of the small library; the cheerful pre-tea din told them where all the others were, and assured them that their solitude here was safe for a little while.

Tossa laid the spray of wilting lilac flowers in the girl's lap. 'We found these this afternoon. We were looking for you before the session, to show you. These are the same kind you had in your hair yesterday, when we met you. We know now where you'd been. Not just along the path to the bridge. You'd been by the grotto, with Lucien. Hadn't you?'

Felicity looked all round her in a last convulsion of protest and despair, and shrank into herself and sat still, her eyes on the flowers. She didn't try to deny anything.

'You'll have to tell us what you know, Felicity. You understand that, don't you? It isn't any use trying to pretend you know nothing now. We *know* you were there.'

Felicity melted suddenly from her frozen stillness and began to shake uncontrollably. She linked her small hands together before her, and gripped until the slight knuckles were blanched like almonds.

'Yes,' she whispered, the word jerking out of her like a gasp of pain. She looked up at Tossa in desperate appeal, and asked in a small level voice. 'What happens to people who're accessories before the fact? Of murder, I mean? Supposing someone caused someone else to kill a person, but without meaning to?' Her face shook, and as resolutely reassembled its shattered and disintegrating calm; she wasn't crying, and she wasn't going to cry. What was the use now? 'Or suppose they *did* mean to, but never really believed it could happen? What do they do to people like that? Do you know?'

They looked at each other over her head, shaken to the heart.

'I think,' said Dominic, with careful, appalled gentleness, 'we'd better go into the warden's office and wait for my father. You'll have to tell him, you know. *We* don't matter, but we'll stay with you, if you want us to. It's *him* you have to tell. You go and sit in there with Tossa, and I'll go and find him.'

CHAPTER 6

'You tell it,' said George reasonably. 'You know what happened, and nobody's interested in tripping you up or trying to make you say something you don't want to say. Just tell us exactly what happened, and don't be afraid that we won't understand. Yes, Tossa'll stay with you. Don't worry! You'll feel better when you've told us all about it. Take your time. We won't interrupt you.'

They were all in the warden's office together, the door safely shut, the room quiet and confidential, nobody to worry them or interfere with the desperate sympathy of their communion. Felicity sat shrunken in the armchair, her hands tightly clasped; the pressure seemed to help her to concentrate a mind which otherwise might fly apart from pure overstrain. Tossa sat beside her with an arm laid round the back of the chair, ready to touch the child or let her alone as the need arose. Nobody would have suspected that Tossa had so much patience and forbearance in her, least of all Tossa herself; but then, it had never been called into use until now. Dominic sat withdrawn on a rear corner of the desk, willing to remain unseen and unnoticed as long as possible; he was hardly more than an extension of Tossa at this moment.

'Lucien went out alone into the grounds yesterday afternoon,' George prompted gently, 'and then you went out on your way to look at the swan's nest, and saw him ahead of you, and you ran and caught him up. Tossa and Dominic saw you go down towards the footbridge together. Go on from there.'

'It wasn't quite like that,' said Felicity, in a voice small, hard and clear. Now that she had reached the point of speech there were going to be no prevarications; there was even the faintest note of revulsion in her tone for this too fastidious consideration. She straightened her slender spine, and looked fairly and squarely at what confronted her, and didn't lower her eyes. 'I didn't care a damn about the swan's nest. There *is* one there, of course, but I wasn't going to look at that, I was just following Lucien. I watched him go out, and then I went after him. I wanted to be with him. I wanted to get to know him really, properly, and for him to get to know me. Because I loved him. I *do* love him! I did, in a way, even before I ever saw him in the flesh, and as soon as I saw

165

him I knew it *was* love. I knew I was the right person for him, and so I went straight for my objective, and I was sure he couldn't help but feel the same way.'

Carefully, nobly, they all sat without stirring a muscle or drawing a hastened breath, nothing to suggest amusement, censure, or surprise. But Felicity knew her grown-ups, even those who were only a few years ahead of her. Faint, proud colour rose in her cheeks. She looked George fiercely, if wretchedly, in the eyes, and said with dignity:

'People think that at fifteen one has no deep feelings. They forget about girls like Juliet. It just isn't a matter of age. And in any case women are always much more mature and formed than men of the same age, and *much* more likely to recognise the real thing when it happens to them. Look at Tatiana, in *Eugene Onegin*. She was the young one, and he patronised and talked down to her, and treated her like a child, and wouldn't take her seriously, but she was right, all the same, and he lived to find it out when it was too late. And this was...rather like "Onegin" over again. Lucien just didn't realise how important it was, what was happening to us. He didn't want anyone then, I suppose. He surely didn't want me. He didn't try to send me away, he only walked on

166

and took no notice of me. We went along the ride there, on the other side of the river, and then we came to that gate, and he pushed it open and went on down to the grotto. He sat on the bench in there, looking at the river, and I sat by him and tried...I wanted him to *understand*, not to make a terrible mistake, but he didn't understand at all. He was like all the rest, he thought I was just a kid. It was "Onegin" all over again.'

All quite predictable, thought George sadly, but quite innocent. And yet something happened down there that wasn't innocent, and she knows it, and is forcing herself towards it inch by inch. But he didn't prompt her again. However she delayed, however deviously she approached what she had no intention now of softening, it couldn't be long in coming. Only a quarter of an hour or so later, Tossa and Dominic had met her coming back towards the house.

For the first time it occurred to him as a serious possibility that Felicity had killed Lucien Galt with her own hands. Her situation must have been disastrous enough, and her disillusionment bitter enough, and a moody and impatient young man, getting up to prowl along the water-side without a thought for the lovesick child who meant no more to him than a persistent mosquito, would have been a very easy victim indeed. All that talk, faithfully reported by Dominic, about accessories before the fact, about causing somebody else to commit murder, without meaning to, all that might be mere talk at random, fending off the horrid fact itself. Or so he would have been tempted to believe, if this had been any other girl but Felicity. Felicity didn't talk at random, didn't toss about terms like 'accessory before the fact' without knowing only too well what they meant. Her solitude had been peopled from books, and her vocabulary, at least, was an adult's. No, wait for the truth to emerge, don't anticipate. She didn't push him. Nothing so simple.

'I told him,' she said, moistening her lips, 'that I wasn't a child, and he couldn't solve anything by telling me to run away and play, I told him outright that I loved him, and he'd better think carefully before he threw away what he might never be offered again. And I said I'd prove it in any way he chose, because there wasn't anything he could ask me that I wouldn't do for him.'

She looked at her locked hands in faint surprise, suddenly aware for a moment that the tightness of their grip was hurting her. She relaxed them a little, and they remained steady at first, and then began to shake; the thin fingers clamped tight again and held fast.

'And then he turned on me,' she said in a precise, drained voice, 'quite suddenly and viciously, and said: "All right, then, prove it. If you're ready to do anything, then do *this* for me. Go and find Mrs Arundale, and tell her where I am, and tell her I've got to talk to her alone. *Got to,"* he said. "Ask her to come to me as soon as she can, he said, and I'll be waiting for her here. *And give her my love!"* '

The brief silence hung blankly expectant, shocked but still braced for greater shocks, waiting for what was to follow. This was brutal enough, but no more than they might have expected; and yet there was something in the air that warned them that here the path twisted, and the place of their arrival, when they reached it, would be very far from where they had reckoned on finding themselves. The faint click of the door-latch drawing back hardly seemed to break the stillness; only the distant babel from round the tea-trolleys, gushing in through the opening door, made them turn their heads.

Audrey Arundale stood in the doorway, her eyes large and startled in her pale face, looking from one to another of them without comprehension, but with a remote and immured intelligence as piteous in its way as Felicity's.

'I'm sorry,' she said. 'I didn't know you weren't alone. I'll come back later.' And she was actually withdrawing, her eyes fixed upon George, when he called her back. Of course she had heard her own name. What was the point of shutting her out now? In any case, she had a right to hear this, it might even be helpful to have her there, to watch the impact of her presence on Felicity, and of Felicity's words on her.

'Don't go, Mrs Arundale! If you're free, please stay. I think you should be present at this.'

'If you think I ought to,' she said, her eyes opening wider; and she closed the door quietly, and sat down in the chair Dominic hurriedly drew out for her from behind the desk. Felicity had given her one long unreadable look, and returned to the painful contemplation of her own rigid hands.

'But if you don't mind, I should be glad if you'd make no comment or interruption until Felicity has finished what she had to tell us.'

'Of course,' said Audrey, 'I won't say anything.' Her voice was light and plaintive, as though the weight of events was too much for her, and she had lost the thread; but her behaviour would always be gentle, coherent and dignified. If there was something tougher and shrewder, and altogether more passionate, beneath that bland, bewildered and charming exterior, she had it under absolute control.

'Go on, Felicity. I'm sorry if we've broken the thread for you.'

'It's all right,' she said bleakly, 'I can't lose my place. I wish I could. Well, that was what Lucien said to me. And it was so cruel and so wicked, and I was so terribly hurt, that I just looked right back at him and said all right, I would. And I walked away from him, and away from the grotto, and latched the gate after me, and came straight up to the house. That was when you met me.' She flashed one grey glance towards Tossa. 'And Uncle Edward and Aunt Audrey were still sitting over their coffee in their sitting-room. So I delivered Lucien's message.'

Something vengeful was still left in the thin voice of hopeless despair and regret. At first they didn't understand fully; she saw the faint, cloudy questioning in their eyes, and made full and patient explanation.

'Word for word, just like he'd given it to me, I recited it aloud in front of both of them. I said: "Aunt Audrey, Lucien's down at the grotto by the river, and he says he's got to talk to you alone, and will you please go down to him there as soon as you can, and he'll be waiting. And I was to give you his love".'

In the instant of horrified comprehension the silence was absolute. Then Audrey Arundale's long, elegant hands made a sudden abortive motion of protest and pain, groping forward along the arm of her chair; her fair head arched back, and speech came bubbling into her throat, but never reached her lips. George gave her a sharp glance and a warning frown, and she subsided into her old apparent calm, even sighed the worst of the passing tension out of her soundlessly, and continued watching her niece with nothing in her eyes but a grieved and helpless sympathy.

'I see,' said George, in the most impersonal of voices. Possibly Felicity had wanted to shock, not wantonly, but to ease the burden of her own horror, and to reassure herself that this crisis of hers was indeed something large and dreadful, even by adult standards, and not a triviality of childish spite of no significance to anyone but her. That would make her anguish even sharper by making it pointless. She needn't have worried on that score, he thought ruefully. What was done to her was a truly cruel and ferocious thing, and what she did in return was large enough even for a Shakespearian woman scorned, or one of those

172

ballad heroines whose wrongs and revenges Liri Palmer sang.

'And then?' he said, in the same neutral tone.

'They sat there staring at me like stones, both of them. It was terribly quiet, you can't imagine how quiet. And then they both turned, ever so slowly, and stared at each other, and Uncle Edward got up, and put his coffee-cup down on the table very carefully, as if it was full and might spill over, but it was empty. He thanked me, and told me I could go. You know? Just as if I'd come to say tea was ready. So I did. I went out and closed the door, and left them there.'

'And you knew then,' asked George, 'what you'd done?'

'I knew what I'd done. I'd even meant to do it, and yet in a way I hadn't, but by then I couldn't undo it. You can't, you know. The very next minute is too late. I wanted somewhere to hide, so I went up into the turret and on to the roof, the side where I couldn't see or hear anything from the river. I stayed there until tea, hoping nothing would happen, hoping everybody'd appear as usual. But Lucien didn't come. And then I knew I'd done something terrible, but I couldn't tell anyone. I was afraid to.'

She raised her eyes to George's face, and

173

from behind the windows of her glass prison he saw her staring out at him in awful panic, while her slight body sat demure and still.

'It's all through me,' she said with terrified certainty, 'that Lucien's dead, and Uncle Edward's on the run.'

Audrey uttered something between a gasp and a cry, and put up her hands to her face. Her eyes appealed wildly to George. How could this child possibly know about Edward being missing? Nobody had known but the three of them, George, Henry Marshall, and Audrey herself. And now Felicity brought out this flat, fearful pronouncement as though its certainty was not in question. George shook his head at her, just perceptibly, and she clutched at the hint of reassurance with unexpected quickness of apprehension. Of course, Felicity was merely drawing an inference which seemed to her self-evident, not speaking from knowledge at all. Audrey sat back wearily, one hand shading her face, her long-drawn, aching breaths shaking her whole body.

'We don't yet know,' said George sensibly, 'that anyone has died, or that anyone has any cause to run. It may very well turn out that we're all worrying without cause, and that goes for you as much as for any of us. Whatever you did, and whatever you think may have followed from it, don't jump to any conclusions yet. Wait and see. Mr Arundale isn't due back from Birmingham until this evening. It won't be time to conclude that he's on the run, as you put it, until he failed to do as I hear he always does, come back right on schedule. Give yourself and him the benefit of the doubt until tomorrow, and don't be in too big a hurry to think you've caused a tragedy. Who knows? You may find yourself sitting opposite Lucien at breakfast.'

He seemed, Dominic thought, to be choosing his words with some care, and he could not be sure if it was for Felicity's benefit, or for Audrey's; or, in some more complicated process, for both of them, and in different ways. Felicity looked at him doubtfully, afraid for a moment of disbelief or disparagement; but though his voice was dry, reasonable and quiet, his face was grave. He contemplated her without a trace of the indulgence she dreaded; she believed that she had let loose a death, and he acknowledged the validity and solemnity of her belief.

All he was doing now was reminding her that evil sometimes misses its target. So that was all right, in so far as anything so monstrous could ever again be made all right; and there was now nothing more she could do. Unexpectedly, Felicity began to cry; she had had neither time nor energy to spare for it until then. Between her sheltering hands she said indistinctly: 'Is there...anything else you want to ask me?'

'Not now. But later I would like to talk to you again. What I suggest is that you three skip the next lecture, and go and have some tea by yourselves, in the small library, perhaps. And you come to me here, before dinner, Felicity, say seven o'clock, and I may have one or two questions to ask you then. Thank you for telling me all this. In the meantime, don't think about it more than you can help. If you have no objection, you and I will think about it together, this evening.'

'I'll go and grab a tray,' said Dominic, picking up his cue, 'before they clear everything away. I'll see you in the library.'

Felicity reached the door in Tossa's arm, her brief tears already spent. She was not a crying girl. She turned a pale, drained face to look back at George, with fixed attention and a degree of wonder; the bleakest of smiles, like a ray of winter sunlight, pricked its way through her clouded despair.

'Thank you,' she said, 'for believing me.'

'But you don't believe her,' said Audrey Arundale tiredly, 'do you?'

'I keep an open mind.' George saw her look round vaguely for the cigarette-box on the desk, and leaned to offer his own case. 'I'm glad you came in when you did, it saves a lot of explanation. And thank you for letting her tell her own story in her own way. Now I should like to hear your version of the same episode.'

'You're quite satisfied, then, that it happened?' She stooped her fair head to the lighter he offered, and drew in smoke hungrily.

'It happened. She didn't in the least mind your being here while she told it. I'm quite satisfied that it happened just as she described it.'

'I'm afraid,' said Audrey sadly, leaning back in her chair, 'she rather enjoyed my being here. It can't have escaped you how much she hates me.'

'You think so? If you want to dispute anything she said, now's your chance. I should be very glad to listen to your account of what happened.'

She looked up at him in a way that reminded him for a moment of Felicity. There was no coquetry in her, he found himself thinking that she would not even know how to begin to use her prettiness and femininity to influence a man; and yet he could never encounter her directly. She, too, was immured within a self which was not of her own choice or creation, as difficult to reach as the child.

'It's strange,' she said, and it was probably her weariness speaking, 'not to be able to guess at all what you're thinking about me.'

What he was thinking at that moment was that she seemed twice as large and twice as real as she had seemed to him yesterday, perhaps because she was a day farther removed from the shadow and the support of Edward Arundale.

'*Do* you want to dispute the facts?' asked George, avoiding the pitfall.

'Not the facts. Only their implication. She did burst in on us just as she said, and came out with that...that rigmarole. I believe it was pretty well word for word as she reported it. And certainly Edward and I were utterly shattered by it. But it was by what we'd just learned about Felicity, not by anything else. If there was a message, it couldn't have been phrased like that, you may be certain. Maybe he did send to ask for me...after all, I was responsible for starting this course in the first place, and there could have been things any of the artists might want to bring up with me. But if he did, it was in very different terms. Much more probably, I'm afraid, Felicity was angry with him, and made the whole thing up out of malice.'

'Against Galt?' asked George. 'Or against you?'

'If you ask me to guess—what can it be but guesswork?—I think both. It seems that Mr Galt was the occasion. If you'd seen her efforts to ingratiate herself with him on Friday night, and his rather strained tolerance, you'd understand. But occasion and cause are two things. Mr Felse, this is entirely a private matter between us? I must tell you, then, that Felicity has been a problem for quite some time now, with a special animosity, I'm afraid, against me. That wasn't news to me. But this display yesterday was shocking. Edward showed great restraint in getting the child out of the room, because we simply had to discuss what was to be done with her. Sylvia sends her here every holiday, but with all our goodwill the experiment has been a disastrous failure. We never quite realised how disastrous, until yesterday. We were wondering if it would be any use suggesting to Sylvia that she sent the child abroad *au pair* for a year or so, and see what quite fresh companions and surroundings can do for her. But we didn't have much time to talk about it, because Edward had to leave just before three, on his way...'

She wrenched her head aside in a gesture of pain and revolt from the futile mention of the place where Edward had never intended to go, and the thought of the innocent engagements he had deliberately cancelled before setting off only he knew where. 'I don't understand!' she said. 'I don't understand anything!'

'You can't tell me for certain,' said George, 'whether there actually was some quite innocent message behind Felicity's apple of discord?—intended apple of discord, at least, even if it didn't come off. You didn't, I suppose, feel enough interest to go down to the grotto and find out?'

'I didn't! I was too upset to do anything of the kind, and then, it would have been, in a way, a capitulation to her. Wouldn't it? Personally I think she made the whole thing up.'

'And your husband didn't go there, either?'

'Of course he didn't! We were together, talking anxiously about what on earth was to be done with her, until he had to leave. His car was already out in the courtyard at the back...I expect you've seen the lay-out of the house by now.'

'But you didn't actually see him drive away?' For their private rooms were at the front of the house, and did not overlook the drive.

'Well, no, I didn't, of course. But we know

that he did leave...'

'We know he didn't leave for Birmingham. At least, not for the two meetings he was supposed to address.'

She put up her hands to her forehead in a gesture of hopeless bewilderment.

'But I don't believe, I don't believe for a moment that he went down to the river. I simply don't *believe* that he was attaching the slightest significance to what Felicity had tried to suggest. Wouldn't he have said so to me, wouldn't he have asked me about it, if he'd believed it? Even if he'd had the least doubt? I don't believe he ever for a moment treated it seriously, or felt the least need to investigate.'

'I appreciate your confidence. But you can't,' he insisted delicately, 'testify of your own knowledge that he didn't?'

'I can't prove it, no. All I know is that it still seems to me quite impossible.'

'Yet he did change his plans, and call off his engagements, and he did it then, immediately after this incident.'

This was not a question, and she did not offer an answer, or even a protest.

'He may, of course, have had other and quite legitimate reasons for that. If he comes back this evening he'll answer such questions for himself, no doubt. You'll understand that there are certain obvious things I can't avoid asking you, however, in view of what has emerged.

'Yes,' she said with weary distaste, 'I understand that you must.'

'How long have you known Lucien Galt?'

'About six weeks now.'

'How did you first meet him?'

'At a cocktail party given by his recording company. Peter Crewe was at the same party, that's where I got to know him, too.'

'Were you acquainted with any of the other artists who're here now? Prior to this course, I mean?'

'Yes, with all of them. I've been interested in the subject for a long time. I told you, I was the one who first suggested this week-end, and of course the ones we invited were the ones I knew slightly.'

'Has there ever been anything in the nature of a love affair between you and Lucien?'

She said: 'No!' so fiercely and disdainfully that it might have been a different woman replying, after the flat exchanges of a moment ago. He looked at her mildly and steadily, caught and deflected by the change.

'Nothing at all improper? Nothing to justify the interpretation Felicity obviously placed on what he said to her? An interpretation I think anyone would have placed on it, to be honest.'

'Nothing improper has ever taken place between us. And we have only Felicity's word for what he said to her, as of course you know.'

But Dominic's word, he thought but did not say, for one tiny incident of far from tiny significance, in the circumstances. A small straw, but swayed in a gale-force wind, and a detached, observant and deeply reluctant witness. Dominic couldn't have been greatly surprised by Felicity's story, after that glimpse of passion.

'And—forgive me!—just one more question. Why didn't you tell me about this incident, when you accounted to me for your afternoon, yesterday?'

'It was wrong of me,' she admitted wretchedly, 'but I couldn't. It didn't seem to me relevant, not then. And one doesn't advertise one's family problems if one can help it. It was for us to solve this matter of Felicity. She isn't our child, but she is our kin. I didn't want to expose her...or us. One just doesn't do that.'

And that was perfectly good sense, and fitted the known facts without a flaw. He sat thinking about it, and about her, long after she had left him to go to her duty. She would be some ten minutes late for the opening of Professor Penrose's five o'clock lecture, but she had the gift of materialising into some quiet corner without disturbing lecturer or audience. One of her allies in this exacting life was silence, and another was unobtrusiveness. Both useful in an illicit love affair, if she ever did undertake one. She couldn't, of course, have been expected to reckon with the possibility that some day her perverse partner would be exasperated into turning on a pathetic adolescent who pestered him too far, and striking her down with the naked truth, which she, given the necessary fury and valour, could carry straight to the oblivious husband. No, such things don't happen.

In any case, when he came to think back over the conversation he had just had with Audrey, he found it increasingly difficult to believe that she was the cool kind of woman who could produce such sound and simple parries on the spur of the moment. Whereas Felicity undoubtedly had the force, fervour and ingenuity to take circuitous revenges when bitterly wounded.

But as often as he came near to conviction, he was visited again by the vision of those two hands meeting and closing warmly in the folds of Audrey's skirt, while her husband walked in blissful ignorance on her other side. And from there it was so short a way to accepting Felicity's story. No want of motive then!

Believe that, and you could not but believe that they did indeed meet and clash, there in that smug little artificial pleasance by the flooded river. Once visited by that relevation, nobody ever had a more immediate stimulus to murder in hot blood, almost in a state of shock. Put that evidence before almost any jury, and their instinct would be to find a verdict of man-slaughter.

But for one significant fact, of course. Edward Arundale had telephoned to cancel his appointments at about three o'clock, immediately after Felicity's bombshell, *before* he went to meet Lucien in his wife's place. That one point alone made this, if it was a crime at all, a more calculated and less excusable crime. For why should he do such a thing, unless he was already consciously contemplating murder and flight?

CHAPTER 7

'After dinner, if you're not bored with the subject by now,' promised Professor Penrose, switching off the record-player, 'we'll go on considering this odd question of historical

185

origins, and try to find out why some of the events celebrated found their way straight into folk-song, and why others, some of the bitterest, too, on occasion, became "innocuous" nursery rhymes. It's a far cry from a feudal social tragedy like "The trees they do grow high" to "Ring a ring o' roses", you might think, but which of them came into being as catharsis for the more unbearable memory? Or didn't you know about "Ring a ring o' roses"? The ring of posies was the bunch of herbs you carried to try and ward off infection, the sneezes were one of the initial and ominous symptoms, and once you'd got that far you all fell down and stayed down until the cart came along to collect. And some inspired Tom Lehrer of the plague year turned it into a nursery game! Well, after all, you all know what happened to "Gulliver". It's a way we have with the unendurable, to give it to the children to play with.'

He could afford to invite them to suppose that they were bored, because he knew they were not. Professor Penrose was not a boring man. He slammed his notebook shut, not having glanced at it throughout, and waved his arms at them as at refractory chickens.

'Out! Shoo! Go and get a breath of fresh air before dinner.'

And out they went, vociferous, argumentative and contented, at least as far as the walled garden and the terraces, there to continue with even greater animation the discussion which would be resumed on its scholarly plane after dinner. On the terraces even the non-singers burst into song. At times they sounded like a choir tuning up on several different test pieces at the same moment.

'I always knew I'd be good as a filibuster,' remarked the professor complacently, finding himself shoulder to shoulder with Liri Palmer on their way out. 'Nobody's ever *encouraged* me to try how fast and how long I could talk, before.'

She gave him a clear look, and said unexpectedly: 'You're a wicked old man. I like you.' She looked, as always, in full possession of herself, her secrets and her thoughts, but the signs of strain were there, once you knew what to look for; her air of withdrawal, the austerity of the set of her lips, the sombreness of the steel-blue eyes that were not interested in illusory hopes. He liked her, too; he liked her very much, but there was nothing he could do for her, except talk fast enough to divert attention from her when she was not singing, and listen to her with gratitude when she was.

'Only one more day,' he said, 'and we can

send them all home.'

She said: 'Yes,' with a brief and shadowy smile, and went away from him with her lithe, long walk, down the back stairs and along the stone corridor, and out into the evening light just beginning to turn misty and green. Once through the courtyard it was only a dozen yards into the fringes of the ornamental shrubbery, and thence into the trees. She looked round once to be sure that she was alone, and then dug her hands deep into the pockets of her jersey jacket, and set off rapidly towards the river. It was easier to keep close to the bank on the farther side, where the trees were thinner, and the paths followed the course of the Braide with reasonable faithfulness. She crossed the footbridge, and went striding along the leafy ride, past the young redwood, past the huge, scrolled iron gate behind which she knew there must be a policeman on guard, though he had not showed himself at noon, and did not show himself now. No use searching within that enclosure, in any case; they would have done that already, very thoroughly. There could be no further trace of him to be found there.

She had begun her hunt, therefore, in the brief interludes between today's sessions, where the enclosure ended, and in two such forays she had reached a point somewhat below the stone bridge. There were no more weirs now between her and the massive wall of the Follymead boundary, less than a quarter of a mile away.

Liri knew nothing at all about the behaviour of drowned bodies, and nothing about the currents of the Braide, and the places where anyone lost in these reaches of it would be likely to cast up. She could see that there was a strong and violent flow of water, and that it would carry anything committed to it with speed and force; but the only way she knew of searching it was by walking downstream from the point of entry, and watching for any sign in the water, along the banks, among the swamped alders, and the lodged debris of the flood. She did it, as she did everything, with all her might.

The police, of course, must also be looking for Lucien, but she had seen no sign of them in these reaches. Let them search in their way, with all the aids their specialist knowledge gave them; she would search in hers, with no aids at all but her ignorance, which would not allow her to miss a single yard of undercut bank or a single clump of sallows.

Here, so close to the boundary, the artificiality of Follymead relaxed into something like a natural woodland. Where the view from the windows ended nature was allowed in again, still somewhat subdued, and the river surged away from the planed curves of its man-made vistas in an unkempt flood. Here for a while it rolled through open meadow and in a straight, uncluttered bed; she looked at the brown, smooth water, quiet and fast, saw the shallow, whirling eddies swoop past her, and felt sure that nothing would ground here. Ahead of her trees and bushes closed in again, leaning together over the water. These tangles of willow and undergrowth must have gone untended for a long time. She left the path and clung to the bank, and clambering through bushes, shouldering her way through sliding, whistling, orange-coloured sallows, she found herself suddenly marooned on a soft and yielding headland, with water before her and water on either hand. On her right the main flow coursed along sullenly, little checked by the lush growth; but the floodwater had spilled over among the trees and drowned the low-lying ground as far as she could see ahead through the twilight of the woodland. Before her and on her left it swirled in frustrated pools, and lay still, dappled with grasses. When she moved a foot, the water which had gathered slowly about her shoe eased away again into the spongy turf. She could go no farther, as close to the river as this. She would have to turn back

190

and skirt the sodden ground at a greater distance.

But before she retreated she made a careful survey of the flooded area as far as she could see. Lodged in the stream on her right, ripping the water into a dozen angry spurts of sound and fury, a fallen tree, or perhaps only a branch from a larger tree, lay anchored with its tattered trunk wedged fast in the soft ground, and its splayed branches clutching and clawing ineffectively at the fast current that slipped hissing through its fingers. She peered into the seething fistful of water, half dirty brownish foam, and among the hundred fleeting, shifting pallors she thought she saw one pallor that remained constant, only nodding and swaying a little while the Braide boiled past it and swirled away downstream.

She had thought she had seen something so often by then that she felt nothing, except the compulsion to know. She set foot testingly on the torn bole, and shoved hard, and it remained immovable, deep sunk in the mud and wedged into place with all the driftwood it had arrested. She straddled a stubborn cross-branch, and felt her way out on the rough bark, holding by the alder wands that sprang through the wreckage and held it secure. Two, three yards gained, and the support under her grew slender, and gave a little beneath her weight but still held fast. The water was rushing under her feet now, she looked down into it with fascination, finding something in it of music, in the melting of eddy into eddy, and current into current, the flow endlessly unfolding, able to plait into itself every thread that came drifting down the stream. Only the small, lax pallor hung idle and unchanging in the heart of change, and shook the pattern of unity to pieces round it.

Another yard, and she would be nearly over it. The branch bowed under her, the water touched her shoes, arched icily over one toe in a hiss of protest, and poured back into the flood. She dared not go any farther. But this was far enough. She stooped carefully, holding by the thin, swaying extemity of a branch, and looked steadily and long at the trapped thing in the water.

She must have heard, though in her preoccupation she had not identified, the small sounds that did not belong to the rhythm of the river. Nevertheless, she was startled when she turned to draw back from her precarious outpost, and found herself staring at Dickie Meurice.

He was a yard out on the tree-trunk after her, clinging and reluctant, but grinning, too, pleased at having crept up on her so closely without being detected. He must have been following her right from the house. He must have frozen into stillness, somewhere there in the arch of the courtyard, when she had paused to look back from the rim of the trees. It didn't matter now. Nothing mattered. Let him come, let him see something, at least, if not all, enough to assure him he hadn't come out for nothing.

'Oh, you!' she said, her voice flat and neutral. 'I might have known.'

'You might have known! Who else would be so considerate? I thought you might need help...if you found anything.'

'You're so right,' she said, moving back upon him without haste, knowing he could not pass her, sure even that if she abandoned him here he wouldn't dare to venture out where she had been. For one thing, he was heavier than she was, he'd be ankle-deep in the Braide. For another, he was more careful of himself than she was, not having her stake at risk. 'I do need help. I need somebody to stay here with it, while I go and raise the alarm.'

He didn't believe it for a moment; he hung still clutching precariously at the still green but dilapidated branches of the wrecked tree, and staring at her narrowly and doubtfully. She laughed on a hard, high note, moving steadily nearer, breast to breast with him, forcing him backwards. He looked over her shoulder, and he saw the floating, languid whiteness, articulated, apparently alive, drifting at the end of its dark sleeve. He uttered a small, strangled sound, and gave back before her gingerly, clawing his way towards the soggy, yielding ground under the trees.

'Yes,' she said hardly, 'that's a hand you're looking at. With fingers.' Saturated grass sagged under her foot as she stepped from the tree. Water seeped into her shoe, and she never even noticed, beyond shifting her stance brusquely to safer ground. 'What's the matter with you? Can't you understand? Are you afraid of a dead man? He's there. I *have* found him.'

Between the thrusting alders and the penning branches of the derelict tree, the pale, flaccid hand gestured and beckoned on a sudden surge of water, and flicked its fingers at them derisively, demonstrating beyond doubt its quenched but unquestionable humanity.

'Stay here with him,' she said peremporarily, and thrust past towards the drier ground, fending off alders with a wide sweep of her arm. He saw her face closely as she passed him, intent and fierce, incandescent with excitement.

194

'I'm going up to the house to tell Inspector Felse.'

He caught at her arm, but half-heartedly, almost confused into obeying her without protest. 'Stay here, nothing! I'm coming with you.'

'Don't be a fool!' Liri spat at him over her shoulder, tearing her sleeve out of his hand. 'Stay here and keep an eye open, and mark the place for us. We don't want to have to hunt for him again, there's a quarter of a mile of this wild part. And suppose the river dislodges him? At least you can tell us. And if anyone else comes near, get them away from here. I won't be long.'

She was away before he could stop her, weaving like a greyhound between the clinging sallows, stooping under branches, running like an athletic boy. And so positive and compelling was her authority that for some minutes he stayed where she had stationed him, his gaze fixed uneasily on that small, idling whiteness in the surge of brown. He could not forget the burning blue of her eyes, so intense as to sear out all expression, and the taut lines of her face, drawn so fine that the bones showed through in fiery pallor. He had never understood her, and never would. Something unsuspected within him, something almost old-maidish in its respect for the proper forms, was scandalised by her composure. Hadn't she just found her black-haired true-love drowned in the Braide? Wasn't that his hand playing horribly with the dimpled currents there, snared in the branches of the tree? Only an hour ago she had been singing, with shattering effect, about another lost love slain by the braes of another river:

'Oh, Yarrow braes, may never, never rain
Nor dew they tender blossoms cover,
For there was basely slain my love,
My love, as he had not been a lover.'

Suddenly he wanted to understand her, he wanted to know, his normal inquisitiveness came to life again and shook off her influence. He always had to probe into everything that came his way, in case there might be something in it for Dickie. He cast one rather reluctant but still avid glance at the elusive thing he was supposed to be watching. It idled on the current like a skater, swayed in a slight, rhythmic movement. *He* wasn't going anywhere. Fixed as the Rock of Gibraltar.

Dickie Meurice could move very rapidly indeed when he chose. He made better time than Liri herself over the obstacle-strewn course to the stone bridge. By the time he reached it, and

196

paused on the edge of the open parkland on the other side, Liri was well up the slope towards the house, and running strongly. He kept to the edge of the trees instead of following her by the direct route, until she came to the steps that led up to the south terrace. She didn't climb the steps. He saw that, and hugged himself. She was up to something, or she would have taken the direct and open way in. Instead, she was circling the wing of the house to enter by the courtyard, as she had left it. Dickie let her slip from sight, and then abandoned his shadowy shelter, and set off at his fastest run across the open ground, and in at the front doors. By the time she had threaded the passage into the house from the rear, he would be hanging over the rail of the back stairs, ready for her.

The gong for dinner had not yet sounded, but everyone was gathering into the public rooms in readiness for it; he could hear the babel of voices from the gallery and the libraries, high and merry, as he slid through the quiet corridors and leaned over the well of the back stairs. Any sounds from below would come up to him clearly here; he would know when she arrived, and whatever her intentions, she would have to cross that quiet lobby below him.

The staircase was old, solid and tightly

wound, and made a wonderful funnel for rising sounds, especially as the lower corridor was of stone. He made his way down perhaps a third of the flight, to a point where he would still be well out of sight of anyone approaching from below, and have time to make his escape into the labyrinth of public rooms before she reached this upper landing. Follymead might have been designed for monstrous games of hide-and-seek. He leaned cautiously over the oak rail, and peered down the coiled, enclosed space, as into the whorls of a shell.

He could see beneath him the stone flags of what had once been the central lobby of the service floor and was now a cool, indoor spot for summer days with a fantasy of plant stands, tapestry-draped walls, a few white-painted wrought iron seats, and two pay telephones discreetly tucked into the corner under the stairs, and walled round, but not roofed, with reeded wood shells just six feet high, painted ivory-white. They provided adequate insulation on their own level, and an excellent sounding board to carry conversation up the well of the staircase. No one involved in the redesigning of Follymead as a college had thought of that; none of them had envisaged a future clientèle, addicted to listening in on other people's telephone conversations. Their mistake, thought

Dickie Meurice, speculating pleasurably on one possibility.

The crisp, chill sound of Liri's footsteps, walking briskly, came along the stone passage ahead of her, and rang hollowly up the stairs. Low heels, but narrow and sharp, tipped with metal. Kitten heels, they called them; appropriate enough for that young tigress. Their rhythm didn't slacken or turn aside towards the staircase. He saw her foreshortened figure cross below him, the dark brown head so erect and beautifully balanced, the impetuous outline of brow and nose, the great braid of hair lashing like a tail for the tigress. Straight towards the telephones! He heard the soft clash of the swing door closing, reed to reed, snug as the seam of a dress.

He dropped one turn lower, sliding down the rail of the stairs eagerly. Almost above her head now, and though she was out of his sight he could hear and time every turn of the dial. Two revolutions, one long, one short. For the operator, so what she wanted was not a local call; but he had never supposed that it would be. And blessedly, that meant she must ask for her number. Things could not have been going more smoothly his way.

'I'd like to call a London number, please. Valence 3581. This is Belwardine 640.'

Every word clear and unmistakable so far. Coins rattled into the slot, below him. They waited for what seemed a longer time than the two minutes it actually was, and in the interval the gong sounded for dinner. That was the signal for the whole hungry party to come milling along the gallery from the small drawing-room, from the terraces, from all the corners in which they were disporting themselves, and converge on the dining-hall. It was on the same main floor, situated above the special level of the great drawing-room, and those once-menial regions where the telephones had been installed. Meurice could maintain his place on the stairs brazenly, and nobody would bother him. But the cavalcade of joyous voices drowned out Liri's first words when the distant party, whoever he might be, answered her, and blotted into meaningless murmurs half of what passed afterwards. It was hard enough making sense of one half of a telephone conversation; trying to make something of half of that one half is a job for the cypher experts.

'Never mind that,' he heard her say clearly, her voice low and guarded, but sharp with impatience and strain, 'there's no time...' And again, after a maddening moment when nothing was audible but the Rossignol twins marching along the gallery to the loud, gay strains of 'Auprès de ma blonde': '...just *get out, fast. The body's been found...*'

There was more, a hard silence on her part, the distant voice inaudibly pouring words at her, never a name to identify him. Why must they sing even when they weren't getting paid for it? There went Andrew Callum, leading half a dozen disciples in 'The Boy from Killane,' and away went a burst of words from Liri, down the wind with the heroic lament for Douglas Kelly:

'Tell me, who is the giant with gold, curling hair,
    He who rides at the head of your band?
Seven feet is his height, with some inches to spare,
    And he looks like a king in command...'

And on the diminishing echo, clearly: 'Damn you, I've *told* you, forget all that, and *go. Good-bye.*'

The receiver clashed in the rest, and the door swung before her thrust, she was out, and at the foot of the staircase.

He turned and took the rest of the stairs three at a time, in long leaps. By the time Liri came out on the main landing, he was away along the gallery and out through the great front

201

doors, and bounding down the steps from the terrace towards the dimming slopes that led to the Braide. He ran like a hare, in exuberant leaps, back to the duty Liri had laid on him. The vacant, wandering hand was still languid and easy on the thrusting current. Meurice found himself a dry place to stand, and waited; it was certain he wouldn't have long to wait.

★ ★ ★ ★

'I wish I hadn't done it now,' said Felicity, as many another has said before her with as little effect, and many another will certainly say in the future. 'If I'd known...' She stopped there, jutted a dubious lip at what it had been in her mind to say, and rejected it ruthlessly. Whatever she lacked, she was beginning to discover in herself a rare and ferocious honesty. 'I should, though,' she said, 'the way I felt, even if I'd known how it would turn out.'

'None of us knows that yet,' George reminded her crisply. He had placed a chair considerately for her, so that no too acute light should touch her face, and no too direct glance put her off her stride. Oh, there was stuff in Felicity of which she knew nothing yet, even if she was finding out some things about herself the hard way, and too rapidly.

'No,' she conceded, 'but we know the pro-
babilities. I did know them, even then, or I
could have if I'd been willing.'

'I doubt,' said George, doing her the justice
of showing a like honesty, 'if you anticipated
that much success.'

She looked up quickly at that, a little startled, and considered it gingerly. The faintest and
briefest glint of a smile showed in her eyes, and
as feebly withdrew. 'You're not trying to make
me think I haven't done something dreadful,
are you?' You, of all people! Her tone implied.

'No, I wouldn't do that. But I am telling you
that something like that happens in most lives.
Most of us, when it does happen, are lucky
enough, clumsy enough, or scared enough to
make a mess of our opportunity for malice. You
were the unlucky one. You had the perfect ex-
plosive put into your hand, and the perfect fuse
for it into your mouth. Even then, for some
of us, it would have failed to go off. But we
shouldn't have been less guilty. Having something to regret leaves you anything but unique
or particular in this world, Felicity, rather con-
firms you one of the crowd.' He saw her braced
to think that out, and resolute to kick the argument to pieces, and saw fit to divert the event.
'Look; suppose I ask you my questions first,
and then we can talk.'

'All right,' she agreed. 'But I've told you everything I can think of now.'

'Yes, this is a matter of something you did tell me. You said you left Lucien there by the river, and came away, "and latched the gate after me." Did you mean that literally? Not just pulled the gate to after you, but latched it?'

She was staring at him now alertly and brightly, momentarily deflected from her own problems. 'Yes, latched it. Of course! Why, is that important?'

'It's a detail. They all help. The latch was still in position then?'

She nodded emphatically. 'You couldn't very well miss it, it's nearly as long as my arm.' An exaggeration of course, what she was really indicating with a small flourish was her forearm, from elbow to fingertips. 'It hasn't had any rivets, or whatever they are, holding it for a long time, it just hangs there in the slots, you can pull it out if you want to.'

'Yes, I see. And Lucien didn't think better of it, and come after you? Try to stop you?'

'No,' she said sombrely, 'why should he? He didn't know what I was going to do. He didn't care about me one way or the other. I suppose there wasn't really any reason why he should. He never even looked round. He was sitting in the grotto, glad I was gone. I realise now that

204

he must have been at the end of his patience, to do what he did to me.'

'I suspect,' said George, 'that his patience was always on the short side.'

'Maybe. I didn't really know much about him, did I?' She said bleakly. 'And neither did he about me.' She looked up earnestly into George's face, and asked simply: 'What am I going to do?'

Outside, the gong for dinner was bawling merrily, but they didn't notice it, or hear the noisy parade to the hall.

'Live with it,' said George with equal simplicity, 'and make the best of it. I can't absolve you, and you wouldn't be grateful to me if I tried. I can't charge you with anything, and there isn't any penance to be found anywhere, if that's what you're looking for. No, you'll just have to hump the memory along with you and go on carrying it, like the rest of us, and learn to live with yourself and your mistakes. It's the one way you find out how to avoid more and greater failures.'

'But if I've killed him?' She said in a whisper, her eyes frantic but trusting.

'Whatever happens, *you won't have killed him*. Not unless you'd been responsible for living their two lives as well as your own, for all the qualities in them and all the things they'd ever done or thought that eventually made it impossible for yesterday to end without a tragedy—only then would you have killed the one and made the other a murderer. Your contribution was bitter enough to you, but only the spark that set off a fire already laid. Don't claim more than your share, Felicity, you'll find your fair share quite enough to carry.'

After a brief, deep silence she said in a low voice: 'Thank you! At least you haven't treated me like a child.'

'You're not a child. Let's face it, you're not grown-up yet, either, not quite. But I'll tell you this, you're a great deal nearer to being a woman than you were yesterday, when I first met you.'

Her lips tightened in a wry and painful smile that was very close indeed to being adult, and she said something no child could have said. 'That doesn't seem much for Lucien to die for,' said Felicity, and finding her own utterance more horrifying than she had expected, rose abruptly to leave him. 'There isn't anything... useful...I can be doing?'

'Living,' said George, 'and perhaps for the moment just living, without any thinking. And don't think that isn't useful. For a start you can go in to dinner with the rest of them, and help to tide Follymead over tonight.'

Faintly she said, the child creeping back into her voice and eyes uninvited: 'Do I have to? I'm not hungry.'

'You will be. The least useful thing you can do is make yourself ill. And you're needed, don't forget you're part of the household, a bigger part than ever before.'

'All right,' she said grimly, and took a step or two towards the door. The weight of the house came down on her appallingly for a moment. She looked back at him in sudden piteous appeal, she didn't know for what.

'Somehow it wouldn't be so bad,' she said in a muted wail, 'if only I wasn't so damned dull and *plain*...'

'Plain!' George echoed incredulously. *'Plain?'* he repeated in a growl of exasperation. 'Child, did you never look at yourself in a mirror? *Plain!* Come here!' He took her by the shoulders and turned her about, and trotted her sharply across the room to the high mantel and the Venetian mirror above it. It hung so high that at close range only her head came into view, with George's impatient face above. He cupped a hand under her chin and tilted her face up to the glass. 'My dear little idiot, for goodness sake *look* at yourself. What do you want, in heaven's name? Do you have to be coloured like a peony to be worth looking at?

What if you haven't got your aunt's milk-whiteness and roses, and a pile of fair hair? *This*...this pale-brown, baby-fine stuff you have got was made to go with *this* face. You find me a more delicately-drawn hairline than this, or a better-shaped head. And as for your face, I'd like to know who put you off it in the first place. Look at the form of these eye sockets, look at this line, this curve along your chin and neck. *Plain!* You haven't finished growing yet, and the peak's still to come, but if you can't see it coming you must be blind, my girl. Don't you realise you've got bones that are going to keep you beautiful until you're eighty? The prettiest colouring in the world won't stand by you like these will.'

Felicity stood transfixed with pure astonishment, her hands raised to touch the cheekbones his fingers had just quitted. Her eyes, huge with wonder, stared unrecognisingly at the face in the glass. Her lips moved very faintly, shaping distantly and incredulously the word 'beautiful.'

The sudden rush of feet outside the door, the rap of knuckles on the wood, never penetrated her stunned senses. Even when the door opened upon Liri Palmer's roused face and glittering eyes, with Dominic close to her shoulder, Felicity only turned like a creature in a dream, still lost to every shock but one.

'Can you come?' Liri's blue stare fixed urgently upon George. 'There's something I want to show you.' She had bitten back, at sight of Felicity, the blunt announcement she would otherwise have made. 'I'm sorry if I'm interrupting you, but it is important.'

Her voice was mild, but her eyes were imperious. Liri's maturity extended to sparing the children; or perhaps she was merely concerned with keeping them from under her feet.

'Felicity was just on her way to dinner,' said George, and started her towards the door with a gentle push between the shoulder blades. She went where he urged her, obediently, like a sleepwalker. They moved aside from the doorway to let her pass, and she looked back for a moment with eyes still blind to everything but the distant vision of her own beauty, incredible and yet constant. She trusted George. There had been very few adults in her young life whom she had been able to trust.

'Thank you! I'll try...I'll do what you said.'

'Good night!' said George.

'Good night!' said Felicity remotely, and wandered away with a fingertip drawing and redrawing the line of her cheekbone and jaw, which George had found beautiful. *Beautiful!* She followed the beckoning word towards the dining-hall and her duty. She was enlarged, she contained and accepted even her guilt, even her inability to erase it. She had something to live for, so unexpected that it loomed almost as large as the death she had precipitated.

As soon as she was gone they all three came into the room and closed the door carefully after them. He should have known that where Dominic was, Tossa also would be.

'Well?'

'I've found the body,' said Liri, point-blank.

It couldn't have been anything else, of course; he had seen it in her braced and motionless excitement. So there wasn't going to be any blessed anticlimax, any apologetic reappearance. They had a body, they had a crime. And Follymead had the prospect of ruin. George looked at the dusk leaning in at the window, at the clock that showed five minutes past the dinner hour, and reached into the desk drawer for his torch.

'Where is he?'

'Caught in a fallen tree in the river. Below the stone bridge, in the wild part. I'll take you there.'

'We ran into Liri at the top of the stairs,' said Dominic, 'and she told us. I hope that's all right. You're going to need somebody, if only to run the errands.'

'That's all right. Anybody keeping an eye on him now?'

'Dickie Meurice,' said Liri, her voice suddenly shaken out of its calm by the surrender of her responsibility, as her legs shook beneath her for a moment. 'He wasn't with me...he just showed up. I told him to stand by.'

'Good! Tossa, you run across by the footbridge, will you, and find Lockyer, and tell him to meet us downstream. Tell him to bring some ropes down with him. And an axe or a hatchet, something we can use on the tree.'

'Right!' said Tossa, dry-mouthed with excitement, and whirled and ran.

'Come on, then,' said George. 'Lead the way, Liri.' And they followed her out across the terrace, and down the slope of turf towards the distant stone bridge.

It took them half an hour to get him ashore, and not a word was said in all that time but for the brief exchanges that were necessary to the job in hand. If they had tried to hack away the driftwood that held him before they had a line on him, he would have escaped them again, for once dislodged, the flood would have taken him headlong downstream out of their hands. It was Dominic, as the lightest weight among the men present, who clambered out barefoot on the swaying barrier of branches,

211

and secured a rope round the shoulder that just broke surface, cased in sodden tweed that was now of no colour at all but the river's mud-brown. The driftwood under him dipped when he ventured too far; the ice-cold darkness rushed over his feet and tore at his balance. He thought of nothing as he worked; his mind had shrunk into his numbed hands.

'All right, come ashore.'

George reached a hand to retrieve his saturated son. Lockyer carefully took in the slack of the rope, and tested it with a gradual pull downstream; the arm that was all they could see of the dead man rose languidly along the surface, like the arm of a man turning in his sleep, but the body did not float free.

George looked along the tangled arms of the tree, and found the one that pinned the body in its clenched fist, half out of the water. 'All right, we'll bring him in branch and all, it'll make a useful brake. Meurice, give me that hatchet.'

Dickie Meurice handed it eagerly. He would not for anything have forfeited his place here. He was only guessing, of course, but if his guess was right the pay-off would be worth a little discomfort.

'And the other rope.'

There was still a cloudy daylight out on the

212

open sward, but here among the trees they had to peer to see even one another. The girls stood well back on drier ground, their faces two pale, still ovals in a green monochrome. Nobody had tried to send them away. What was the use of banishing Liri, who had been the one to find this pathetic thing they were trying to bring ashore? In any case, she would not have gone. She stood silent and intent, and her composure was impenetrable.

George climbed out himself this time. There was no need to go so far that his weight would be a handicap. He made the coil of rope fast round a fork in the branch, and passed the ends back to Dominic's waiting grasp.

'Give him a hand, Meurice. Everything may come loose with a rush when this gives.'

He hacked at the branch, below the fork where the rope was secured. The wood was still green and young, clinging to life; it took him a few minutes to chop his way through it.

'Dig your heels in, it's going.'

They had heard the first ominous cracking, and were braced and ready. The whole branch suddenly heaved and turned like a live thing, tossing the body momentarily out of the water, and dropping it again in a flurry of dirty foam; then the tangle of wood broke loose from its moorings, and would have surged out into

213

midstream at once, but the two ropes, drawn in gradually hand over hand, coaxed it sidelong into the bank. Torn foam seethed through the lattice and sodden leaves. George scrambled back to the muddy ground, and helped them to draw him in, and disentangle him from the tree. Ankledeep in cold spill-water, they hoisted the dead weight clear, and laid him on the higher ground padded with last year's leaves and starred with this year's late anemones.

The sagging, shapeless shadow that had been a man lay flattened to the moist earth by his mud-heavy clothes. Lank hair of the universal river-colour plastered the pallor that was his forehead. George said in a voice suddenly sharp and intent. 'Give me the torch.'

The cone of light sprang out of the dimness and brought shapes of life again in this twi-lit world that had no shape. The long body sprawled awkwardly, so weighted down with water that it seemed to be dissolving away from them into the ground. A massive, large-featured face, smooth and austere and once impressive enough, gaped up at them through soiled trails of river-water.

The single muted whimper of a cry came from Tossa. Liri Palmer made never a sound. Dickie Meurice drew in breath with a long-drawn hiss that might have been pure horror and excitement, but sounded horribly like glee.

'But *that* isn't...' blurted Lockyer, amazed, and let the sentence trail away helplessly into silence. He had a teen-age daughter; in her vicinity there was no possibility of avoiding acquaintance with the features of the current pop and folk idols.

'No,' agreed George grimly, staring into the pool of light at his feet, 'no, it isn't Lucien Galt. It looks as if we've got to hunt farther afield for him. No...*this* is Edward Arundale.'

CHAPTER 8

'Perhaps,' suggested Lockyer blankly, after a long moment of silence, 'they *both* went into the river.'

'You think so?' George switched off the torch, and the deepening dusk fell on them like a cloak. 'And who drove Arundale's car away? It was there, in the yard, with his overnight case and his books in it, at three. It was gone before four, and nobody else had gone missing. Oh, no, they didn't both go the same way.'

'They didn't both go down the river, anyhow,' said Dickie Meurice softly, and they heard and felt him stirring in the darkness, again with that curious suggestion of pleased malevolence. 'Because just before Liri came to tell you she'd found this one, *she was talking to the other one on the telephone.*'

He had his sensation, and it was everything he had hoped it would be. Only Liri herself let the revelation pass without a sound. She had made one sharp movement, however, that did just as well. However stolidly she sat out questioning, after that, he'd know that he'd hit her where it hurt. She'd had her chance to have his goodwill, and done rather more than turn up her nose at the offer. Now she could try it the other way.

'How do you know that?' demanded George, 'if you were here keeping an eye on the body?'

'I wasn't. I had a hunch she was up to something, so I let her get a head start, and then followed her up. If she'd been on the level she'd have come straight in by the terrace, but she didn't. She went off round the back of the house, to the passage from the yard. So I came in by the front and beat her to the back stairs, and I was there to see exactly what she did. She went straight to the telephone call box under the stairs, and asked for a London number.'

'Dear Dickie,' said Liri quite gently, as if

neither he nor anything he did could matter to her now, 'always so true to form. Where were you? Hiding in the next box?'

'In the presence of the police,' he retorted maliciously, 'I shouldn't be too witty about eavesdropping, if I were you. They have other names for it in the way of duty. I can demonstrate that I heard all right, and I can repeat every word I heard, too. Including the number!'

'And including a name?' asked George dryly.

'No, I didn't get a name. But the number was Valence 3581. You can check it easily enough, but I wouldn't mind betting you'll find it's the number of Lucien's London flat. That would be the first place she'd try, even if she didn't *know* where he'd be—and maybe she did, at that!'

'And why didn't you tell me about this at once, as soon as we arrived? Instead of behaving as if you'd been here all the time and had no information to offer?'

'Because I couldn't make out just what it was all about, not until I realised *whose* body we'd found. And what mattered first was to get him out. *She* wasn't going to run.'

'So in fact you didn't actually know whose number it was, or to whom she was talking?'

'No, not then. I don't know, for that matter,

217

but listen to the text, and draw what conclusions you like. I didn't hear everything, people were just coming chattering along the gallery to dinner. When someone answered her she said: "Never mind that, there's no time." And the next I got was: "...just *get out, fast. The body's been found...*" Then whoever was at the other end was doing the talking, until she cut him off. "Damn you," she said, "I've told you, forget all that, and *go*. Good-bye!" '

'That was all?'

'Isn't it enough? I didn't know whose body she'd found, but *she* did. She was climbing out on the tree when I came on the scene, she'd had a good look at him. But maybe she'd known all along which of them went into the water. Maybe she even helped in the job, or at least helped Lucien to get away afterwards. Stay here, she says, and keep an eye on him, while I run and tell Mr Felse! You have to hand it to our Liri, she's quick on the draw. She couldn't suppress the discovery, because I happened on her just at the wrong moment. But she could and did run like a hare to warn the murderer, before she gave the alarm. And she found me a job to do that would keep me quiet while she did it, or so she hoped. Only as luck would have it I'd already begun to smell a rat by then.'

He smiled, the well-known smile that charm-
ed the tele-viewers regularly on Thursday
nights, his fair head cocked towards Liri; and
though the smile was now invisible, they felt
its weighted sweetness probing her.

'But in any case, you don't have to take my
word for it. Ask her! Ask the operator who got
her her London number.'

'All in good time,' said George impassively,
'we'll ask everything that needs to be asked,
but not, I think, here. I should be grateful if
you would all keep this to yourselves, just as
you have done until now. Lockyer, stay with
him, I must go and telephone. The rest of you,
come on, let's get back to the house.'

They made their way back in single file to
the dry pathway and the glow-worm twilight
that was left in the park, George lighting them
until they were out of the trees. At the end of
the line, Dominic and Tossa linked hands and
drew close, shivering suddenly with the chill
of the river, and the cold oppression of darkness, malice and death. She whispered in his
ear, anxiously, that he must go straight up
and change. The suggestion, mildly maternal,
pointedly possessive, seemed to be left over
from another world, but at least indicated the
possibility of recovering that world, when all
this was over. Dominic, the shivers warmed

219

out of him by her solicitude, pressed her hand impulsively and wondered again at the terrifying diversity of man.

'Come up to the office with me,' George said to Liri as they climbed the steps to the terrace. 'I must talk to you.'

'Of course,' said Liri. Her voice was curiously easy now, aloof and contained still, but something more than that. The word that suggested itself was 'content.' George understood that. They had their body and their case, a pretty substantial case now, though still circumstantial; but she had done everything she could, and it was no longer up to her. 'But it *will* be you talking,' she said gently. '*I've* got nothing to say.'

In the yellow drawing-room, as they passed through the gallery. Andrew Callum was singing, in a voice achingly muted and raw and sad:

'The judge looked over his left shoulder,
He said: "Fair maid, I'm sorry."
He said: "Fair maid, you must be gone,
For I cannot pardon Geordie." '

'So that's the way it is,' said Duckett heavily. 'Well, we can put out a general call immediately for the car, and turn on everything to find it. That's no problem. About the boy I'm not

220

so happy. We'll get all the airports covered, and have a watch kept on his flat—though if the girl was lucky enough to catch him there, that's one place he'll have written off. We've nothing to lose by avoiding a public appeal. There still *could* be another answer.' But he sounded exceedingly dubious about it. 'I suppose it's practically certain he did take the car?'

'I'd say a hundred per cent certain,' said George. 'He knew, as everyone here knew, that Arundale wouldn't be expected back until tonight. He could give himself many hours grace by making off with that car.'

'Well, since she's tipped him off about the body being found...you say she hasn't admitted anything about that?'

'She won't say anything at all. She's done what she could for him, now she doesn't care what happens to her.'

'You don't think she actually *was* in it with Galt? After the fact, say?'

'I'm certain she wasn't. If she had been, the last thing she'd have done was to go looking for the body. She'd just have sat back and prayed for us not to find it. But she did go looking for it. According to Meurice, she's been hunting it at intervals all day. Oh, no, it wasn't Arundale she expected to find, it was Lucien. That's why she's so calm now, almost happy.

221

He may be in trouble, but at least he's alive.'

'Then why won't she talk about any part of it?'

'Two reasons, I think. First, because she knows nothing herself, and isn't sure how much I know, so that even by opening her mouth on something that seems innocuous to her she may be handing me another little fact that makes damning sense to me. And second, by refusing to say anything at all, she may be able to leave us in some doubt about her, and divert a bit of our attention from him.'

'I thought she hated him?' said Duckett.

'She thought so, too. She knows better now, and so do we. One more point, he certainly has a valid passport, because in three weeks time he's due to leave for a tour of Latin America. First destination Buenos Aires. And since she caught him successfully at his flat, he's undoubtedly pocketed his passport. Most likely that's what he went there for. And possibly to raise some quick cash.'

'You think he was heading out in any case?'

'I think so.'

'Right, airports, then. Ports, too, but less likely. For the car we'll put out a general call immediately. Where d'you want the wagon to come? That drive's too public by far.'

'We're lucky there. Have them go on along

222

the main road, past the lodge and over the river bridge beyond the edge of the estate. Just beyond the bridge there's a gate, and a cart-track crosses two fields—it's drivable, all right—and reaches Follymead ground at a third gate by the riverside. Lockyer's down there on the spot, and I'm going back there now. No point in viewing the place where we got him out, it's pure chance he got held up there. The doctor can have him right away.'

'*Did* he drown?'

'Unlikely. If so, the water won by a very short head. His skull isn't the right shape. I didn't do any close investigating, there were too many spectators, and the doctor will do it better. But something hit him.'

'It couldn't have been a fall?'

'Could have. Pending closer examination, of course. But in that case, why run for it? It looks as if Arundale went hopelessly wild when the ground reeled under him. It looks as if he was the aggressor. And lost. They've been married twenty years, and never anything, not a shadow.'

'It happens,' said Duckett, and drew in breath gustily through the moustache that would have done credit to a Corsican *maquisard*.

'It does, I only wish it hadn't.'

'You can say that again, George…they're due out tomorrow evening, this folk-music party?'

'There's a final concert after tea, five to half past six, then they disperse. We can hold it that long, if we have to. I'd prefer it, too.'

'Keep it wrapped, then, and I'll manage this end. If the lid has to blow off, let it be when they've gone home. We may save something.' His hard breathing rattled in the receiver. 'But…*Arundale!* My God, George, he was impregnable. Do you reckon Buckingham Palace is safe?'

'Think of me,' said George bitterly. 'I've still got to break the news to the widow.'

The class came chattering and singing from the after-dinner session at a quarter to ten, and headed for the small drawing-room to continue their discussions over coffee. Every evening the noise had grown, and the gaiety, and the exhileration. Professor Penrose must have surpassed himself, in spite of being deprived of the services of Liri Palmer and Dickie Meurice. It was extraordinary how the two dramatic productions being staged at Follymead had run parallel all the way, even in their crises and accelerations, apparently unconnected and without communication. Only Liri linked them now, or rather, moved from one to the other freely, and had a part in both. Meurice, thought George, reluctantly but clearly, was largely irrelevant. He stirred up a little mischief in passing, but he was of no importance. In a sense he never had been. His malice frayed the edges of events, but never determined or even deflected them. He was the mouse gnawing at the exposed root of an oak tree already split by lightning.

When Audrey Arundale passed along the gallery—and he noted that she had so arranged matters as to move as long as possible alone—George was waiting for her. He saw her pause for a moment outside the open door of the small drawing-room, and brace herself to enter and put on her hostess face.

'Mrs Arundale…'

She turned and saw him, and her look was almost glad. Whatever business he had with her would be preferable to going in there and making pleasant talk. But she didn't know, of course, what it was going to be.

'Can you spare me a few minutes? There's something I have to tell you.'

'Of course. Shall we go into the office?'

There is no easy way to tell anything as heavy as bereavement, and the spiral approaches are worse than the straight. The victim has so long to imagine and fend off belief. George was only just back from seeing the body removed from the Follymead grounds by the police ambulance, and was very tired. Everything he could do tonight was done, every inquiry he could set in motion was already on the move. By this time all the airports were alerted to look out for Lucien Galt, and the number and description of the stolen Volkswagen were being circulated on all the police transmissions. They had reached a dead point where there was nothing for them to do but pause and draw breath. George and Audrey looked at each other across the hearth of Arundale's office with a shared exhaustion, not enemies, not even opponents.

'Mrs Arundale, I think you must know that ever since I was called in here we've been accepting it as a possibility that a death was involved, and in fact have been looking for a body. I'm afraid what I've got for you is not good news. This evening we've found it. We took him out of the river about an hour and a half ago.'

She set her hands to the arms of her chair, and rose. Her eyes, wide and fixed, held steady on his face. She said nothing at all, so plainly waiting that there was nothing to do but complete the half-arrested blow.

'It isn't Lucien Galt, as we'd expected. It's

your husband. I'm very sorry.'

Her lips moved, saying automatically: 'I understand,' but there was hardly a sound, only a faint rustling of her breath. She turned her head questingly this way and that, and put out her hand with that remembered gesture, feeling for Edward, her prop and mentor; but Edward wasn't there, and would never again be there ready to her hand, and there was nobody now to tell her what to do. She was alone.

He saw the blood drain from her face, and her eyes roll upward in her head. As if she had indeed leaned on the arm that unaccountably failed to be there, her balance forsook her. She swayed, and then, like a shot bird, collapsed in broken, angular forms at his feet; and he lunged from his chair on one knee, and took her weight in his arms as she fell.

George drove home to Comerford through a sudden squall of rain, and his eyes were full of Audrey Arundale's reviving face. When she came round she had apologised for her lapse, and resolutely refused to have anyone fetched to her, or to concede that she might be in need of help. 'I'm quite all right now!' How often he'd heard it, hurried and insistent and forbidding, from people who were anything but all

227

right, but dreaded above anything else being the centre of a fuss. If you over-rode them, you sometimes precipitated the total collapse you most wanted to avoid. And besides, he had detected in Audrey a kind of relief, a kind of relaxation, that meant she wouldn't break. After you have been living with horrible uncertainties, even the definition and finality of death come as an almost welcome change.

Now at least she knew. And what was there he could do for her? Not bring the dead man back to life again, certainly; and not, in his present state, even attempt to assess her degree of guilt or innocence.

So George drove home, and Bunty fed him and asked him no questions. She never did, but he sometimes confided. It might not be exactly approved procedure, but given a discreet and intelligent wife and an appropriate case it would have seemed to him a waste, even a dereliction of duty, not to use *all* the means to hand.

She looked him over from head to feet with alert eyes the image of Dominic's, noted the river-slime coating his feet and ankles, and probably got as much out of this instantaneous physical examination as ever he did on looking over a witness. But all she said was:

'Our two all right?'

'Very much so. I'm afraid they may even be

enjoying themselves.' It was clear to her that George was not. Lesson One, do not become involved. But the effective text of Lesson Two, *how* not to become involved, no one has ever yet supplied. Perhaps as well. The best policemen are those who walk rather more in other people's shoes than in their own, and never lose sight of the relevance of the grace of God. 'That place is a Disneyland fantasy,' he said, looking back suddenly at the monstrous bulk of Follymead, and astonished at the impact it made when viewed from homelier fields.

'We ought to go and spend a week-end there, some time,' said Bunty, busy with whisky and water. In a single hazel glance she estimated the amount necessary, in his present state of tiredness, to knock him out for the nine hours of sleep he needed. 'They're having a course on Mozart's wind music next month, it could be good.'

'We will, some time,' agreed George without conviction. If it's still functioning, after this earthquake that's brewing, he added in his own mind. The whisky was hot and strong and very welcome; buds of warmth and sleepiness opened in him like accelerated shots in some botanical film. 'I'm going to bed, I'm bushed. Get me up early, won't you?'

'With what?' said Bunty rudely. 'Dynamite?'

But she didn't need dynamite; the telephone did it for her, rather too early, to her mind. George had awakened once with the first light, and stayed awake just long enough to enjoy the realisation that he need not move yet, his wife's long, soft breathing beside him, and the sudden awareness that one thing of significance had certainly been said last night between them, though not by him.

'Our two all right?' Indeed!

Here had he been treading cautiously and watching the weather in the house, wondering what it would be like for Bunty to awake to the fact that her son had brought home a remarkably positive and permanent-looking girl friend; and all the time Bunty had it weighed up accurately and fairly, and was giving him the nudge, in case he had missed the significance of what was going on. 'Our two' sounded large enough to set at rest more minds than his. He fell asleep again smiling. When he awoke again to the clamour of the telephone, it was half past seven, and Bunty was downstairs preparing breakfast. He reached for the instrument beside the bed, before she could pounce on the one downstairs and silence it.

'Sorry to wake you,' said Duckett, 'but I wanted to make sure of getting you before you left. I've got an interim report from the

230

doctor for you.'

'Already?' George sat up abruptly wide-awake. 'That's quick work.'

'He didn't drown. No water in the lungs. He was dead before he ever went in.'

'The head wound?'

'Fractured skull. It turns out he had rather a thin one, but not one of those extreme cases. Somebody hit him a lot too hard, from almost behind him, slightly to his left. He'd be dead in minutes.'

'And the weapon? Has he got anything on that? Kind, shape, material? He must have been up all night,' said George with compunction.

'He *was* up all night. He wants to know why you can't find 'em at a civilised hour. We can't give you proper details yet, but I asked him for a long shot. And here it is. Traces of rust in the wound. Iron, he says, and narrow, say half an inch thick at the most. Width might be as much as two inches or so. Squared-off edges to it. It penetrated so deeply that it must have been swung at him pretty desperately, edge-on. Doc argues a fairish length, eighteen inches to two feet, maybe even more. Something like a flat iron bar, or a very large file. Does it make any sense?'

'It makes a lot of sense. Now I've got a

231

request for you. Can you borrow me a frogman, and get him to Follymead during the morning? The sooner the better.'

'I can try. Where d'you want him?'

'Have him brought in the same way the ambulance came last night, and I'll have Lockyer on the lookout for him at the boundary.'

'All right, you shall have him. And one more item of interest for you. Arundale's Volkswagen has been found. Abandoned at a parking meter in Mayfair, locked, unrifled, everything intact. He took it to London, George. He went to his flat, the girl's phone call proved that. But he can't have been there long, there's no word so far of anybody seeing him. In any case, he won't go back there now he's warned. Where d'you reckon he'll turn up next?'

'Rio, probably,' said George, and reached for his dressing-gown. 'I'll call you from Follymead.'

'Oh, and George...'

'Hullo?'

'Those blood-samples you brought in earlier, from the ground there. Arundale was an AB, a universal recipient. Your specimens are A. They may be Galt's, we don't know his group yet. They're certainly not Arundale's.'

Duckett's police frogman was a wiry Blackcountryman who had dived in these parts before. He barely made the minimum height requirement, and had a chronic cigarette-smoker's cough, but he was tougher than leather, all the same, and had a lung capacity abstemious athletes might well have envied. He stood at the edge of the bank where Edward Arundale had almost certainly entered the water, and looked down into the black pool above the third weir. The surface water whipped across its stillness so impetuously and smoothly that it appeared still itself, to break in a seethe of white foam over the fall. Beneath the surface it would be mercilessly cold; he was going to need his second skin. The colour of the pool was perhaps more truly olive-green than black, and opaque as the moss-grown flags that floored the grotto.

'Soup!' He said disapprovingly, and trod out his cigarette into the soft ground. 'How am I supposed to see through that?'

'That's your problem. We've tried fishing for it with hooks, but it's deep here, deeper than you'd think.'

'I should have thought anything going in here would be carried over the edge. You've got some force running there.'

'That's what we thought, too, and why we looked for him well downstream. Too far downstream, as it turned out. But what we're looking for now would go down like a stone, and stay down.'

'Yeah,' said the diver, dabbling a toe thoughtfully, 'What is it I'm supposed to be looking for? I might as well know, I suppose.'

George told him. Shrewd, deep eyes set in nets of fine wrinkles in the sharp face visualised it, measured, weighed. 'If that went in here, it's still here, all right. Any idea what the bed's like?'

'Mucky. Maintenance isn't what it once was. But there doesn't seem to be much weed.'

'All right, let's go.'

It was about half past ten when he lowered himself into the pool, and submerged, plunging promptly beneath the rushing surface water. In the yellow drawing-room at the house the first session of the day was still in progress, and even when the students emerged for mid-morning coffee, at eleven, the interval wouldn't be long enough to allow them to stray. The operators by the river had the grounds to themselves. Given a less absorbing subject and a less expert persuader, there would have been truants by this time. George had half-expected two truants, as it was, but it seemed that Dominic and Tossa were doing their duty.

So there were none but official witnesses

when the diver rose for the third time, breaking the surface tension in a surge of unexpected
silver in the day's first watery gleam of sun.
The Braide streamed down his black rubber
head and shoulders, and pulled at him viciously. George had insisted on having a line on him,
in case of accidents; small river though the
Braide was, it could be dangerous even to an
expert when it ran as high as this. But in the
issue he had needed no help. He hoisted himself ashore, black and glistening, with a lizard's
agility, and pushed up his mask.

'Got it! Half sunk in the muck down there.
I hit something else, too, that I'd like to have
another go at, but this is your prize.'

He unhitched it from the cord at his belt, and
held it up to be seen.

Felicity hadn't been exaggerating, after all,
it was a good three inches longer than the span
of her forearm and stretched fingers. The
laboratory guesses weren't far out: half an inch
thick, roughly two inches wide at the business
end, which still retained traces of its last coat
of paint, and possibly traces of haemoglobin,
too, in spite of the river water; somewhat
thicker and wider where it had rested in the
wards, and this central part of it was a dead
ancient-iron colour, since paint couldn't reach
it, and nobody had used oil on it for years. And

235

at the other end, a huge, coiled handle to balance its weight, decorated with a flourish of leaves. An ideal handle fcr grasping to strike a blow edge-on. With a thing like that you could hit out and fell an ox. And there it had hung in the wards of the gate, where Felicity had been the last to drop it home when she walked away from Lucien on Saturday afternoon, and went to set light to the fuse and fire the charge that was to blow Follymead apart. Ready and waiting for the hand that would be next to raise it, the hand that drew it out of the wards to use as a weapon of vengeance. Trees were set round in a screen between the gate and the waterside, thirty yards away; the waiting victim would see nothing.

'That's it,' said George, 'just a gate-latch, right there on the spot, waiting to be used.' The weight of it was formidable, and yet not too great for even a scholar's arm to be able to swing it effectively. 'That fills the gap. Thanks!'

'I'm going down again. Maybe it's nothing, but I'd like to make sure while we're on the job.'

He slid down from the bank again, feet-first into the water, and dropped from view. They were left contemplating the length of wrought iron that lay on the slippery turf between them.

'It looks straightforward enough now,' said Lockyer. 'Arundale came down here pretty well in a state of shock, without thinking what he was going to do. And when he bore down on the handle, he felt the latch loose in the socket. And took it on the spur of the moment. You could say it was this thing put murder in his mind.'

'And then what?' Asked George dispassionately. 'It was Arundale who got his head stove in and his body slung into the river.'

'He was up against a much younger and fitter man. There was a hand-to-hand struggle, and this thing changed hands in the fight, and the boy hit out at him with it, and found he'd killed him.'

'A case of self-defence. Could be. He might still panic, get rid of the body and run. People do do such things.'

'Especially as he might not get away with a manslaughter verdict, if his misconduct with Mrs Arundale was taken into consideration.'

'In any case,' observed George, brooding, 'even if you're being attacked, there are limits to what you're entitled to do. Getting your enemy's weapon away from him is one thing, bashing his head in with it when you've disarmed him is another. Watch it, here he comes.'

A coil of wet rope surfaced like a languid

snake, and Lockyer furled in the slack. The diver broke surface in a fountain of spray, and they eased him in to the bank and leaned to help him ashore. For this time he carried something in his hands. He uncovered his face and drew in air greedily, and held up his prize triumphantly.

'Look at that! Maybe it's nothing to do with your affair, but don't tell me it's proper place is in the slime down there. Or that it's been there long, either.'

A black walking-cane, with a chased metal knob for a handle; the shaft an appropriate length for a fairly tall man, perhaps rather thicker than pure elegance would have decreed, but tapering away to a fine metal ferrule. The diver balanced it in his hand curiously. Not so heavy. I'd say if that was just tossed in and happened to fall flat, it would go downstream. It was speared deep into the mud, ferrule down. I kicked the knob, groping for the other thing. What's the wood—ebony?'

'It looks like it.' George took the stick from him and turned it in his hands. He rubbed with an inquisitive thumb at the metal of the ferrule, and it brightened suggestively under the friction. 'I believe this is silver. Looks as if it must have come from the house.'

He took out his handkerchief, and wrapped

it about the knob, which was traced all over with coiling leaves. Not much possibility of getting any prints off the thing, after it had been at the bottom of the pool, but the action was automatic. He had the knob lightly enclosed in one hand, and the other hand holding the shaft of the stick, when he felt a slight play between them, as if the handle had worked loose. Gingerly he closed his fingers and tried to move it; it would not turn, but it did shift uneasily in his hand, drawn out a fraction of an inch from its socket.

'Wait a minute! Look...look at this!'

He drew stem and knob apart, and they gave with a slightly gritty resistance. Inch by inch the long, fine blade slid into view, until he drew it completely from its sheath and held it out before them. A blue runnel of light, edged with the dulled rainbow colours of tarnish, ran down the steel like captured lightning and into the ground.

'Good lord,' said Lockyer, fascinated, 'what is it?'

'A sword-stick, I suppose they'd call it. Sort of city gimmick the members of the Hellfire Club would carry and use for kicks.'

'That's me all over,' said the diver, staring admiringly, 'always a whole-hogger. You ask me for one weapon, I find you two. All zeal, Mr Easy!'

'Well, but,' blurted Lockyer, 'if Arundale brought *that* with him...'

They looked at each other over the thin blade, that gleamed sullenly in the sun, and down the wind went one plausible theory. The man who had had the forethought to cancel his engagements had also taken care to provide himself with a weapon. And not even a would-be murderer needs a bludgeon in his left hand when he has a sword in his right.

CHAPTER 9

'Why, that's the sword-stick from the collection in the gallery,' said Marshall, as soon as he saw it. 'It always hangs in a display pattern of curios on the wall there. The Cothercotts amassed quite a museum of these things. How could it have got into the river?' It was a silly question; he saw it as soon as he'd spoken, and wished it back again. Who knew better than the warden of Follymead where to find a killing weapon, if he wanted one?

The handsome, deadly thing lay between them on the desk, a bit of fashionable devilment from the eighteenth century, probably never meant to be used. The blade had been sheathed fully before it was thrown into the water, and its point was engraved with fine vertical grooves; it might very well preserve traces of haemoglobin still, if this was what had drawn that blood that was not Arundale's blood. Another job for the laboratory.

'Was it in its place on Friday evening, when the party assembled and was shown round the house?' George asked.

'I can't say I noticed particularly. Perhaps someone else may have done. I didn't comment on it to my group, there are so many things to be seen.'

'And of course, no stranger would have the slightest idea what it was, unless he was told.'

'No, I suppose not.' That brought it still more closely home to the few who were not strangers, and did know what it was. Mr Marshall went back to his duties a very unhappy man. He cared about this place, he cared about music, he cared passionately about the Cottercott collection of keyboard instruments. Who was going to maintain them properly, as living things for use and pleasure, if the college folded? For them a museum would be a coffin.

It was a quarter to twelve; still three quarters of an hour before the class would come bursting out from the yellow drawing-room, hungry and vociferous, heading for lunch. Better get this thing out of the house now, thought George, while everything was quiet, and let the lab men worry about it, while he got on with some of the inevitable and tedious routine work that waited for him here in Arundale's desk.

He rolled the sword-stick in soft paper, and took it down to Lockyer, who was smoking a cigarette in a quiet corner of the stableyard at the home farm, neatly screened from the house by a belt of trees. The tenant farmer was used to seeing overflow cars from the house parties parked here, and took no interest in them. Nor was it unusual for Midshire students, who knew the lie of the land, to go in and out by the back way, and so save themselves a mile or more on the way into Belwardine. Lockyer had his motor-cycle tucked away under the stable arch. The sword-stick would be in headquarters at Comerbourne in twenty minutes.

George went back to the warden's office, and began to turn out the drawers of the desk one by one. In all probability for nothing, but he wouldn't be sure of that until he'd gone through everything. Extraordinary how one weapon too many could make nonsense of an otherwise perfectly sound theory. The thing could have happened exactly as Lockyer had outlined it, the wronged husband coming to confront his wife's lover, the heavy instrument presented almost accidentally to his hand, and then the struggle in which the younger and more athletic man wrested the weapon away from him, and struck him with it; the appalled realisation that he had killed him, the disposal of the body and the latch in the river, the opportune recollection that the victim's car was waiting and ready, and he was due to leave at this very hour, the subsequent flight to London, the abandonment of the car there, everything fitted in. Except this one grotesque thing, this Georgian whimsy that yet was not a toy, this fop's gimmick that could kill. And this one thing threw everything out of gear.

He had still to find out whether it had been in its usual place on the wall on Friday evening; possibly Dominic could help, there. But whenever it had been taken from its place, one thing was certain, Lucien Galt had not taken it to the grotto. Felicity had been with him from the time he left the house until they parted by the riverside in exasperation and offence; if he had had any such bizarre thing with him then, she would certainly have mentioned it. Nor was there any suggestion that at that time he had been thinking in terms of danger or violence. No, it was not Lucien.

But if Arundale had taken it with him—and if he had, it was one more proof that he went with intent to kill, sanely if not calmly—then what did he want with a heavy iron latch? And if *he* did not take it from its place, who did? Lucien, to defend himself? Rather a clumsy defence against two and a half feet of steel, but better than nothing. But there were considerable objections to that theory. One weapon too many, and nothing fitted snugly any longer. Better, for the moment, concentrate on these personal papers. And nobody ever had them in more immaculate order.

The records of Follymead were here from its inception, press clippings, photographs, a full list of all its courses, concerts, recitals, lectures. And the total was impressive. Music is one of the fundamental beauties, consolations and inspirations of life, a world without it would be unthinkable. This crazy, perverse, slightly sinister house had never in its history served so useful and beneficient a purpose as now. And that was largely Arundale's work, and it ought to be remembered to him. He had certainly loved it; the proof was here to be seen. For the first time George felt an impulse of personal warmth and pity for that elusive figure, now never to be better known.

He had adored his wife, too, that was to be

seen everywhere. Perhaps with the possessive fervour of a husband who looked upon his wife as an extension of himself, but he wasn't alone there, and the passion was no less real for that. The last drawer of the desk yielded a harvest of photographs of her. George worked backwards through them, and experienced the eerie phenomenon of watching Audrey grow younger and younger before his eyes, dwindling to the nervous young wife, the frozen bride, refrigerated among her trappings of ice, the blooming debutante, the schoolgirl... Here in his private drawer Edward had preserved the complete record, decently hidden from alien eyes, the entire history of a love affair, the passion of a man not given to passions.

Here she was in full evening splendour for some grand event, very beautiful, very austere. And here at some function at Bannerets, being gracious, adequate and charming with parents. Too handsome, perhaps, for a headmaster's wife, but that air she had of being always at one remove from the world stood her in good stead. It was impossible to suppose that Audrey did not know she was considered beautiful; it was equally impossible to believe that she realised what that meant, what power it gave her, or should have given her. She looked out from her many photographs, a creature manipulated

245

by circumstances, always filling her role well, always withdrawn from it in the spirit. And defenceless. Why should the camera be the eye to discover that quality? If ever there was a sad woman, here she walked, successful, influential, well-off, envied and admired; and always lost, anxious and alone.

He had worked his way back to her younger days now, the twenty-year-old with her new engagement ring discreetly displayed, the fiancée photograph posed specially for her distinguished in-laws. Then an even younger girl, with Arundale in some restaurant booth, the kind where souvenir pictures are taken. Somehow not quite typical of either of them. And then, almost abruptly, the schoolgirl. Three pictures tied together with a pink tape, the last of the collection, evidently taken during the first year of his acquaintance with her.

The first showed her in school uniform. How old? Sixteen? Surely no more, and already a beauty, indeed perhaps she had never been so beautiful since. No puppy fat here, a slender, ethereal, glowing girl, not at all awkward or immature, indeed with a lustre upon her like a woman already admired and coveted and glad of her femininity. She must have been a thorn in the flesh of the others at that exclusive school to which her shopkeeper parents had sent her at such cost. On her, adolescence, so often a torment and an affront, hung like an apple blossom splendour, fragrant and joyous.

None of the subsequent pictures of her had this look.

George turned the half-plate portrait, and found the imprint of the photographer in blurred mauve type:

Castle Studios
E McLeod, A.R.P.S
Auchterarne 356.

Yes, of course. Nineteen-forty-two or thereabouts, this must have been, and Pleydells had been exiled into Scotland, like so many British institutions disseminated into the wilds to avoid bombing.

The second of the three pictures was of Audrey in tennis clothes, laughing, with her racket in her hands. The same imprint was on the back, the girl was approximately the same age. Probably all these Scottish pictures were taken within a few months. And the third...

The third was of Audrey in a white, virginal party dress, impeccably suitable for a school festival, with small puff sleeves and the Pleydells version of a décolletage, pretty liberal for its time and circumstances. The same in-

247

definable aura of bliss hung about her; it might have been merely youth and health, but it seemed to George to be more than that, a sort of radiant fulfilment rare enough at sixteen. Mr McLeod had done well by her. A good photographer, not concerned with glossing the lines of a face and showing up in immaculate definition every detail of a costume, the focus faded at her sleeves and the neck of her dress, leaving the face brilliant and surely almost untouched as the centre of attention. So successfully that George had returned the picture to its fellows and was re-typing the pink tape before he realised what he had seen depending from the silver chain round her neck.

He uncovered it again in a hurry, and stared disbelievingly. The fading definition blurred the design, but that was probably what had nudged his memory. This had been taken twenty-four years ago; the armoured saint in the nutshell helmet had been sharper and newer then, the hazing of his outlines only brought him nearer to what he was today. The spread eagle on his shield was faint but recognisable. Saints have their hallmarks, exclusive for all time. Saint Wenceslas had his copyright in this princely armour and heraldry, and once noted, could not be mistaken for any other sanctity in the calendar. So Dominic had said, and the books bore him out.

There couldn't be two of these things circulating among these few people. This was the same medal Lucien had worn. It was from Audrey he had got it!

There had been altogether too much and too conflicting evidence about that small disc of worn silver. Audrey swore that she had known Lucien only six weeks, Liri, on the other hand, testified that he had worn this medal round his neck ever since she had know him, which was a matter of two years. Lucien had said, according to Liri, that he had got it from his father. And now this picture said clearly that the thing had belonged to Audrey, and Audrey must have given it to him. So how many of them were lying?

Or, wondered George, the premonitory quiver of intuition chilling his flesh, *or were none of them lying?*

He had to hunt out a road atlas and gazetteer to find out where this Auchterarne place was. Stirlingshire. He'd never yet had any communication with the Stirling police, but they'd be the quickest way to what he wanted to know. Probably the school had been evacuated to one of those Gothic mansions that decorate the Scottish countryside, to remind one that while England is for ever England, Scotland is in many ways Europe. With upland wastes around it on all sides, and every kind of embattled refugee group deployed there, from Scandinavian timber-men to Polish pioneers. Maybe army, he thought, as he lifted the telephone and asked for a line to the police at Stirling; there were a lot of wild and mixed army units waiting their time up there. But more likely air force. That was where the young, the cultivated, the engaging, were, in those strange and wonderful days when life had an enormous simplicity and purpose, and everybody knew where he was going, even if the way there proved uncommonly short.

'I'm sorry,' said the operator, after a few minutes of waiting, 'there'll be a slight delay, but I'll get you through as soon as I can. Can I call you back?'

'Please do. I'll be right on hand.'

He heard the students emerge from their session, and the gong pealed for lunch. Marshall had taken to sending him in a tray as soon as the party were all accounted for and busy. Not long to go now; this evening they would disperse, he hoped with only pleasant memories of this extraordinary week-end at Follymead, and then the survivors could look round without secrecy, and see what could be salvaged.

George propped up before him the photograph of Audrey in her party-dress, and sat waiting, eye to eye with all that youth and innocence and happiness. He wondered if she'd ever looked like that for Edward Arundale.

Ten minutes later the telephone shrilled, and he reached for it eagerly, expecting his Scottish connection. But the voice that grated amiably in his ears was that of Superintendent Duckett, in high feather.

'George? We made it in time, after all. You can relax. They picked up Lucien Galt at London Airport half an hour ago.'

'Nothing to it,' Duckett was elaborating happily a minute later. 'Came in by taxi and checked in as if nothing had happened. Best thing he could do, of course, only he didn't do it quickly enough. Yesterday morning he could have flown out like a V.I.P and no questions asked.'

'Why in the world didn't he?' George wondered. 'Inexperience?'

'Money. It takes a little time to knock together about three thousand pounds in notes.'

'That's what he had on him?'

'In his case. As much as he could turn into cash in the time, obviously. He had a ticket for

251

Buenos Aires. They're holding him at the airport for us, and I've started Price and Rapier off to fetch him back. On the car charge, of course—taking away without owner's permission. And even for a holding charge that must be the under-statement of the year.'

'How did he react when they invited him to step aside and talk things over?' asked George. He'd seen that moment walk up behind so many men and tap them on the shoulder, and he had a pretty clear picture of this young man he'd never yet seen, proud to arrogance, impetuous, used to respect and adulation, even if he thought he despisd it.

'Quietly. From what I hear, he looked round smartly for a way out, and might have tried to make a break for it if he could, but he sized things up at once, and went along without any fuss. He hadn't a chance, and I fancy he'd hate to make an unsuccessful scene. Now the question is, how do we handle him. It's your case, George, you know the people and the set-up there, you're up with all the new developments, if there are any since you fished up that queer affair the boys are working on. You suggest, I'll consider.'

So now it was up to George, and he had to make up his mind a shade too early, before he really had anything but a hunch to go on. It was a gamble, and he was no gambler, and yet all his instincts told him to trust the conviction in his blood.

'All right, I'll tell you what I'd like done. Have him brought straight back here to me, to Follymead. I'll be waiting for him, and I'll be responsible for him.'

Duckett digested that in hard silence for a moment, and then said: 'Right, I'll do that.' Duckett was an admirable chief even in his acts, George found himself thinking, but better still in his abstentions. Not everybody could leave a subordinate alone to do a thing his own way. 'How do you want the boys to handle him meantime? Press him, let him alone, what?'

'Don't discourage him, don't press him. Just let him stew, and if he wants to talk, caution him, but then let him talk. It might be very interesting.'

'You think he *will* talk, don't you?'

'It wouldn't surprise me.'

'Just a minute, George...hang on, here's Phillips in from the lab...'

'Yes?'

'There's a positive reaction on the blade of that sword-stick affair. It seems to be A, the same as your specimens from the ground.'

'Good, thanks! No prints, of course?'

'Not a ghost of one. What did you expect,

after being in the water all that time? In any case that knob's so finely chased it breaks up all the lines,' said Duckett philosophically, 'and nobody's going to hold a sword by the blade... not while he's using it.'

The second time the telephone rang George pounced on it like a hunting leopard, assured that it must be Stirling this time. But it was Scott, reporting from London at last.

'Well, about time,' said George, round a mouthful of chicken sandwich. 'What's been keeping you?'

'Mobile people, mostly,' said Scott crisply, the light tenor voice buoyant and detached. 'I struck unlucky at that children's home of yours. The old house-parents—Stewart and his wife—they retired just about a month ago. There's a couple named Smith in possession now, brand new. Naturally they know some of the past kids as names, but no other way. The only people about the place who know young Galt know him only from his visits since he left. Nobody there knows a thing about this medal of his.'

'Did you follow up the Stewarts? They must have retired somewhere around London. Londoners don't go far away.'

'I did. They've got a little house in Esher,

all very nice and accessible. But they've got time on their hands, too, for the first time in years, and they've gone off to Italy for an early holiday. Can't say I blame 'em. They'll be back next week, but next week doesn't help us now. Well, that took a fair amount of time without much result, I grant you. So I took off for that garage and service station where the kid started work. Purley and Sons, Highbury. Quite a nice chap, Purley, old-fashioned paternal style. Good little business, and still personal. Garages can be, even in London.'

'And they remember him?'

'They remember him. Give him quite a good name as a worker. Didn't mind how mucky he got, and loved cars nearly as much as guitars. And you know he was only a kid when he started with them? Well, this is the one pearl I've got for you with all this diving, George. Purley took a real interest in the kids he employed, and was a stickler for the regulations. And you know the birth certificate juveniles have to produce when they start work?'

'Of course, what about it?'

'Just that in his case it wasn't a birth certificate. It was an adoption certificate.'

So he had known, of course, he had known all

along. It is, in any case, the modern policy to ensure that they know, and so avoid future shocks. He had always known; and this was the one fact he had always refrained from mentioning, if not suppressed. He talked freely to interviewers about his upbringing in public care, he went back to his old home regularly as a visitor. No sore places there.

But never, never did he tell anyone, even Liri Palmer, that John James and Esther Galt were only his adoptive parents. That was a spot he was careful never to touch.

For fear of pain?

A quarter of an hour later the telephone rang for the third time, and this time it really was Stirling. By that time the inquiries he had to make there seemed almost unnecessary, but he set them in motion, all the same. It would take a little time to get hold of details from so far back, names, dates of death, and so on, but the services kept everlasting records. He would get what he wanted, though perhaps not in time to affect or simplify the issue.

And now there was nothing left to be done, except sit back and wait for Lucien Galt to come back to Follymead under escort.

In the back of the police car, purling steadily along the M1 at seventy, Lucien Galt sat closed into himself like a locked house, but like a locked house with someone peering through the curtains, and possibly a gun braced across the sill of a just-open window. He had said hardly anything since the large, civil men closed in on him at the airport, and wafted him smoothly aside into a private room. If he had seen the slightest hope of giving them the slip, then or afterwards, he would have risked it, but they didn't take any chances, and they didn't give him any. No use looking back now and cursing the mistakes he had made. He had a situation to deal with here. Nothing else mattered now.

He was horribly tired, that was the worst thing about it. He needed to think clearly and carefully, and he was in no condition to do it, but he had to try. This perfectly decent and pleasant person beside him, and the other one, driving, they were human, they had treated him throughout with slightly constrained civility and consideration. It was an extraordinary feeling, being wound about with chains of forbearance and watchfulness, like a mental case, like a psychopath under observation. But it did mean that they would listen to him and report on him with all the detachment of which they were capable.

'I'd like to tell you how it happened,' he said

257

abruptly, breaking the silence which had been largely of his own making. At first he hadn't known what to do, or how to conduct himself, and though he had despised the normal bluster and pretence with which the guilty cover up their guilt, it had seemed to him that a profession of non-understanding was the only course left to him, and after that, silence, and such dignity as he could find a way of keeping. I know nothing, I understand nothing, I am a citizen of substance and some importance, *(am I?)* but I am certainly not going to make a fuss in this public place. Since you apparently have a duty to do, by all means let's go back and sort out this misunderstanding in private. All very well, but it made this blunt and exhausted opening now seem very crude. He shrank from the sound of it, and yet he was aware that it made a credible beginning. The guilty first protest (at least he had done that only once, and briefly), then sit back and think, and begin to worry, and break into a sweat of anxiety, and finally come to the conclusion that a half-admission may get them something. What he had said must have that ring to this solid, quiet person beside him, who looked like a merchant skipper on leave, brown-faced and far-sighted, and at ease anywhere.

The eyes had shortened their focus upon

him, along a broad tweed shoulder. The good-natured teak face gave nothing away. 'How you drove the car away, you mean?' asked Detective-Sergeant Rapier placidly.

'All right, I did drive the car away, if you want me to say so.'

'I don't want you to say anything you don't want to say. We're not asking you for any statements.'

'I know that. I'm offering you one. If you want to take it down, you can. But even if you don't want to, you can listen. I'm tired of running, anyhow, I want it straightened out.'

'If you want to talk,' said Rapier philosophically, 'who's to stop you? But I feel I ought to remind you that there are two witnesses present, whether there's a record or not, and that anything you say may be used in evidence. Maybe you should take another long, quiet think—about as long as from here to Comerbourne. There'll be time there to do all the talking you'll need to do.'

'I have thought,' said Lucien bleakly. 'I should have done better to think before I ran. What has it got me? I don't suppose I ever had much chance of getting out, but what chance I had I seem to have muffed. Talking can't make things worse now. It might even make them a shade better. Because I never meant to

259

kill him, of course. If I hadn't had the most hellish luck he'd be alive now.'

In the small, pregnant silence, shatteringly apparent even while Price continued to direct the car calmly at the same smooth speed, Lucien observed his two escorts exchanging in the mirror a speaking glance that was yet very careful not to say too much.

'I didn't know,' said Rapier mildly, 'that anybody'd mentioned a death.'

'Oh, for God's sake,' said Lucien in a spurt of nervous fury that left him trembling, 'let's pack in this pretence that you're after me for running off with a car. People don't try to skip out to South America for that, and you fellows don't have the airports alerted to stop them. That's not what all this is about. You know as well as I do that Mr Arundale's dead, and if you weren't as good as certain I killed him, you wouldn't be here taking be back with you to Comerbourne. So why put on this act with me!'

'Have we asked you any questions about Mr Arundale's death, sir? I don't recollect that we have.'

'You don't have to ask me, I'm telling you. I want to tell you. I'm sick of being the only one who knows.'

'It's a free country,' allowed Rapier considerately. 'But no charge has been made against you formally yet on any count. I shouldn't be in any hurry to make statements, if I were you.'

'But if I do, you'll keep a record of it? Not that I care, except that I'd rather get it over in one. I'm so damned tired.'

'Very well, sir, if that's what you want. But you will bear in mind that I've cautioned you.' And with the minimum of movement and fuss, suddenly the sergeant had his notebook on his knee, and his ball-pen in his hand. Probably wise to the fact that I'm one of those contra-suggestible types, thought Lucien bitterly. If they seem to be heading in the direction you want them to go, push like the devil the other way, and they'll persist. If you give them a hand, they'll turn back.

'Oh, I give you full credit for that. But it's all right, I want it finished now. It never should have begun. It was all unnecessary.'

He moistened his lips nervously. How much did they know? Better assume they knew most of it. How could Felicity keep her mouth shut for long, once she realised what she'd unleash-ed. And even if they hadn't yet recovered everything the river was supposed to conceal, they soon would when the level went down. No, better leave out nothing that was there to be found.

'I was down by the river,' he said, and shivered as if he'd plunged into its coldness, 'and the kid had followed me there, the warden's niece, the Cope girl. She'd been round my neck ever since I'd got to Follymead, I couldn't shake her. And I was in a miserable way because I'd quarrelled with my own girl, and she was around, too, and things were pretty bad with me. I wanted to get somewhere by myself, and think, and there was this silly little thing bleating about love, when she didn't know she was born yet. I stood it a long time, and then blew up. All I wanted was to get rid of her, and I wasn't particular how I did it. I'm not proud of it now. I suppose it was about the cruellest thing I've ever done. I gave her a message to take to her aunt...to Mrs Arundale...as if there was something between us. There wasn't, of course, I only met the lady a couple of times before. It was just that Felicity was already mad jealous of her aunt, that's why I made it her. It cut deeper. And it worked, too. She took offence and walked off and left me there, and that was all I wanted. I never thought she'd go and deliver the damned message, right out in front of both of them...or just to him, I don't know...to him, anyhow, because he came. I'd said to tell Mrs Arundale I was waiting for her there. But it was her husband who came.'

The sergeant's hand seemed to do no more than idle over the paper, spraying shorthand symbols like rain. But he wasn't missing anything. And he could still spare one eye, occasionally, for a quick glance at his prisoner's face.

'Must have been a bit of a shock, when you expected Mrs Arundale,' he said sympathetically.

'I didn't expect anyone. I told you, all I meant to do was shoo the Cope girl away. I never thought she'd have the devilment—I don't know, though, I asked for it!—or the guts, either.' Lucien shivered, a nervous compulsion that ran through his bones in a sharp contraction of cold. 'He was there before I knew. I wasn't paying any attention to anything. I was just glad to be alone, and then there he was coming out of the trees, with this thing in his hand...' A compulsive yawn followed the chill; he smothered it is his hands, and shook himself violently. He wasn't through the wood yet, he had to keep his mind clear.

'This thing...?' said Rapier, patiently nudging.

'Maybe you don't know it. It hangs in the gallery there, among a lot of other exotic junk, Victorian, maybe older. The Cope kid showed

263

it to us when we went round the house, the first evening, It's a black walking-stick with a silver handle, but really it's a sword inside an ebony sheath. I knew it as soon as I saw it, but I never thought... He just drew it out and came at me. Never said a word, simply ran at me with the blade. I tried to talk to him, but there was no time at all, and anyhow I doubt if he could even hear. He looked quite mad...stone-cold mad. I couldn't believe in it, I nearly let him get me because I couldn't take it in. But then I knew he meant killing, and I just put the rocks between us in time, and ducked aside into the trees, hoping to beat him to the gate and get away. But he saw what I was about, and cut back there as fast as I did. I got my hand to the latch, and then he was on top of me, I jumped round and put up my other arm to fend him off, and the tip of the blade ripped my finger...' He flexed them painfully, and there indeed was the sliced cut, imperfectly healed, crossing all four fingers diagonally between second joints and knuckles. 'And the latch had pulled half out of its place, so I knew it was free, and I pulled it out.'

He shut his face tightly between his palms, trying to suppress the sick yawns that were tearing at him now like bouts of pain. Queer the way you reacted when the time came, mentally calm but physically disrupted, a rash of nervous symptoms with a tensed and wary mind. This pause he prolonged in the hope of eliciting a question, anything that would make things easier for him, and give him a signpost, but Rapier waited politely with his ballpoint suggestively poised, and said not a word.

'But I had to spring away from the gate to get out of range. And then he was between me and it, and even if I had a weapon I couldn't match his reach. He drove me down towards the water again, and all I could do was try to parry his strokes. But then it was no good backing any more, I should have been in the river, so I had to try and jump him. I'm no more good at that than he was, and I was in a state by then, and...I don't even know exactly what happened. We were struggling together there, and I hit him... He went down. I didn't know I'd hurt him badly, the only thing I thought about was to grab the sword, while he was stunned. But after a few minutes, when he still didn't move, I got scared, and took a closer look at him. His head was like a ploughed field, and yet there was next to no blood. He wasn't breathing, and with a head that shape he wasn't going to breathe again. I knew I'd killed him. And all for nothing. I never wanted to, I hardly knew him... What was I supposed to do, with that on my hands?' he appealed passionately.

'The right thing,' said Rapier, accepting this literally, 'in a case like that, would be to leave everything as it is, call the police, and tell them the whole story.'

'And how many ever do the right thing, when they get into a jam like that? Try it, some day, and see if you don't do what I did—run. There wasn't a thing I could do for *him*. He was dead. I pulled him to the edge of the river, and threw him as far out as I could, into the current, and I saw it take him downstream over the weir. I threw in the sword-stick and the latch in the pool there. And I remembered that he was supposed to start for Birmingham, and his car was out in the yard ready. So I took it. Nobody'd look for him again until Sunday night. But you can't get money out of banks or turn other assets into cash on a Sunday, I had to wait over until today. If it hadn't been for that, you wouldn't have caught up with me.'

'And how,' asked the sergeant mildly, 'did you know that we were inquiring into this death, then? You say nobody'd be expecting him back until last night, and nobody'd panic at one extra night, would they? Or did somebody tip you off? Did you hear from somebody that his body'd been found?'

Lucien took his hands away from his drawn face, and stared him steadily in the eye. 'No, how could I? I thought I was still ahead of you until they dropped on me at the airport. After that, I couldn't help knowing you'd either found him, or found traces that were just as good. You wouldn't have known about the car being stolen, otherwise. And what you didn't know before,' he said wearily, 'you know now. Have you got it all down?'

'Yes, Mr Galt, I've got it all down.'

'Good! I should hate to go through all that again.'

'I'm sure you would, sir,' agreed Rapier serenely.

'I don't want anybody else to be pestered,' said Lucien, leaning back in his corner with a drained sigh, 'when nobody but me had anything to do with it. I didn't have a thing against him, I hardly even knew him. But *I killed him.*'

'Yes, Mr Galt,' agreed Rapier, accommodatingly, watching the stillness of the pure, dark profile against the streaming world outside, 'yes, you've made that quite clear.'

CHAPTER 10

Audrey Arundale emerged from her privacy to preside at the final gala tea. She wore black, but like many primrose-and-silver blondes, she very frequently did wear black, and there was nothing to remark on in that. She was pale, her eyes a little remote, and shadowed by bluish rings that made them look larger and more lustrous; but there was nothing in her appearance to give rise to comment or curiosity. Her manner was as it had always been, but at one remove more, and the wall of glass that separated her from the rest of the world, even while she touched and conversed and was patently present in the flesh, was so thin and clear that happy people never noticed it.

She was about again on Follymead's business, and had a couple of calls to make. On her way to the small drawing-room she looked in at the deputy warden's office. Henry Marshall looked up from his laden desk as she entered, and came to his feet in quick concern.

'Mrs Arundale, I'd no idea... You're not going in to tea?'

'Yes, I must. I'm quite all right, I assure you, there's no need to worry about me. I just wondered if there was anything I could help *you* with. I'm so sorry to have left everything to you, like this.'

'You mustn't trouble about the running of the place at all, that's what I'm here for.'

'I know,' she said, 'and I know how well you can do it. I hope... I hope they'll give you the job, Harry.'

'Thank you!' he said uncomfortably. He hadn't thought of her bereavement, until then, as his opportunity. 'I think we've got everything in order. It's lucky that we had no special fixtures for the next few days. We're circulating all the people who've booked for the course next week-end, and cancelling the arrangements. I thought it would be impossible to go through with it. I have it from the police that no statement will be given to the press until tomorrow, and I very much hope it will only affect the local and regional press at the moment.'

'But there'll have to be an inquest, won't there?' she said, contemplating the complexities of death with eyes of stunned distaste.

'It's to open on Wednesday morning, I'm told. But Inspector Felse says it will be only a formal opening, and the police will be asking

269

for an adjournment. At least that will allow time for the public to forget about us a little.'

'And find some newer sensations,' she said with the blanched ghost of a smile. 'Yes... And what about the subscription concert, on Monday evening of next week? So difficult to cancel a thing like that, when all the tickets have been sold, and then it's hardly fair to the artists...'

'I think we ought to go through with that. A whole week will have passed, and the public who do use Follymead will know by then what's happened here, and I think they'll be reassured to find that the work is to go on. I'm sure the governors will approve.'

'Good,' said Audrey. 'I'm glad you feel that way about it, too. I thought myself we ought to honour the arrangements. It's certainly what Edward would have wanted us to do. I'm so glad you're here to look after everything, Harry. I see you don't need me at all. Now I must go along and have a word with Inspector Felse before tea.'

He sprang to open the door for her, his anxious eyes searching her face, but there was nothing to be seen but a white calm. 'I don't think you should attempt too much. The social load is taking care of itself, you know, you've only to listen to them. And it'll soon be over now. You weren't thinking of attending this last concert, were you?'

'Yes, I feel I must. Edward would have wished it.'

She went along the corridor from the gallery to the warden's private office. George Felse was sitting behind the desk with his head propped in his hands, the telephone stilent now, the photograph of Audrey in her party-dress, Audrey at sixteen, leaning against a trough of Edward's books. George could look from the girl to the woman, and feel time whirl past her over his head, and she, since the picture was hidden from her, would not even be able to guess at the reason for the look of wonder and compunction in his eyes.

'Mr Felse, I hope I haven't done something I shouldn't have done, but it seemed to be my job. I've told Felicity, in confidence, that her uncle is dead; and I've telephoned her mother, and told her that I'm sending the child home by the half past five train. Wilson will drive her to the station. If you have no objection? I know you'll probably need her, later on, but you'll find Mrs Cope's address there in the book, and Felicity will be available whenever necessary.'

'I'm glad,' said George. 'It's the best thing you could have done. You may be sure we shall spare her as much as we can. It may not even be necessary to bring her into it at all. If we

271

can avoid it, we will.'

'I know. She told me…she said you've been very kind to her. She…we have never understood each other, I know that. I feel guilty towards her.'

'So does she,' said George quietly, 'towards you.'

'Yes…we can hardly take a step, it seems, without infringing someone else's liberties. I've suggested to Mrs Cope that she should try sending Felicity abroad for a time, perhaps even to school abroad. A completely new environment, new companions…'

'It would be the very best thing for her. And I believe she could make good use of it, now.'

'I believe she could. Thank you, I'm glad you think I've done right.'

She closed the door gently after her, and went towards the hubbub in the drawing-room. And there she dispensed tea, and made conversation, and was everything the hostess of Follymead should be, always with the invisible and impenetrable veil between her and reality.

'Such a delightful week-end, my dear,' said Miss Southern, balancing a china tea-cup as old and fragile as her own thin, bluish fingers. 'So wonderful to get away from this awful modern world and enjoy an island of such *peace.*'

272

'I'm so happy,' said Audrey, 'that it's been a success.'

'Oh, it has! Everyone's enjoyed it *so* much. That charming little girl with the harp... I do think the harp's such a *graceful* instrument for a woman, don't you?'

'Mrs Arundale,' shrilled the girl with the butterfly glasses, bounding between the chattering groups with a cucumber sandwich in one hand and a tea-cup in the other, 'it's been *fab!* I can't *wait* for the next one.'

'I'm so glad you've enjoyed it. We must try to fit in another one as soon as we can.'

'I'm only sorry Arundale's missed most of it,' said a thin gentleman in a dog-collar. 'Do tell him, when he gets back, what an enormous success it's been.'

'I'll tell him,' said Audrey, and her glass smile never wavered.

Felicity came down the stairs from her room at a quarter to five, carrying a coat over her arm and a suitcase in her hand. She cocked an ear towards the small drawing-room, but on reflection did not go in. Instead, she looked round the recesses of the gallery for a secluded spot, and there in a cushioned corner of one of the built-in seats was Liri Palmer, sitting alone.

'Hullo!' said Felicity. 'I was just thinking of

273

going to look for you, only I was a bit scared, too. Do you mind if I sit with you? I've got ten minutes, and then I've got to go.'

'You're leaving?'

'My aunt's sending me home.' Felicity put down her case, and dropped into the cushions. 'I think she thinks the children should be kept out of the way of crime and the law, and if there's going to be unpleasantness, Felicity must be shipped off to more sheltered places. Very correct, very conventional, is my Aunt Audrey.' She looked along her shoulder at the clear, still profile and the glorious, envied hair. 'You know my uncle's dead, don't you?' Her voice was low, level and determinedly unemotional, but her face was solemn and pale.

'I found him,' said Liri simply. 'How did you find out?'

'Aunt Audrey told me. She knew I was in it already, up to the neck, so she told me how it turned out. I was grateful to her for that. It's horrible to know bits...too much, but not enough... And to have to find out the rest maybe from a newspaper. Now at least I know where I am, even if I don't like it much.'

'Who does?' Said Liri.

'No...nobody, I suppose. But *you* haven't *done* anything.'

'And you have?'

'Yes, that's what I wanted to tell you. You see, the bits you know are different bits from mine. And I only found out today, from Dickie Meurice, that you and Lucien... You were engaged, weren't you? Or as good as, what's the difference? I wanted to tell you, I didn't know that. If I'd known, I wouldn't have tried to make him interested in me, and none of this would have happened. Not that that makes it much better for you, I suppose, because in any case he was playing you false.' The phrase came strangely but without affectation; whatever was on her mind now, Felicity was not pretending, even to herself. 'He was Aunt Audrcy's lover. I suppose you knew that?'

Liri stared straight before her. 'He broke three dates with me, always with a good excuse, always on the telephone. It's easier to lie to somebody on the telephone. Twice I swallowed it, the third time I was a shade low, so I took myself out to dinner at a little place we sometimes used. He was supposed to be at rehearsal for a recording session, but he wasn't. He was there with her. They were glowing like studio lights, and talking like bosom friends, as if they had a lifetime's talking to make up. He was holding her hand, right there on the table. They didn't see me. They weren't seeing anyone but each other. I didn't interrupt

275

them. I waited until the next time he came for me, and then I threw it at him that he'd been standing me up for another woman. He said there was nothing in it, I was making a mistake. But I knew better. We both went mad, and that was the end of it.' She sat up abruptly and shook herself, between anger and amazement. 'Why am I telling you this?'

'I don't know,' said Felicity humbly, 'unless it's because I've grown up suddenly.'

'Afterwards I thought about it, and I thought, no, that was too big a thing to throw away like that, without even trying to straighten it out between us. So I came here to Follymead, because he had this engagement here. I came to make it up with him if I could. and the first person I saw when I got here—no, the second, actually, *you* were the first, through the lighted windows right here in this gallery—the second person I saw was this woman who'd been with him in the restaurant. So then I knew why Lucien had taken this engagement...maybe why the whole week-end course had been thought up. And that was the end of it as far as I was concerned. I *thought!* Actually it turns out things don't just end when it's appropriate, they go on whether you want them to or not. Is that what you wanted to know?'

'It isn't that I wanted to *know*. But thank
276

you, all the same. It makes it easier to understand. Me, I didn't know any of all that, or even about you. All I could see was Lucien. I was in love with him, or I thought I was. I went out after him last Saturday afternoon...' She told that story again, softening nothing; Liri had a right to know.

'That was what he said. And I did it. I went straight back to the house, and Uncle Edward and Aunt Audrey were sitting there together, and I said just exactly what Lucien had told me to say, right out loud to both of them. And that's the part you didn't know. That's all. That's why Uncle Edward went down there to kill him, only he got killed himself, instead. But whichever way it went, somebody died, and I was the cause of it.'

'You did *that?*' Liri had turned to study the girl at her side with wide-eyed attention. 'Went and chucked his private invitation down on the table between them, "where they were sat at meat"?'

'Well, not exactly that,' said Felicity, puzzled. 'They were just finishing coffee, actually.'

'Don't mind me, it was just something that came into my head. It happens in one of the ballads, didn't you know? Just like that.' She stared sombrely at the story that now unrolled before her remorseless and complete. 'It's something I might have done, too, if he'd done a thing like that to me.'

'Oh, might you? Do you really mean that? But you didn't,' said Felicity, clouding over again. 'I was the one who did it, and I was the one who caused Uncle Edward to get killed.'

'You and all the rest of us who've had any part in this affair. And Mr Arundale himself, that's certain. Don't claim more than belongs to you,' said Liri hardly.

'That's what Inspector Felse said,' admitted Felicity, encouraged.

'Inspector Felse is a pretty deep sort of a man.'

'He is, isn't he? There; that's the station wagon for me.' The horn had blared cheerfully in the courtyard. Felicity picked up her coat and her case. 'Good-bye! I wish things could turn out better than they look now. I'm sorry!'

She turned her slender, erect back, and marched away along the rear corridor towards the back stairs. At the warden's office she hesitated for a moment, and then tapped on the door. It would be only polite, wouldn't it, to say good-bye to Inspector Felse?

'Oh, hullo!' said George. 'I heard you were off home.'

'It's all right, isn't it, for me to go? Aunt Audrey said she'd tell you.'

'Yes, it's all right. If we need you, we shall know where to find you. Take care of yourself, and good luck. Better luck,' he said gently, 'than you've had so far.'

'Thank you. You've been very kind.' He saw her glance stray involuntarily towards the glass over the hearth. 'You did mean what you said, didn't you? You do really think I'm going to be...pretty?'

'No,' said George firmly, 'you're never going to be pretty, and that isn't what I said.'

'I was afraid to say the other word,' Felicity admitted simply. 'But you *did* mean it, didn't you?'

'I meant it. You'll see for yourself, before very long.'

'It's not that it makes any difference to what's happened,' she explained punctiliously. 'But it's something to start from—like having capital. You know!' She picked up her case sturdily. 'Good-bye, then, and thanks!'

'Good-bye, Felicity! You'll be all right?'

She understood that in its fullest meaning, and she said: 'I'll be all right.'

The station wagon taking Felicity away to catch her train left the courtyard and circled the house to the front drive just two minutes before Price drove in by the farm road. The tower

279

clock, which was several minutes fast, was just chiming five. In one and a half hours the students would be dispersing, by car, by bus, by the house transport and the local trains, to homes scattered over the whole of the Midlands, and some even farther afield. Let them, at all costs, get off in peace. An extra car suddenly appearing at Follymead was nothing to wonder about at normal times, but better to take no chances now. Price parked carefully in the obscurity under the archway, where they could not be seen from the windows.

Lucien awoke from a wretched and uneasy doze with the exaggerated alarm of nightmare, and stared round wildly to find the familiar and unwelcome apparition of Follymead enclosing him. He could face what he had to face, but he shied at the idea of added ordeals.

'Why have you brought me here?' he demanded, roused and resentful. 'I thought we were going to the police station at Comerbourne.'

'I don't remember that we mentioned exactly where we were going. Inspector Felse has been working from here, and this is where we shall find him.' Rapier got out of the back seat, and locked the car upon the two who remained; not that he thought the boy would try to make a break for it now, but, there was no point in leaving him even the meagre opportunity. The sergeant climbed the back stairs, and let himself into the warden's office.

George looked up from the report he was compiling, short as yet of a few details, a date or two, a name, but by this time essentially complete. 'Well, how did it go?'

'No trouble,' said Rapier complacently. 'He's below in the car.' He laid his notebook on the desk, and flicked through the close pages of shorthand. 'There you are! He insisted on making a statement, didn't seem able to rest until he had it all in order. I'll send it up to you as soon as I can get it typed. He's made a full confession.'

'Ah,' said George, with a faint smile that Rapier found, in retrospect, more than a little puzzling. 'Yes, I thought he might.'

'He says Arundale attacked him, and he killed him in self-defence. You won't have any trouble, he's filled in all the details, and they all fit.'

'Oh, yes, I quite thought he'd make a good job of it.' The smile was still present, wry, private and sad, and yet understandably touched with the pride and satisfaction of a man whose judgement has been vindicated by events. 'And what about Mrs Arundale?'

'She had nothing to do with it. I will say that

281

for him, he went out of his way to make that clear. He hardly knew her. He says he used her name to shock the kid, because he knew she was jealous of her, anyhow, and the kid must have gone and told her uncle. Oh, he's made your case for you.'

'All right,' said George, 'bring him up.'

Rapier went back down the staircase and unlocked the car, dropping the keys into Price's hand. 'Ready for you now, Mr Galt. Up the stairs, that's right.'

Lucien heard the distant, starling clamour from the great drawing-room, and reared his head in a wild gesture of mingled ardour and revulsion. 'But they…do *they* know about this?' He climbed the tight spiral flight, tensed and suspicious, his ears stretched. They surely couldn't know. The high-pitched din was eager and innocent, untouched by death.

'You'd better ask the inspector that. In here.'

Lucien entered the warden's office, and the door was closed quietly behind him.

George rose from behind the desk. 'Sit down, Mr Galt. You must have made very good time. I was reckoning on this final concert being over, or nearly over, by the time you arrived.'

It was like coming into a familiar room which had been emptied of its furniture, and was no longer familiar. All the echoes were wrong, all the tones distorted so acutely that Lucien felt his balance affected, and spread his feet aggressively to grip reality more firmly. Even in the car he had this feeling of disorientation, but now it went over him as acutely as panic, and left him sick and frightened. He had made a detailed statement admitting his responsibility for the death of Arudale, why wasn't he under arrest? Even if his escorts from London had been instructed only to deliver him safely to the man in charge, here, presumably, *was* the man in charge, and still nothing seemed to be about to happen. He gripped the back of the chair that was offered him, and stood taut and distrustful, his eyes roving the room.

'I don't understand. Why did I have to come back here? Was that fair? I haven't made any trouble for your men, I've co-operated as well as I can, I'm not disputing anything I've done. So *why...?*'

'Sit down,' said George.

It wasn't worth arguing about; Lucien sat. George came round the desk and sat on the front corner, looking his capture over with interest. Black as a gypsy, strung fine as a violin, a slender, dark, wild creature, with arrogant eyes shadowed now by grief and fear, and a hypersensitive, proud mouth that was ready to curl even at this moment. Like his picture, but even more like the picture his friends and enemies had built up of him for the man who had never set eyes on him until now.

'I've made a statement,' said Lucien. 'It should clear up everything for you. I suppose he has to transcribe it, or whatever. I don't know what more you want.'

'Then I'll tell you. I want another hour and a half of apparent normality here. After that we can be as business-like as you please.' He saw the tired eyes question doubtfully, and smiled. 'Mr Galt, I believe you'll have a certain sympathy with our concern for this place. It may not be perfect, what it does may not go very far, or be very profound. But with all that, it is a pretty remarkable institution. It brings music, and what's more, knowledge and desire of music, to people who've perhaps never really experienced it before. If its appeal fell off as the result of a scandal and a notorious case, or if its enemies—oh, yes, anything that can be called cultural has always more than enough enemies—if its enemies got an effective weapon to use against it, it might be killed for good, and that would be a real loss. There's going to be publicity, inquest and trial can't be avoided. There's going to be a bad period; but if we can minimise the effect as much as possible, Follymead may survive. That's why I want to take no action whatever until this course has dispersed. The next can be called off without too much backwash. So let's at least wait until the house is empty tonight, before we start talking in terms of guilt and arrests.'

After a brief and dubious silence Lucien said slowly: 'I'm not sure what it is you want of me.'

'I want you to give me your word not to try to get away, just to wait and behave normally until the party has left.'

Lucien moistened his lips. His eyes kindled suddenly into a slightly feverish glitter. 'This is a straightforward concert for the finish?'

'Yes. Until half past six. They they all go home.'

'Is Liri taking part?'

'Yes, Liri's taking part.'

He thought of her head bent over the guitar, the great braid of hair coiled on her neck, the suave curve of her cheek and the intent, burnished brow, and of the voice achingly pure and clear and passionate. He thought of a future blank with confinement and solitude, where the voice could not penetrate.

'If you'll let me sit in on this concert, all right, I give you my word I won't cause you any trouble.'

He didn't believe there would be any response to that offer, he was sure they'd never risk him among the crowd. But Inspector Felse had got to his feet briskly, and swept his papers into a drawer.

'Agreed, if you don't mind my company. And in that case we'd better go in, hadn't we? They'll be starting any minute.'

From her place among the artists, Liri saw them come in.

The lights were already dimmed, the hum of voices was becoming muted and expectant, and it was time. There at the back of the great room people moved about gently in obscurity, settling themselves, changing their places, finding comfortable leg-room. For once Professor Penrose came a little late to his place, and in haste, having taken too long a nap after tea; but for that the programme would have begun before the padded door at the back of the room opened again, and her attention would have been on the singers, and not on the two late-comers. As it was, she was gazing beyond the last rank of chairs in the shadow, beyond even the walls of the room, when the opening of the door caused her to shorten her sights, and return to here and now. And the person who came in was Lucien.

Her heart turned in her, even before she saw

286

George Felse follow him into the room, and edge along after him behind the audience, to a seat against the wall. So they had him, after all. He wasn't used to running from things, and he hadn't run fast enough, and now they had him, back here where the thing had happened that never should have happened, the wasted, meaningless thing in which she still couldn't believe. She felt the walls closing in on her, too.

And yet if he was under arrest, what was he doing here? There seemed to be no constraint upon him, even if the inspector had come in with him, and taken a seat beside him on the elegant little gilt and velvet couch against the tapestried wall. They sat there like any other two members of the audience, she even saw them exchange a few words, with every appearance of normality. What was happening? There was something here that was not as it seemed to be, and she could not make out what it was, or whom it threatened.

She looked to the inspector for a clue, but his face was smooth and reserved and quite unreadable, there was no way of guessing what was going on in the mind behind it. If she had gone in terror of the obvious end, now she found herself equally afraid of some other eventuality beyond her grasp. Why bring a prisoner here into this room? She could understand that the police might prefer to get all these people out of here before they took decisive action, but even so, why bring Lucien to the gathering?

A hand jogged her arm. The professor's insinuating voice begged her winningly: 'Your legs are younger than mine, lass. Run and fetch my notebook for me, will you? I went and left it in the warden's office before tea, and forgot to collect it again.'

His notebook was a joke by that time. He couldn't talk without it open before him, and yet he had never been known to consult it for any detail, however abstruse.

'You've never needed it yet,' protested Liri, her eyes clinging to the distant pair at the back of the room, lost now in an even dimmer light. Someone had turned out the strip-lights over the pictures. 'You're not likely to start tonight.'

'There has to be a first time for everything. Go on, now, like a good girl.'

And she went, impatiently but obediently, flashing to the doorway and running along the corridor. Her heels rang on the polished wood with a solitary and frightening sound, for outside the great yellow room the house hung silent and deserted. Nothing now was quite real, so much of her mind laboured frenziedly with this crisis she could not comprehend. She pushed open the door of the warden's office, which for the past three days had become an extension of police headquarters, while the house went about its blithe business oblivious of all evil. The massive folder of the professor's notes lay on a walnut table near the window. She tucked it under her arm, and turned to the door again, and then as abruptly turned back, and crossed to the desk.

Would he leave anything, any unconsidered trifle, where she could find it and make sense of it? She had to know; there was a feverish pulse beating in her blood that insisted it was imperative for her to know.

She put down her portfolio on the desk, and began trying all the drawers one by one, but they were fast locked. She should have guessed that. There was nothing here for her.

But there was. Her eyes fell on it as she straightened up with a sigh from her useless search. There it was, propped against Arundale's rack of reference books, eye to eye with her, the half-plate photograph of a young girl in a white party-dress. She had never seen the living face joyous like this, but she knew it at once, as she knew the little silver disc that hung round the girl's neck on a thin chain.

Lucien's medal, the one he had worn ever since she had known him, long before he met Audrey Arundale. The one thing that had been his father's. And yet here it hung round the neck of the sixteen-year-old Audrey, how many years ago, how many worlds away?

Now she did understand. Intuitively, without need of details or evidence, she understood everything. Yes, even why Lucien was sitting there among the audience in the dresssing-room, under no restraint, though he surely expected arrest afterwards. Liri knew better. She knew what was going to happen afterwards; she knew what went on behind George Felse's unrevealing face.

She caught up the portfolio and slipped from the room, to run like a wild thing through the silent libraries, and along the corridors to the warden's private quarters. But there was no one there. The lights were out and the rooms deserted. And she must go back, she couldn't hunt any farther. Too late now to make any amends, too late to look for Audrey, too late to warn her. A minute more, and someone else would be out hunting for *her*.

She went back to the yellow drawing-room, back to her place on the dais. She gave the professor his notes, which of course he would not need or use. It was no use now; there was no way of reaching her. Liri raised her eyes and looked carefully over the array of attentive faces, little moons in a mild twilight. Those two at the back, side by side on their crazy little gilded perch, looked improbably at ease. The professor was talking about the summing-up of all that they had experienced together, the relationship of folk-music to the wider and deeper field of music itself. Presently the Rossignol twins were singing, two angelic voices, eerie and sweet.

The long range of windows that led out on to the terrace brought the dim and cloudy day in upon them in tints of subdued violet and green. Not even dusk yet, not by a couple of hours, and yet the low and heavy cloud hung like a pall, turning this after-tea hour into night.

The most distant of the long windows, down there at the back of the room, stood ajar. A while ago they had all been closed. The last chair at the end of that row, certainly empty then, was occupied now. Someone had come in by the window, and moved the chair aside into the embrasure, drawing a fold of the heavy curtains round it to screen her from at least half the room. A dead black dress, the sheen of pale, piled hair.

Edward Arundale's widow, still chatelaine of Follymead, had come to the final concert. They were there in the same room together, there was only about fifteen yards of air between them, and yet they could not communicate.

Or was there still a way? That curious conversation with Felicity had started a tune running in Liri's head, and it would not be quieted. It plagued her with reminders of the rogue page who tossed just such an apple of discord in among Lord Barnard's household 'where they were sat at meat.' The verse ranged through her head, in the light of what she had just learned, with a new and terrifying aptness. If they talked to her, they could talk to another person, one, the only one except George Felse and Lucien Galt, who knew the whole story, and would recognise only too well the full implications. She might still misunderstand; but that had to be risked. Liri could not leave her to step over the edge of the pit without so much as reaching a hand to her. Whatever her own wrongs, she owed Audrey that and more. She was indebted to her for a world, and she could make so little repayment now.

Liri folded her hands on her guitar, and waited. She knew now what she had to do.

CHAPTER 11

Past six o'clock. The darkness was purplish, thundery, the air still as before a storm. It must be her turn soon. Why had the old man kept her until last?

'And now for Liri. She promised to sing us "The Queen's Maries" in the full text, which is by way of being a marathon performance, so I've reserved enough time for her to do herself justice. But now she's whispering in my ear that she'd like to change her choice. It's a woman's privilege. So I'll leave any introduction to Liri.'

'I thought,' she said, clearly and quietly, 'that everyone knows the story of Mary Hamilton, and there are so many fine stories that very few people know. I warn you, this is a marathon performance, too, but I hope you won't find it dull. I'd like to sing the ballad of "Gil Morrice." Anybody know it?'

Thank God, nobody did. She knew the proud, proprietary emanations of those who find themselves one up on the rest, and here there was nothing like that, only pleased expectancy. It's still true, people love to be read to, to listen to stories. Even those kids who are so with it that they've completely lost contact with most of it—'it' being the total body of mental and spiritual fulfilment and delight, the mass of music, the body of books, the entire apparition of art—even they will shiver and thrill to this blood-stained tragedy, though they won't recognise their excitement as something dating back into prehistory. They'll think it's because this is 'folk,' of all the odd labels. This is human, which is more than being folk.

'Here goes them. "Gil Morrice".'

She curled over the guitar, felt along its strings with a sensuous gesture, and raised her face, filling her lungs deep. The guitar uttered one shuddering chord, and that was all. She began in the story-teller's level, lilting voice;

> 'Gil Morrice was an Erle's son,
> His name is waxed wide;
> It was not for his great riches
> Nor for his mickle pride,
> But it was for a lady gay
> That lived on Carron side.'

So much for the introduction, and straight into the story. The guitar took up a thin, fine line of melody, low beneath the clear voice, that had as yet no passion in it, but remained a story-teller, uninvolved, unwrung:

' "Where shall I find a bonny boy
That will win hose and shoon,
That will go to Lord Barnard's hall
And bid his lady come?

"And you must run my errand, Willie,
And you may run with pride,
When other boys gae on their feet
On horseback ye shall ride."

"Oh, no, oh, no, my master dear,
I darena for my life.
I'll not go to the bold baron's
For to tryst forth his wife.

"But oh, my master dear," he cried,
"In greenwood ye're your lane,
Give o'er such thoughts, I would you rede,
For fear ye should be ta'en," '

The guitar had enlarged its low comment, the thick chords came in rising anger. A stillness began to bud in the centre of the audience, and opened monstrous petals in the gloom. A little more, and she would know she had them; but whether she had Audrey she had no way of knowing. The pulsing excitement of the telling took her like a trance. She heard her own voice deepen and grow harsh, and she had done nothing at all, issued no orders:

' "My bird Willie, my boy Willie,
My dear Willie," he said,
"How can ye strive against the stream?
For I shall be obeyed.

"Haste, haste, I say, go to the hall,
Bid her come here with speed.
If ye refuse my high command
I'll gar your body bleed."

"Yes, I will go your black errand,
Though it be to your cost,
Since you by me will not be warned,
In it ye shall find frost.

"And since I must your errand run
So sore against my will,
I'll make a vow, and keep it true,
It shall be done for ill." '

The guitar came crashing in now with the dark themes of the page's hate and love, and the rapid, rushing narrative of his ride to Lord Barnard's castle. He swam the river and leaped the wall, and burst in upon the household at table. She had them in her hand, and the instrument sang for her, passionate and enraged beneath the far-pitched thread of her voice stringing in the words like pearls. Oh, God, let her understand what's coming before *he* does, let her listen with every nerve. All I want is that she should have time to get her armour on, and be ready for him.

The page was in the hall now, striding in upon the assembled company. The voice sang full and clear, almost strident to ride over the meal-time talk:

    ' "Hail, hail, my gentle sire and dame,
My message will not wait.
Dame, ye maun to the good greenwood
Before that it be late.

"See, there's your sign, a silken sark,
Your own hand sewed the sleeve.
You must go speak with Gil Morrice,
Ask no bold baron's leave."

The lady stamped with her foot
And winked with her ee,
But for all that she could say or do,
Forbidden he wouldna be.

"It's surely to my bower woman,
It ne'er could be to me."
"I brought it to Lord Barnard's lady,
I trow that you are she."

Then up and spake the wily nurse,
The bairn upon her knee:
"If it be come from Gil Morrice
It's dear welcome to me."

"Ye lied, ye lied, ye filthy nurse,
So loud I heard ye lee.
I brought it to Lord Barnard's lady,
I trow you are not she."

Then up and spake the bold baron,
An angry man was he.
He's thrust the table with his foot,
So has he with his knee,
Till silver cup and mazer dish
In flinders he gar'd flee.

"Go bring a robe of your clothing
That hangs upon the pin,
And I'll go to the good greenwood
And speak with your lemman." '

Her mouth, as always when she attempted
these appalling feats, was sour and raw with the

myriad voices that spoke through it, and the bitterness that century upon century could not sweeten or abate. There was sweat running on her lips, and until this moment she had not been able to raise her head and rest, letting the guitar speak for her again. Now it sang softly, unalarmed, waiting in serenity, and she cast one urgent glance towards where Audrey sat beside the open window. There was a tension there, something braced and ready and wild, to which her own heart rose with answering passion; but whether it was really more than the tension that held them all was more than she could guess. There was so little time, because the thread of this compulsion rested in her, and she must not let it flag. The sylvan song had been prolonged enough, and here came the ultimate test of her powers, the key verse that must reach Audrey before the rest had time to aim at understanding:

'Gil Morrice sat in good greenwood,
He whistled and he sang...

It had dawned upon George already that for some reason of her own Liri was re-telling the whole story of what had happened here. Perhaps not to the end, for how could any ballad encompass everything that had happened? And this was genuine, no doubt of that. The effort he had to make to tear himself out of its spell for an instant was like tearing the heart out of his body. This girl was marvellous. Listen to her now, the voice light and careless again, and yet with an indescribable overtone of premonition and doom disregarded:

' "Oh, what mean all these folk coming?
My mother tarries lang."
The baron came to the greenwood
With mickle dule and care,
And here he first spied Gil Morrice,
Combing his yellow hair...'

The word, the unexpected, the impossible word, had passed George as it had been meant to do, drawn away before his mental vision in the tension of the story. But suddenly as it slipped away from him he caught it back, and the stab was like a knife-thrust into his consciousness. 'My mother...'

My mother!

What did she know, and what was she about? How *could* she know? This couldn't be accidental, it couldn't be purposeless, and it couldn't be wanton. What Liri Palmer did was considered and meant, and he doubted if she ever took anything back, or regretted much.

300

He cast a quick glance round into every corner of the room, but everywhere the tension held. She had them all in her hand.

' "No wonder, no wonder, Gil Morrice,
My lady loved thee weel,
The fairest part of my bodie
Is blacker than they heel.

"Yet ne'er the less now, Gil Morrice,
For all thy great beautie,
Ye'll rue the day ye e'er were born.
That head shall go with me." '

The rage and grief of the accompaniment remained low and secret, hurrying bass chords suppressed and stifled.

For a few moments she let her instrument brood and threaten, and looked down the room. Inspector Felse was sitting forward, braced and aware. Beside him Lucien was shadowed and still, very still; there was no way of knowing, with all her knowledge of him, what he was going through now. After all, it was not Lucien she was trying to reach.

But there was a movement now in the folds of the half-drawn curtain at the last window. Audrey's little solitude lay in comparative light, but the curtains were of heavy brocade, and lined, there would be no shadow to betray her. Softly she got up from her place, and softly, softly, with infinite caution, she slipped back step by silent step from her chair, towards the unlatched window. Audrey had understood.

Now cover her, whatever happens. Don't let any of them look round, don't loose their senses for an instant. Cry out and cover her with the steely shriek of murder and the savagery of the mutilation:

'Now he has drawn his trusty brand
And whatt it on a stone,
And through Gil Morrice' fair bodie
Has the cauld iron gone.

And he has ta'en Gil Morrice' head
And set it on a spear,
The meanest man in all his train
Has gotten that head to bear.

And he has ta'en Gil Morrice up,
Laid him across his steed,
And brought him to his painted bower
And laid him on a bed.

The lady sat on castle wall,
Beheld both dale and down,

And there she saw Gil Morrice' head
Come trailing to the town...'

The clamour of violence died into the lamen-
table threnody of death. The guitar keened,
and the voice extended into the long, fatal
declamation of that which can never be put
right again. The tension, instead of relaxing,
wound itself ever tighter until it was unendurable. The singer's face, sharpened in the
concentrated light upon her, was raised to look
over the heads of her audience. The lady was
at the window, easing it silently open, melting
into the outer air.

And this might well have been her voice, if
things had gone differently, high, reckless and
wild, as she came down from her tower to
welcome her lover, her life laid waste about
her for ever:

' "Far better I love that bloody head,
But and that golden hair,
Than Lord Barnard and all his lands,
As they lie here and there."

And she had ta'en her Gil Morrice
And kissed him cheek and chin.
"I was once as full of Gil Morrice
As the hip is of the stane.

303

"I got ye in my father's house
With mickle sin and shame..." '

To the last moment Audrey kept her face
turned towards the singer; and as she slipped
back through the window the freer light found
her face, and showed Liri its white and resolute
tranquillity, and the already irrelevant tears on
her cheeks. The two women who loved Lucien
exchanged one first, last glance of full understanding and acceptance, that paid off all the
debts between them.

The spell-binding voice soared in fearful
agony to cover the moment of departure:

' "I brought thee up in good greenwood
Under the frost and rain..." '

Audrey was gone, lost to sight at once, across
the blind end of the terrace, and down the
steps.

George felt the boy beside him strung tight
to breaking point. He saw the bright lines of
Liri's face drawn silver-white in the light of the
lamp on the dais, the huge eyes fixed and frantic. Something was happening, and yet nothing
was happening, not a movement anywhere in
the room, she wouldn't let them move, that
long, strong hand of hers that plucked the

strings was manipulating them all like mario-
nettes, the generous, wide-jointed fingers that
drummed a funeral march on the body of her
instrument held them nailed in their places.

' "Oft have I by thy cradle sat
And fondly seen thee sleep,
But now I go about thy bier
The salt tears for to weep..." '

In the changing temperature of the evening
the normal small dusk wind arose, as suddenly as was its habit here over the open sward.
It took the unlatched window and swung it
wide against the curtain, seized the folds and
set them swinging. A chill draught coursed
along the wall, and fluttered the skirts of gold
brocade at every window embrasure.

George heard and felt the abrupt, cold whisper from the outer world. He came to his feet
with a leap, lunged silently along the wall, and
whisked round the curtain to the open window,
now swinging fitfully in the fresh currents of
air. Far down the slope of grass he saw the fair
head receding. The curtain shook, and he, too,
was gone, down the steps and after her in a
soundless run. And Lucien, the thread of his
passionate concentration broken by the sudden
movement beside him, came out of his dream

to the sharper and more personal pains of the real world. She saw him rise, and felt the belated shock of knowledge and realisation sear through him; but there was nothing she could do, as he groped his way blindly after George, except sing on to the end, prolong the postlude, cover the slight, the very slight disturbance, and make those few who had noticed it forget it had ever been.

' "And syne she kissed his bloody cheek
And syne his bloody chin:
"Oh, better I love my Gil Morrice
Than all my kith and kin."

"Away, away, ye ill women,
And an ill death may ye dee.
Had I but known he'd been your son,
He'd ne'er been slain for me." '

Five minutes more, to preserve the integrity of the course, and nobody, certainly not the professor, would dream of filling in with something smaller after this monstrous *tour-de-force*. Liri knew her worth. But don't let them go yet, hold them fast, keep them from looking out of the windows yet, tie their feet from following. She didn't know what she had done, but she knew there must be no interference with it now, no well-meaning unlookers, no witnesses to tell the story afterwards.

She raised the volume and passion of her instrument to a crisis of anguish, improvising in a galloping rhapsody that bore the fortunes of Lord Barnard and his lady and Gil Morrice racing to ruin together, away down the wind and into the distance of antiquity, where old hatreds and old agonies lay down together between the four lines of a ballad verse as in a bed, and slept, and dreamed. The threnody sobbed away beneath her fingers, diminuendo, and died on a mere breath, one muted quiver of a single string.

She felt the sweat cold on her forehead and lip, and the silence came down on her stunningly, like the fall of a roof. It seemed to last for a long time, while she could hardly breathe or stir for weakness; and then a sigh like a gust of wind went through the room, and they were all one their feet roaring and clapping together, and Professor Penrose had his old arm round her shoulders and was shaking her in a joyful embrace, while out of the contortion of her mouth that passed for a smile she was howling at him over and over, under cover of the din:

'Get them away, quickly! Get them out of here...get them out...*get them out!*'

After they were gone, with all that merry racket of cars and voices and horns, like a wild hunt of the twentieth century—and some of them still singing—the house was awesomely quiet. So quiet that it was hard to remember that somewhere downstairs some dozen or so resident staff still remained, few of them ever seen by visitors.

Celia Whitwood had tucked her harp lovingly into the back of the huge old car she drove, and set off westwards for home with Andrew Callum as a passenger. The Rossignol twins and Peter Crewe had clambered gaily into the station wagon, bound for the London train, and after them the professor, embracing his inevitable notes and leaving behind in his bedroom the same case of recording tapes he had forgotten at Comerbourne station on Friday evening. Even Dickie Meurice was gone with him, edged competently and civilly into the transport by the deputy warden, with his consuming curiosity still unsatisfied. From his front seat, for once in the audience, he had not seen Lucien appear or Audrey disappear. To him it was only a matter of time, of a little patience, and Lucien's arrest was a pleasurable certainty. Let him go, let him sit and gloat in town, waiting for the flare headlines he was never going to see. He had never been of much importance;

now, in this immense calm after the whirlwind, he was of no importance at all.

Liri sat in a deep chair in the gallery, her eyes half-closed, exhaustion covering her like a second skin. She saw the growing dusk take away the small possessions of the Cothercotts one by one into shadow, the fan that concealed a dagger, the empty place where the sword-stick had hung, the silver-chased pistols, the miniatures on ivory; and then whole pieces of furniture, the love-seat with its twisted arms, the spinet, the inlaid cabinets, the entire end of the long room. Darkness crept in upon her, and was welcomed. She seemed to have been there alone for so long that it was strange to hear a movement in the room with her. It could have been Felicity's fictional ghost; but it was only Tossa Barber, sitting just as quietly on a high-backed chair by the library door.

'It's only me. It's all right,' said Tossa simply, 'I'll go away when they come.'

'I don't mind. I thought everybody'd gone.'

'We have to wait for Mr Felse. We're driving back with him, if...' She let that fall. Nobody knew when George would be ready to go home. 'Dominic went down to see if he... to find them...' Every sentence flagged into silence. All they were really doing was waiting.

It must have been nearly eight o'clock when

they heard the first footsteps crossing the terrace, the clash of the window-latch, a heel on the sill, stumbling, uncertain. Two people, the second closely following the first, but never touching him. A hand reached over an oblivious shoulder to the light-switches at the end of the gallery, hesitated, and chose the single lamp that made only a faint pool of radiance in a corner of the twilit room. Nobody said anything; but Dominic caught Tossa's eye, and Tossa rose softly and slipped past Lucien Galt, who neither saw nor heard her. Dominic took her hand, and drew her away with him, and Lucien and Liri were left together.

He saw her, and his eyes came to life in the shocked grey mask of his face. He pushed himself off from the doorway, and walked into her arms without a word, and without a word she opened them to him. He slid to his knees at her feet, and she held him on her heart, along with the chill and the dank smell of the river; and she knew where Audrey had gone. After a while he stopped shivering, and locked his arms tightly round her body, and heaved a huge sigh that convulsed them both; and neither he nor she would ever know whether it was of grief at his loss, or involuntary relief at this vast and terrible simplification of his problems, or both, and in what measure.

'I called to her,' he said presently, in a voice drained and weary. 'She was on the parapet. I wanted to tell her that we...that you and I...that we didn't care, that it didn't matter any more...'

'It wouldn't have been any good,' said Liri. 'It *did* matter to her.'

No, it wouldn't have been any good, even if she had listened to him. How can you convince a person like Audrey Arundale that she no longer has to sacrifice everything to respectability, to public reputation, to what the world will say? What's the good of arguing with her that her parents are dead now, and Edward's dead, and the people she has left simply don't look at values that way, simply won't care, that they would welcome her back even after years of prison, and damn the world's opinion? How do you set about convincing her of that, when she's been trained to subdue everything else to appearances all her life? She couldn't be expected to change now. This way there wouldn't be any murder trial, there needn't even be much publicity of any kind. The police are not obliged to make public the particulars of a case which is closed to their satisfaction, when the person who would otherwise have been charged is dead, and the public interest wouldn't be served by stirring up mud. They simply say the

311

case is closed, no prosecutions will be instituted as a result of it, and that's the end of it. General curiosity only speculates for a very short time, till the next sensation crops up. This way everything would be smoothed away, everything hushed up, everything made the best of, just as it had always had to be. Maybe they'd even succeed in getting an open verdict on Edward's death, and the locals would evolve improbable theories about a poacher or a vagrant surprised in the park, and hitting out in panic with the nearest weapon that offered. Audrey wouldn't care. Audrey had observed her contract and her loyalties as best she could to the end. Edward would have wished it.

'I got her out,' Lucien's labouring mouth shaped against Liri's heart. 'They've been all this time trying...trying...'

Yes. Trying to revive her, of course; but Audrey, it seemed, had made quite sure.

'All I meant to do was warn her,' Liri said. 'I'd just found out that *he* knew... It was the only way I had...'

Her voice flagged, like his. They had no need of explanations, and speech was such an effort yet that they could afford to use it only for the ultimate essentials. With her cheek pressed against his wet black hair: 'I love you,' said Liri gently, and that was all.

312

★ ★ ★ ★

'She was my mother,' he said, 'and I can't even bury her.'

The ambulance had come and gone. Henry Marshall had had a fire lit for them in the small library, and left the handful of them there together in the huge and silent house. Lucien had bathed and changed, and put on again with his fresh clothes a drained and languid calm. Liri sat across the hearth from him and watched him steadily, and often he looked up to reassure himself that she was there. Two dark, reticent, proud people; in the intensity of this unvoiced reconciliation their two young, formidable faces had grown strangely alike, as though mentally they stared upon each other with such passion that each had become a mirror image of the other.

'I've got to sit back and let Arundale's relatives do it for me, because I can't compromise what she wanted left alone. All her life keeping up appearances, doing the correct thing, and now she has to die the same way.'

'She chose it,' said George.

'She never had a choice, being the person she was. If my father hadn't been killed...'

'You do know about your father?'

313

'Do *you?*' challenged Lucien jealously.

And neither of them was speaking of John James Galt, though he had done his part well enough, no doubt, during the year or so he had been in the place of a father.

'I know the Galts re-registered you as theirs when you were only a few months old, presumably as soon as the adoption proceedings were completed. I'm reasonably sure that your real father must have been one of the Czech pilots who were stationed at Auchterarne during the war. I guess that he must have been killed in action in 1942. But adoption certificates carry only the Christian names given to the child, and the name of the adoptive parent. *His* name I don't know yet. I shall get it eventually either from Somerset House of from the service records. But that's unnecessary now,' said George gently. 'You tell me.'

'His name was Václav Havelka. I know, because *she* told me about him. Václav is the same name we call Wenceslas. That's why he gave her his Saint Wenceslas medal. He hadn't got anything else to give her. He hadn't even got a country, then, only a job and a uniform. He was twenty years old, and she was sixteen, nearly seventeen, and they met at some innocent local bunfight when her school was up there in Scotland. There wasn't a hope for them. Her people were set on her getting into society and marrying a lord, or something, not a refugee flyer with no money and no home. So she did the one thing really of her own that she ever did, she gave herself to him. Maybe she hoped to force her parents' hands, and maybe she might even managed it, but it never came to that, because my father was shot down six months before I was born. After that, she didn't put up much of a fight for me.'

'How much chance did she have?' said Liri in a low voice.

'Not much, I know. With my father gone she hadn't got anybody to stand by her. She had to tell her folks, and they took her away from school quickly and quietly, and then set to work on her, for ever urging her to have it all hushed up, to spare them the shame, to think of her future, when she hadn't got any future. She gave way in the end. She'd have had to be a heroine not to. She let them hide her away somewhere to have me on the quiet, and then she let me go for adoption. But she insisted on meeting the Galts before she'd sign. They were decent, nice people who badly wanted a child, she knew I'd be all right with them. So she asked them to make sure that I kept my father's medal, and then she promised never to trouble them again, and she never did. And after the war they married her off to Arundale, a big wedding and a successful career, every thing they'd wanted for her. You know how *he* first met her? He gave away the prizes at her school speech-day, the last year she was there. It must have been only a few weeks before my father was killed.

A school speech-day, George thought, dazzled, why didn't I think of that? The white dress, the modest jewellery permitted for wear on a ceremonial occasion, the radiance in her face— Arundale must have had that vision on his mind ever afterwards. And she without a thought of him, or of anything else but her lover, the bridal gift round her neck, and the child that was coming.

Liri was frowning over a puzzling memory. 'But you know, what I don't understand is that Mr Arundale practically told me that his wife *couldn't have* any children. Not in so many words, but that was what he meant.'

'Felicity told me the same thing,' said George, unimpressed. 'That's not so strange. Can you imagine a man like Arundale being open to the idea that the fault might possibly be in him?'

'No,' she agreed bitterly, 'you're right, of course. Even in the Bible you notice it's always barren *wives.*'

'And how,' asked George, returning gently to the matter in hand, 'did you come to meet your mother again?'

'It was at a party the recording company gave, about six weeks ago.' Lucien turned his face aside for a moment, wrung by the realisation of how short a time they had had together. 'She'd lost sight of me all these years, but after I started singing she began to follow up all the notices about me. I kept my own name, you see, so she knew who I was. She began to edge her way into the folk world, to get to know people so that she could get to me. And I...it's hard to explain. I'd grown up happy enough. After the Galts were killed it was the orphanage, of course, but that was pretty good, too, I didn't have any complaints. They told me I'd been adopted, naturally, they always do that, because you're dead certain to find out one day, anyhow. We had one committee-woman who'd known the Galts slightly, and she told me how this medal I had had belonged to my father, who was dead, and my mother had let me go for adoption. I never had anything against my father, how could I? But there was always this thing I had about my mother, pulling two ways, wanting her because after all you're not complete without one, and hating her because she just gave me up when the going got rough.

317

And then this one day, at this party, there I was suddenly alone in a corner with this beautiful, fashionable woman, and she said to me: "I've been trying for ages to meet you. I'm your mother." '

He doubled his long hands into fists and wrung them in a momentary spasm of anguish, and then uncurled them carefully, and let them lie still and quiet on his knee.

'You can't imagine it. Not even you, who've seen her. She wasn't like she is...was...here. The way she said it, with a terrible kind of simplicity, sweeping everything that didn't matter out of the way. I thought I hated her, I even felt I ought to hate her, but when it happened it wasn't like that at all. It was like falling in love. The way she was, it wiped out everything. She wasn't courting me now because I was a lion, she'd just found her way back to me because she couldn't keep away any longer. All she wanted was to be with me. Edward—that was a contract, and she must keep it. You know? She was even very fond of him, in a way, and very loyal. But loving...I don't think she'd loved anyone or anything but me since my father died.'

'And you?' asked George with respectful gentleness.

'It was queer with me. If I'd always had her
318

I should just have loved her casually, like anyone else with a mother, and that would have been it. But getting her back like that, quite strange, and beautiful, and still young...and so lost, and to be pitied! Sometimes I didn't know whether I was her son, or her brother, or her father. I knew I was her slave.'

Yes, of course, from the moment he saw that she was his. Her adoration might well have disarmed Lucifer, pride and all, grievance and all. She had loved her Gil Morrice better than all her kith and kin, how could he help returning her devotion?

'We had to meet sometimes, we couldn't help ourselves. We had so much time to make up. But then there was Liri...Liri broke it off with me, and I knew it was because of *her*, but I couldn't explain, you see, it wasn't my secret. We could never let it be known what the real connection was, my mother's whole life, and his, too, all this build-up, would go down the drain if we did. We must have been mad to start this week-end course, and bring the thing right here into the house. And it was awful here, always so many people, we never could talk at all. And I had to talk to her, I *had* to. Because when Liri followed me here I saw she wasn't absolutely finished with me, I was sure I could get her back, but only by telling her the truth. And I couldn't do that, even in confidence, without my mother's consent.'

'So the message you sent by Felicity,' said George, 'was a genuine message, after all?'

Lucien shook his head, wretchedly. 'It was a lot of things...I don't know...I'm not proud of that. It was a vicious thing to do, but there she was offering to do anything for me, and I wanted her out of my hair, I needed to think and she wouldn't let me think. And I did want my mother to come, while the whole place was nearly empty. I thought *he'd* be away by then, safely on is way to town. So I told Felicity what she could do for me, if she meant it. I knew what she'd think, I knew what she'd feel, I knew I'd hurt her. I meant to, though I wished afterwards I hadn't. But I did believe she'd give the message to my mother, and I was sure she'd come.

'And instead, it was Arundale who came, with that damned murderous toy. It was like an unbelievably bad film. It was even funny at first, because I couldn't believe in it seriously. I tried to talk to him, but I swear he never heard a word. I think in a way he was mad, then. All he wanted was to kill me, and he'd have done it, but then suddenly *she* was there... She must have heard us right from the gate, because she came running with the latch in her hand, and hit out at him like a fury, almost before I realised she was there. And then he was on the ground, and it was all over. Unbelievably quickly. He was dead in minutes.'

Lucien passed a tired hand over his face. 'She hit out in defence of me. She never thought of killing, only of stopping him from killing. But afterwards she knew she *had* killed him. She was totally dazed, but quite docile. It was up to me. She did whatever I told her. I taught her what to say when you questioned her. But it was partly true, you know, he did behave like she said, after Felicity left them. He did put it all aside as a piece of childish spite, and made out he was leaving for town, just as he'd planned. It was only after he'd gone that she got frightened, and came herself, to make sure...'

'You didn't know, of course,' said George, 'and neither did she, that he'd telephoned to both bodies he should have addressed in Birmingham, and called off the engagements. Yes,' he said, answering the quick, dark glance, 'he was going to make good use of those two days' grace, too. He intended murder.'

'My own fault, I snatched the world away from under his feet. But that was something *I* never intended. I told her to go back to the house, and to be sure not to be seen on the way. And she did whatever I told her. Ever since her heart broke, between my father and me, she's always done what people told her, what they expected of her. When she'd gone I tried to bring him round, but it was no good, and I knew he was dead. I threw him into the river, and the sword-stick and the latch after him. And I sneaked up to the yard and took his car and ran for it. I thought I was taking the whole load of guilt away with me, and she'd be all right. I should have known better, but I was in a pretty bad state myself. How could she ever be all right again?' He shook his head suddenly in a gesture of helpless pain. 'How did you know? Why were you sure it wasn't me? I thought I made out a pretty good case.'

George rose from his chair. It was late and it was over; and if these two could sleep, sleep was what they needed.

'I haven't even read your statement yet, but if it's any consolation, you convinced Rapier, all right. Don't worry, we shall never be asking you to sign it. I knew the latch was still in its place when Felicity left you. And what did Arundale want with it? Like Lord Barnard, he came with a sword. And he was between you and the gate, he and forty yards of ground. You'd never have had the slightest chance of getting to it. No, someone else, someone who followed him there, dragged that latch out of its wards.' He cast a summoning glace towards the corner where Tossa and Dominic had sat silent throughout this elegiac conversation. 'Come on, I'd better get you two home before I go in and report.' And to Lucien: 'You're staying here overnight?'

'Mr Marshall was kind enough to suggest it. Then we can move into Comerbourne, if you still need us. I suppose we'll have to stay within call until after the inquests?'

'Probably, but we can talk about that tomorrow.'

'I realise,' Lucien said abruptly, 'that there must be a good case against me as an accessory after the fact.'

'Then so there is against me,' said Liri at once. 'I warned you, and I warned her.'

She would probably never realise, George thought, how grateful he was to her for that. 'What fact?' he said dryly. 'There isn't going to be any primary prosecution, why should I go out of my way to hunt up secondary charges? Much better just get on with the business of living. It may not always be easy, but it's still worth the effort.'

'Is it?' Lucien raised bruised eyes in a challenging stare. 'What did *she* ever get out of it? In her whole life she never had any real happiness.'

'You think not?' said George.

He walked suddenly to the door and out of the room, and they heard his footsteps receding along the passages now populous only with echoes. In a few moments he was back with a half-plate photograph in his hands. He dropped it in Lucien's lap.

'Here you are, a souvenir for you. And you can add me to the crime-sheet—petty theft from Arundale's estate. Incidentally, that makes you a receiver, too.' He watched the flooding colour rise in the boy's dark cheeks, and the warmth of wonder ease the tired lines of his mouth. 'Taken at that last prize-giving, unless I miss my guess. If I'm right, then *he* was still with her, and *you* were on your way. Maybe it didn't last long, but believe me, she had it.'

Lucien looked down in a daze at the Audrey he had never seen before, with the bloom and the radiance and the spontaneity still on her, and caught at their height. If ever he doubted that he had been the child of love, he had only to look at this, and be reassured. And it was, for some reason, almost inevitable that he should look up in suddenly enlarged understanding from Audrey to Liri, whose eyes had never left him.

George wafted Tossa and Dominic quietly out of the room before him, and they went away and left those two to come to terms with the past and the future in their own way.

Nobody had bothered to draw the curtains. Dominic looked back from the courtyard, before he climbed into the car, and there were the last two guests left over from Follymead's folk-music week-end, framed in the softly-lighted window of the small library on the first floor, locked in each other's arms. They must have sprung together and met in splendid collision as soon as they were alone. Their cheeks were pressed together as if they would fuse for all time, their eyes were closed, and their faces were timeless, as though love had fallen on them as a new and cosmic experience, original and unique in the history of man.

Dominic climbed hastily into the car and slammed the door, ashamed and exalted.

George Felse drove round the wing of the house, and out upon the great open levels of the drive, suddenly moon-washed and serene after the thunderous sulks of the evening. Follymead receded, the partial rear view of it grew and coalesced, became a harmonious, and symmetrical whole, making unity out of chaos. Gradually it withdrew, moonlit and magical, a joke and a threat, a dream and a nightmare, deploying its lesser shocks on either side of

325

them as they retreated. Even those who escaped always came back; there was no need to set traps for them.

' "Black, black, black," ' sang Tossa softly to herself in the back set, her chin on her shoulder, 'is the colour of my true-love's hair..." '

MAGNA-THORNDIKE hopes you have enjoyed this Large Print book. All our Large Print titles are designed for easy reading, and all our books are made to last. Other Magna Print or Thorndike Press books are available at your library, through selected bookstores, or directly from the publishers. For more information about current and upcoming titles, please call or mail your name and address to:

MAGNA PRINT BOOKS
Long Preston, Near Skipton,
North Yorkshire,
England BD23 4ND
(07294) 225

or in the USA

THORNDIKE PRESS
P.O. Box 159
Thorndike, Maine 04986
(800) 223-6121
(207) 948-2962
(in Maine and Canada call collect)

There is no obligation, of course.